Dear Reader,

I'd given up my life of crime and settled into a demanding job as a consultant, when this dame walked through my door. P. J. Fitzjames, Jr., was an uptight, upright Bostonian with ethics up to her pretty, plain little earlobes.

"Junior" was just the type of little lady that I try to avoid. But beneath that proper exterior was the perseverance of a bull terrier, and she wouldn't take no for an answer. Before I knew it, I was accepting her magnanimous offer of two hundred fifty dollars a day—my usual hourly rate!

I'm not worried, though. Junior won't be getting everything her way in this caper. I'm willing to help her find out who perpetrated the scam to steal her father's millions—but she's about to learn that I do my best work underhanded . . . and under the covers.

Eli Holder

Massachusetts

MEN MADE IN AMERICA

BETHANY CAMPBELL

Pros and Cons

Massachusetts

Harlequin Books

TORONTO • NEW YORK • LONDON
AMSTERDAM • PARIS • SYDNEY • HAMBURG
STOCKHOLM • ATHENS • TOKYO • MILAN
MADRID • WARSAW • BUDAPEST • AUCKLAND

To Dan and Jan and Fran

HARLEQUIN ENTERPRISES LTD.
225 Duncan Mill Road, Don Mills,
Ontario, Canada M3B 3K9

PROS AND CONS

Copyright © 1987 by Sally McCluskey

ISBN: 0-373-45171-7

Published Harlequin Enterprises, Ltd. 1987, 1993

Printed in the U.S.A.

Prologue

Dr. Nigel Cummings stirred uncomfortably in the high-backed leather desk chair in his home den. He was a self-satisfied man, not often given to guilt, but the young woman seated before him reminded him how deeply the years had changed him. Cummings and her father had once been friends, close friends. But Cummings had not seen old P.J. for years. The two men had both been idealists once. The difference was that old P.J. had remained one. From Nigel Cummings's lofty sphere of influence at the Harvard Law School, there had been half a hundred favors he might have offered P. J. Fitzjames Sr. over the years. Somehow he had always been too busy to do so. Nor had his friend been the kind to ask for special privilege and assistance. Now, after all this time, old P.J.'s daughter was asking one simple favor. Cummings could tell she had forced herself to do it—for her father's sake. All she wanted was information. Cummings had been startled by her question. What was done was done, he thought. But she had looked at him so seriously, and with such hopeful anticipation, that a strange uneasiness had welled up within him.

At last he answered her. "One person—" he locked his fingers with false calm over his prosperous paunch "—one person might have been able to win that case for your father." The young woman looked at him, her blue eyes focused with taut expectancy. "Eli Holder," Cummings said. "If anyone could have done it, it would have been Holder."

"Holder," she said in a low voice. He could tell the name was unfamiliar to her. She paused, then swallowed. "Is he a lawyer?"

Cummings shook his balding head. *Why does she want to know? She has no intention of trying to... No,* he thought, shaking his head. *No. She's too levelheaded a girl to try to do such a damn fool thing. At least she seems to be.* "No," he said, reverting to his hearty professional voice. He had worked years to cultivate that voice, but suddenly he didn't like the sound of it. "Holder's not a lawyer. *He* calls himself a consultant. It's as good a term as any, I suppose."

Like her father, she wasn't one to waste words. She waited, in the same intense quiet, for him to explain. Cummings sighed and moved a silver inkwell on his desk. "What the case needed was an expert on fraud, my dear. And that's what Eli Holder is—the country's foremost expert. He knows it all—from experience." Again she waited in that same disquieting silence for him to go on. He inched the inkwell back to its original spot. "In fraud circles the Holder family was famous. They perpetrated some of the most ingenious scams in the annals of such unhappy business."

He saw her catch her lower lip lightly between her teeth, then release it. "This consultant," she said carefully, "is...a criminal?"

By the Lord Harry, he thought, *the eyes in that innocent face look right through a man.* He shook his head in the sage and professional manner he had adopted over the years. "Was a criminal," he replied. "As a young man he was sentenced to five years in Leavenworth. It didn't teach him a lesson in the moral sense—he's a law unto himself— but it taught him one in the practical sense. He's not the kind of man to adapt well to prison. He managed to adapt instead to selling what he knows about fraud rather than practicing it.''

"He's an informant?" she asked, blue eyes suddenly judgmental.

Just like old P.J., Cummings thought. *The barest scent of wrongdoing and she's up in arms.* "No," he replied. He scratched his smooth jowl. "He's a lecturer and free-lance investigator. He wrote a book on fraud that's used as a primary text in half the criminal-law and police-training programs in the country."

She took a deep breath. She exhaled it. "Why didn't my father consult him?" she asked.

"First," Cummings replied, "he probably wasn't familiar with him—foundation law is a far cry from criminal law."

She nodded grimly. She'd heard that statement before, voiced as a criticism. The case had been far removed from what her father usually encountered in his practice. And he could not afford outside help. He had been unable to spend anything except his own waning strength.

"Second," Cummings continued smoothly, "Holder hasn't been in Boston long. He moved because of the universities and the computer industry here. His next book will be on computer crime. 'The crime of the future' he calls it. He's undoubtedly right."

She raised her chin slightly. She wasn't interested in the crime of the future but in a crime of the past, the very recent past.

No, Cummings thought, watching the determined light in her eyes. *No, she's not thinking of trying to start the whole thing over again. She couldn't be. It would be insane. She isn't even a lawyer—what is she?—a business administrator, if I remember correctly. For the same foundation as her father, of course.* "It's all academic, anyway," he said, as gently as he could. "Holder would never agree to work on such a case as your father's."

"Why not?"

Her question was direct and immediate. Cummings paused, searching for a tactful way to respond. There was none. "He's not interested in causes—only money," he said carefully. "When he gets involved in an investigation, it's large—and expensive. Few can afford him."

"You're saying he wouldn't have even wanted to talk to my father," she said as calmly as she could.

"Yes," Cummings replied, meeting her blue gaze, "to put it bluntly. Holder's brilliant—but hard. He wouldn't have the least interest in an organization like yours. I'm sorry, but that's the truth." He studied the set of her jaw and felt the prickle of that uneasiness returning. *Why is she asking this now? What's she up to?*

"I see." She nodded briskly. "Thank you, Dr. Cummings. You've been very helpful. I'm sorry for taking up so much of your time."

He sighed but was glad to see her leave. She reminded him, painfully, of what it was like to be young and high-minded. They exchanged a few polite and meaningless comments in the ceremony of farewell, and he walked her to the door of his den. Watching her squared shoulders, her soldierly stride, he was reminded absurdly of Joan of Arc listening to her private voices, setting out to do battle.

Curiously lightheaded, she stepped out into the bright August sunshine of Beacon Hill. Eli Holder, she thought purposefully, heading through the dappled sunshine of Beacon Street. Eli Holder would not want to talk to her. She would make him do it. He would help her. He had to. She had to convince him. She didn't care how difficult it was. Her parents had raised her to face difficult tasks. They had taught her the virtue of persistence. They had taught her to fight hard and for the right causes. They had taught her everything she believed in. And she had learned her lessons well. Too well, some had said.

Chapter One

Eli Holder cracked his knuckles in irritation. He didn't know why he had agreed to see the Fitzjames woman unless it was because she was so damned persistent. She had been after him for over a month.

He had quit smoking years ago, but he opened his desk drawer and took out the pack of unfiltered Luckies he kept for the occasional day so rotten it warranted the peculiar pleasureless relief of a cigarette.

From the habit of his prison days, he broke the cigarette in two, put one piece back in the crumpled pack and thrust the other between his lips. He lit it with the gold cigarette lighter shaped like the blindfolded Goddess of Justice. The lighter had been given to him by the Boston Law Association. The association had either lousy taste or a weird sense of humor. To ignite the thing he pushed a button at the statuette's base. Then Justice's head burst into flame as if she had the world's worst migraine.

"Send in Miss Fitzjames," he said brusquely into the intercom that connected him to Miss Goodboddy, his secretary. Despite her luscious name, Miss Goodboddy was far from luscious. She was, however, despite her stoop and wrinkles, efficient and hardheaded and industrious. Furthermore, she wasn't distracting. Eli, who liked to keep life simple, appreciated that.

Miss Goodboddy was also the slightest bit deaf. "Send her in," he thundered again, then mentally added, *So I can kick her back out.*

He didn't take private cases, but the young woman who'd been hounding him couldn't get the fact through her head. He wondered grumpily what kind of parents would name their daughter Junior, anyway. P. J. Fitzjames Jr. Liberated Boston intellectuals, he decided and shuddered slightly.

On the phone the woman had a voice like a stubborn mouse and an accent with Harvard practically engraved in it. He could picture her with unfortunate clarity—the classic dowdy Cambridge type. Low heels, a gray flannel skirt, a white blouse, a navy blazer and possibly, since this was the age of sexual equality, a tie. She would wear no makeup and have her hair cut like a boy's. She would have no discernible figure and a face slightly plainer than a block of cement.

He shook his head and inhaled. The smoke cut into his lungs with satisfying punishment. The walnut door of his inner office opened, and the woman he'd come to think of as Junior walked in, her back straight as a Boston church spire. She couldn't be older than twenty-six—just a kid, really.

She wore low heels, a gray flannel skirt, a white blouse, a navy blazer and a black silk tie. She was without makeup, and her brown hair was cut like a boy's. Beneath her shapeless garments Eli's expert eye noted a figure that was probably very nice indeed. And even without makeup she had the kind of face men usually saw only in their happiest dreams—wide-set blue eyes, cheekbones fit for a princess, an elfin nose and a wide, full mouth that made him think with longing of Sophia Loren. But the eyes were alight with naive idealism, and the slightly pointed chin was set to do battle. She had the air of somebody who's read every book in the library but needs a map to get around the block.

Hell's bells, he thought with disgust, *what a waste.* He took another drag on the broken cigarette. Through the smoke he gave her as unfriendly a look as he could muster. He was a man capable of looking extraordinarily unfriendly.

P.J. THOUGHT IN SWELLING PANIC, *I've never seen a man look so hostile*. But she kept her back straight and set her chin at a defiant angle. It had taken her thirty-four days to get this appointment.

Eli Holder loomed behind a massive walnut desk and offered her an unwelcoming scowl. He clamped the stub of a cigarette between his lips and exhaled smoke through his nostrils like a dragon.

"You," he rumbled, "must be Junior."

"I'm Miss Fitzjames," she said, tilting her chin so high that her neck hurt. "Do you mind if I sit?"

"Yes, Junior, but I have the feeling you'll sit, anyway. Pull up a chair, make your pitch and then get out. I told you, I don't take private cases."

P.J. sat down carefully, crossing her ankles in a studiously ladylike way. She folded her hands primly in her lap. She watched him grind out the cigarette and then stare at her through the smoke that still drifted bluely in the air.

He was a nasty man, and despite the expensive three-piece suit and obviously costly haircut, he exuded danger. She remembered with a shiver that he'd spent five years in prison. She'd never talked to an ex-convict before. But he was her last chance, her only chance.

"It's not exactly a private case," she said, keeping her voice steady. She was a medium-sized woman, but she had a little girl's voice and she hated it. "It involves a foundation. A nonprofit foundation. SOS—Save Our Seas—it's a conservationist group."

He gave a derisive snort. "What's the matter? Is some-body embezzling from the squids? Look, Junior, I'm not interested in the sea. It's big and it's wet and it smells like fish. Why'd your parents do it, anyway?"

"Do what?" she asked, disconcerted. She folded her hands a bit more tightly in the gray pleats of her skirt.

"Name you Junior. Did your daddy want a boy?"

"Mr. Holder," P.J. said, struggling to keep her voice even, "I'd appreciate it if you weren't flippant. This is an important matter. It concerns several mill—"

He raised an eyebrow to indicate that he was fighting an attack of extreme boredom. "I'm not being flippant. I want to know who I'm dealing with. Why'd they name you that? Is that why you've got the boy's haircut, the tie? Nice tie, by the way. I think I have one just like it."

Her hands were now clenched so tightly her knuckles paled. He was making her angry, and that was dangerous. On the few occasions she'd lost control of her anger, she'd frightened even herself.

"My parents married late in life," she said, acidity add-ing age to her voice. If Holder thought he could put her off by playing rough, she would show him otherwise. "It was obvious I was the only child they'd ever have. My parents were not sexists. They believed a girl could carry on her father's name as well as a boy. They also believed in man-ners. I wish *your* parents had. Then we might be able to get down to business without your condescension."

Touché, thought Holder and studied her more intently. He could tell she was frightened, but she had spunk. He liked that, but it made him even more irritable. She was far prettier than she probably realized, even with her severe clothes and haircut, and for some reason that irritated him, too. She met his brown gaze with her blue one, and she didn't blink.

She was sizing him up as carefully as he was her. He was a big man, about thirty-nine, she'd guess, and she couldn't tell if his shoulders were really that wide or if his suit jacket was padded. His face wasn't handsome, exactly, but it intrigued and perplexed her. His hair was straight and light brown, like hers, and one well-barbered lock looked as if it would like to fall rebelliously onto his forehead but didn't quite dare. He had light brown eyes, hazel really, with the slightest tilt at the outward corners. They should have been quite ordinary eyes, but their intensity and the long, slightly arched brows above them made them almost hypnotic. His nose was nothing special, she decided, his mouth was too wide and he had a perpetual crease in one cheek that she had first thought was a dimple, then realized with a shock was a scar. It gave him a permanently satirical look, as if he were secretly laughing. He had an adequate chin, an acceptable jaw, but somehow the disparate features combined into a face that was better-looking than it should have been—and marked by utter cynicism.

"So tell me about yourself. And about SOS," he muttered at last. "Although I don't take fish for clients. I've met enough sharks in my time."

She was sure he had. He had the face of a con artist, calculating and measuring, and he was measuring her now for weakness. She was determined to show none.

"My mother helped found SOS," she said briskly. "She was a marine biologist. She knew some of the first people who were concerned about what's happening to the oceans—Rachel Carson, Jacques Cousteau. She knew something had to be done. She spent the rest of her life working for SOS."

"Touching," said Eli, obviously untouched.

"My father—" for the first time P.J.'s voice wavered a bit, almost cracked "—my father was a corporation lawyer, but he got more and more caught up in Mother's work. He resigned and became the foundation's lawyer.''

"Um," Eli said, rubbing his forefinger against the scar in his cheek. "And probably took a helluva cut in pay." He gave a short laugh and shook his head at such foolishness.

P.J. felt the frustration beginning to well up again. She was driving her sensible squared-off fingernails into her palms. "He did what he thought was *right*," she said tersely. Her father used to tell her when she got angry, he could see blue sparks firing up in her eyes, and she could feel them starting to swirl now. "They *both* did what they thought was right. Money—or lack of it—wasn't an issue."

"Then I'd say they were a little empty in the head," Eli replied easily, leaning back in his chair. He waited to see if she'd explode and then stamp out of his office and his life.

"Maybe you would," she replied, struggling to maintain a veneer of calm. If the man was into insults, she could play the game as well as he. "You might think that St. Francis and Abraham Lincoln were a little empty in the head, too."

"I never discuss religion or politics." He flicked the air idly with one lean hand. "Get on with it, Junior. My time is valuable. So far, you're wasting it."

"I went to work for SOS last year. I'm assistant financial manager and in charge of forming a subcorporation—FUTURE. We're working out marketing ideas to raise funds."

"Oh, swell," mocked Eli, still leaning back lazily in his chair. "So more people will be out on the streets peddling T-shirts with sad little harp seals on them and greeting cards with weepy whales. Just what the world needs. More good-cause airheads hawking schlock. Well, a girl's got to live. Nice little foundation you've got there. Too bad you don't have a bigger family so you could all get on its payroll."

"I have," P.J. said in her steeliest voice, "an MBA from Harvard. I could work anyplace I want. I wanted to work for SOS, and I got the job on my own merits."

Eli shook his head again, his mouth crooking grimly. So the crazy little cookie had the much-prized Harvard MBA. He should have guessed. He'd never gotten beyond the tenth grade himself. His professors had been his father and uncles who'd taught him a thousand kinds of cons. His postgraduate degree was from Leavenworth, where he'd learned about breaking the law from a faculty of experts.

All his life he'd divided people into two classes—the con men and the suckers. The con men were smart, and the suckers were stupid. The only problem was that even the smartest con men got caught. Eli hadn't given up crime out of any high-minded conversion to the virtues of the law. He'd given it up because he calculated he could make a lot of money and stay out of prison. He liked money, and he hated prison the way some people hated snakes.

It was people like the girl sitting before him—the do-gooders—that he could never fit into his tidy system. If he thought of them at all, it was as fuzzy-thinking eggheads who still believed in Santa Claus, the innate goodness of all humankind and kindred improbable myths. They were, in short, ridiculous.

But the woman sitting in such rigid self-control before him was not stupid. Naive, but not stupid. And despite her obvious idealism, he sensed iron in her, a spirit of fight he hadn't expected.

"So, Harvard," he drawled, sounding totally uninterested, "what's your problem? Somebody steal a T-shirt design from you?"

P.J. ground her teeth slightly, then quit immediately. "My problem isn't a little one. It's big."

"How big?"

"Four million dollars big," she said, then sat a bit more stiffly, watching his reaction.

He raised his brown brows. He whistled softly. For the first time he looked slightly interested. "Four million. A respectable sum" was all he said.

She felt a small surge of hope. "Last year a man named Delmer Fordyce died," she said, speaking quickly, trying to fuel Holder's attention. "Fordyce was rich and a little eccentric. But he had a passion for ecology, and he'd told my father many times that he intended to leave his fortune to SOS."

"Throwing his money into the ocean? That's 'a little eccentric,' all right," Eli said with the crooked smile P.J. was learning to hate.

"It was a fine gesture for a good philanthropic cause," she answered, almost snapping the words. "He told my father repeatedly his will was made and signed. SOS was to receive his entire estate—worth four million dollars. And SOS *needs* that money, Mr. Holder. We're hanging on by the skin of our teeth."

Eli kept his hands behind his head and pretended to stifle a yawn. "Let me guess," he mused, looking at the ceiling thoughtfully. "Your dear idealistic daddy got a copy of the will, but then another will popped up and somebody else claimed the four million. Right?"

She looked at him with slight surprise. The case hadn't received much publicity because SOS thought such publicity unseemly. "Did you read about it in the papers?" She frowned. There had only been a few paragraphs and those printed months ago.

"No," he said, returning his troublingly intense eyes to her again. "It just figures. That's why you're here. Who was the lucky beneficiary of the other will?"

She unclamped her hands from her lap and set her arms on those of the chair "Four men in Vermont—they call themselves the Bachelors' Club. Fordyce spent his last summer up there—Leaftree, Vermont. It's a resort town. He befriended them. And a complete and apparently perfectly legal will—more recent than the one that left the money to SOS—was in a safe in an attorney's office in Leaftree.''

"If it's complete and legal, then you've just had yourself about four million dollars' worth of bad luck, Junior. My condolences.'' He shrugged as if dismissing her.

"I said *apparently* legal,'' P.J. emphasized, leaning forward in frustration. "It wasn't even made out by a lawyer—it was done from one of those 'will kits' you get by mail order. Listen, Mr. Holder. Fordyce was more than just a benefactor. He was a friend of the family. He spent the summer in Vermont. Then he came back to Boston. Two weeks before he died, Mr. Holder—remember this: two weeks before—he had dinner at our house, and he told my father *again* that the money was to go to SOS. I heard him. So did six other guests. But the Vermont will was dated in July. Why would Fordyce insist in September the money was going to SOS if in July he'd made arrangements to leave it to the Bachelors' Club? It makes no sense.''

Eli shrugged again lazily, lifting one wide shoulder. "You said he was eccentric.''

"Eccentric. But not crazy and not senile and not forgetful. No.''

The intent brown eyes flicked over her, making her feel prickly. "So maybe he was a liar. Maybe he didn't want to admit the truth to your father. Maybe he was counting on more free dinners.''

"Mr. Fordyce was *not* a liar,'' she said, more sharply than she'd intended. "My father didn't consort with *liars*.''

"Maybe you don't know as much about human nature as you think.'' Eli smiled. The smile radiated his sense of superiority.

"Maybe you don't know as much, either,'' P.J. retorted. "I knew the man from the time I was a child. He was not a liar. He intended that money to go to SOS.''

Holder allowed himself a slight roll of the eyes to indicate he wasn't going to argue with a woman whose mind was obviously made up. He scratched his chin thoughtfully. "So what did the old boy die of?" he asked. "It didn't have anything to do with his brain, did it?"

"Certainly not! And none of us expected him to die so suddenly. He seemed much healthier than my...my father. But his heart gave out. Just stopped. It was terribly sudden. Nobody even knew he had a heart problem."

Eli reached for a pencil, tapped it meditatively on the desktop. "So your father's taking the case to court," he offered, then stopped tapping, his eyes locking with hers again. "Correct? To contest the second will. But he's not having much luck finding hard evidence. So he sent his pretty little Junior to ask me to play detective. I'm not a detective. I'm a consultant. Thanks, but no thanks."

"No," P.J. said with a vehemence that surprised him.

"No what?" growled Eli. She was a pretty little thing and a surprising one, but he wanted her gone. She wasn't his type, and her problem wasn't the kind of problem he dealt with. She meant nothing but trouble, and Eli liked his life easy and luxurious—and complication free. This woman, he sensed, could cause him problems he didn't even want to think about.

"No, my father didn't send me. My father's dead." She bit her lip, and her chin wobbled a bit.

Oh, God, he thought in weary despair, *she's going to cry.* He mentally ran through a litany of swear words.

But she squared her shoulders, and no tears shone in the blue eyes. Only that same fierce determination.

"Sorry," he said coldly, watching her.

She ignored his spurious attempt at sympathy, and he admired her for it.

"And the case isn't being tried in court," she went on grimly. "It's already been tried. SOS lost. The Bachelors' Club got the inheritance. Every penny."

Eli had been slouching in the chair. Now he stiffened and his head jerked up sharply. *"What?"* he asked in disbelief.

"You heard me," she answered, still in stern control of herself. "We lost. Two months ago. My father died three weeks later. He worked like a dog on that case. He was too sick and too old to work as hard as he did, but he couldn't let SOS be robbed by four greedy old men. And I can't, either. That's why I'm here."

He looked at her for a long time until she got that uncomfortable prickly feeling again. Then he gave her his mocking crooked smile and shook his head. "Hard to believe you went to Harvard, Junior. The facts are simple. The battle's over. You lost. Too bad."

He saw that flash in her eyes again. "The battle isn't over until I quit fighting," she contradicted. "There's an important principle at stake here. And I'm not quitting."

"Principle?" Eli laughed.

"Yes," she replied hotly. "Principle. And if you can't understand that, I'll put it in terms you *can* understand. The Bachelors' Club swiped four million bucks from my people. I want it back. Wouldn't you?"

He smiled again. The words "swiped" and "bucks" sounded incongruous coming from that lovely educated little mouth. It was almost as if she were talking dirty. He liked it.

"SOS has given up," she plunged on. "But I haven't and I won't. I want to hire you to prove the Vermont will is false."

Lord, she's as spirited as she is naive, he thought. *Amazing little thing.* "I'm not," he repeated firmly, "a detective. I write. I consult. I lecture. I deal with corporations and law-enforcement agencies and universities. I can't help you, kid."

I'm not a kid, she wanted to scream at him, *I'm twenty-six years old.* Instead, she said. "I talked to Dr. Cummings of the Harvard Law School. He said if anybody could find out if a . . . a scam had been perpetrated, it'd be you."

Eli suppressed a groan. It would be that foggy-headed old dean. A crafty old bastard who liked to pose as a friend of all things right and honorable. He'd probably drooled all over his dentures at the thought of helping Miss Sweet Young Thing by throwing her into Eli's lap.

"Maybe old Doc Cummings should retire," Eli said between clenched teeth. "I believe this is the third time I've said it, but maybe it'll be the charm. I don't take private cases."

"And I said I'd pay you," she retorted. "I'll pay you whatever you usually get. I've got my father's insurance money. Cummings said you were the best. I want the best. I'll pay your price."

His price, he was beginning to decide, might require a little private, personal negotiation because the blue eyes were starting to get to him. But Junior here didn't look like a woman who took that sort of thing lightly. That made him irritable again. He didn't like being got to. He gave her a sardonic look and said, "You can't afford me, Miss Fitzjames. I'm expensive. Very expensive."

She only looked more determined. He had the feeling she was about to play her trump card. She did, and it was a joker. "I am willing to pay you," she said, narrowing her eyes in an unsuccessful attempt to look streetwise, "two hundred and fifty dollars a day."

He restrained the desire to hoot. The woman must have got her idea of investigative fees from an ancient detective novel. His fee was two hundred and fifty dollars an hour—and that was for the easiest of tasks.

"Well?" she said expectantly. She thought she had dangled a juicy carrot in front of him. He felt almost sorry for her.

"Terribly generous." He smiled, watching the fire in her eyes fade slightly. "But no. Flatly no."

It took only seconds for the spark to come back. "You've got to," she insisted. "I mean, a terrible injustice has been done. Fordyce *said* the money was supposed to go to SOS. His first will said it. And there's something suspicious about that Vermont will. One of the witnesses died and couldn't testify, and the second was never located. I have good instincts. Fordyce was a benevolent man, devoted to SOS. Why would he leave his money to four grasping old men he'd just met that summer?"

Ah, mused Eli, the blue sparks were fairly whirling now. Did this prim little thing have any idea how she looked when the passion danced in her eyes like that? He doubted it.

"Look," he said as kindly as he could. It didn't sound very kindly because kindness wasn't an emotion Eli often practiced. "Your father contested it in court. Did the Vermont will seem to be in order?"

"Yes," she admitted, but her chin was tilting up in defiance again.

"Was the signature analyzed? Did Fordyce actually sign that second will?"

"The experts said he did," she said curtly.

"And Fordyce seemed to be enjoying perfect mental health?" he probed.

"Perfect." Her chin was held very high now.

"And," he went on, weariness and cynicism combining in his tone, "he did make friends with these 'Bachelor' characters?"

"Yes," she conceded. "They claimed he was an honorary member."

Eli reached into his drawer and, loathing himself for the weakness, took another cigarette, the broken piece of the first.

"You haven't got a chance," he said, casting aside any attempt to be kind. He wasn't good at it, and it hadn't helped, anyway. "Forget the whole thing. Go back to your T-shirts and greeting cards. Tell the whales hello and to stop beaching themselves on Rhode Island. They stink up my summer place."

She stared at him for a moment. She had worked so hard to see him, had fought so long for this opportunity, been treated so cavalierly by him.... She felt something within her head distinctly snap. It was the lock she kept on her emotions. She knew something usually foreign to her character was not only about to escape but to attack.

"Coward," she said at last, quietly in her small voice. She meant it with all her heart.

"What?" he rumbled, narrowing his eyes at her. He could narrow his eyes so menacingly that it had kept him relatively safe for five long, rough years in prison. But she didn't flinch.

"Coward," she repeated icily. "Invertebrate. *Jellyfish*." She said the word jellyfish with all the disdain of a woman who knows precisely how gelatinous a jellyfish is.

Eli looked at her first in amazement and then in disbelief. "It's a good thing you're a woman," he said at last, smashing out the cigarette, "because the last man who said that to me—"

"Big talk," sniffed P.J., tossing her head. "You roar like a lion, but when a real challenge crops up, you simply turn your back." She looked at him as if he were a cockroach.

He rose, walked slowly around the desk and stood towering over her. The damned woman still didn't flinch. He reached down and took her black tie in his hand. "Junior," he said, a dangerous edge in his voice. "Don't push me. You've got more problems than the Bachelors' Club. You've got a real complex spinning under that little-boy hairdo. You're trying to avenge your daddy and be the son you think he wanted. You even dress the part. Grow up. And try being a big *girl*, not some unisex Robin Hood for a bunch of whales.''

He released her tie with a taunting flip. He expected her to stamp her foot or cry or do some womanly thing, then flounce out of his office for good.

What he didn't expect was that she'd stand so quickly, taking him by surprise. In her flat-heeled, sensible shoes she barely came to his shoulder, but she looked up into his eyes with the same controlled fury he felt, pulled his tie from his vest, then flipped it loose with a gesture far more contemptuous than his own had been.

''Keep your hands off my tie, and don't try to psycho-analyze me,'' she ordered hotly. She was breathing hard.

He glared at her in surprise. ''Keep your hands off *my* tie, and stop trying to psyche me out, amateur,'' he ordered back. A vein began to throb in his temple.

She took a step backward and stared up at him, tossing an errant lock of brown hair from her eyes. ''You can tell the Kiwanis Club how some oily con man sells fake stock to lit-tle old ladies in Dubuque,'' she accused, ''but whatever the men in the Bachelors' Club have pulled off is too sophisti-cated for you, and you know it. I heard you were the best.'' She laughed. ''You must have a really unscrupulous PR man.''

He glowered at her. ''I'm my own PR man.''

''It figures,'' she said, fine nostrils flaring in disdain.

He took a step backward himself. She was too close, and he was either going to give her a good shake or kiss her till he left her as limp as one of her own jellyfish. The latter impulse surprised the hell out of him.

He straightened his tie as she straightened her own. They eyed each other like animals contemplating something primitive.

"I don't take private cases," he said for the fourth time. "And even if I did, I wouldn't take yours. You haven't got a snowball's chance in hell, lady. Stop trying to make up for your father's failure. He didn't have a snowball's chance, either. I think you'd better leave now before one of us ends up hanging dead from a rafter."

"The difference between my father and you, Mr. Holder," she said, adjusting her dark blazer, "is that he was a man of principle and action. And he didn't have an egotistical bone in his body. He may have been old and tired and sick, but he wasn't afraid of a hard fight."

"Neither was Don Quixote," Holder said out of the corner of his mouth. "And as I recall, he ended up fighting a windmill and getting himself nearly spun to death."

"At least Don Quixote had a few ideals," she said with a little catch in her voice. He wasn't sure, but he thought he saw, at last, the barest glint of a tear in her eye, and it did something strange to the pit of his stomach.

Tell her goodbye and to get out, he warned himself. *Be polite, or tell her to go to hell in a hand basket, but get her out of here. Fast.*

He opened his mouth to tell her to leave and was only slightly surprised when he heard himself say, "Oh, hell. It's your money, Junior. I'll take your case."

Her blue eyes widened. She went a bit pale. She seemed to sag slightly, as if she had gotten this far on nothing but raw nerve.

"You will?"

"Yeah," he said gruffly. He turned his back on her and strolled to his desk. He sat down, lazing against the back of his chair again. He put his hands behind his head and studied her with more indifference than he felt, resisting the strong urge to reach into the desk and get another cigarette, a whole one.

"I'll go up there—where is it?" he asked.

"Leaftree," she answered in the voice of a child.

"I'll go up to Leaftree and look around. Ask a few questions. And I warn you now, I don't expect to find anything. You're practically giving your money away, kid."

"It's my money," she replied evenly.

"And if I do find anything," he said, arching an eyebrow unpleasantly, "I'll send for you. You'll have to join me." *There,* he thought, *see how she likes that.*

P.J. blinked hard. "Join you? Why?" Eli Holder was having a strange effect on her, and the idea of "joining" him in Vermont was vaguely unsettling.

"Because," he said smugly, enjoying her discomfort, "my methods aren't always exactly...orthodox. I doubt your late, idealistic daddy would have approved of them. I may need assistance. And unless you want to pay me an extra thousand a week for it, you can come and do it yourself— providing, of course, it isn't too far out of your league, and you're not a coward, an invertebrate, a jellyfish, et cetera."

She swallowed hard and ran a hand over her short, smooth hair. He was challenging her, and she knew it. "How am I supposed to get off work?" she asked reluctantly. "I'm supposed to be setting up this subcorporation. And SOS doesn't even know I'm trying to reopen the case."

"Easy," said Eli with a casual shrug. "I bet SOS is full of bleeding hearts just like you. Tell them you don't feel good. Tell them you've got the nervous whim-whams. Tell them you've got a moral crisis and need time off to work it out. I'll bet dollars to doughnuts your colleagues will fall all over themselves to do yet one more charitable deed."

Damn, she thought, *he's probably right.* She wasn't sure she trusted Holder, but he was her only chance of getting the money back to SOS where it belonged. She wished the idea of working with him didn't seem oddly exciting. She replied with a brisk nod. "Fine," she said. She wished again her voice didn't sound so young, so inexperienced. She stood as straight as she could. Then she reached into her sensible handbag, pulled out her checkbook, went to his desk and scribbled him a week's payment in advance. She handed him the check.

He eyed it doubtfully. "Wow. That's a lot of money," he said.

She wondered why such a strong note of irony vibrated in his voice. She did not know that a week before he had received a check for almost three times that amount from the School of Law at Princeton for three half-day lectures.

"And this is a copy of my father's file on the case," she said, laying a folder on his desk. "It will tell you everything we know about the Bachelors."

He didn't bother to open it. He kept staring at the check and smiling. "You'll be hearing from me within a week, Miss Fitzjames," he said, looking up from the check to her.

They should be such ordinary brown eyes, she thought in exasperation. *Why aren't they?* She suddenly remembered where she had seen eyes like that before—a male wolf at the Stone Zoo. And she remembered an old folk saying: "Never look a wolf in the eyes, for he will steal your soul forever."

Shaken, she made her good-bye as businesslike as possible, but when she left, it took all her considerable willpower not to flee like one pursued.

Eli looked at the closed door after she left. Again he fought the overwhelming desire to reach for a cigarette. Why had he done such a damn fool thing? He was halfway through the book on computer crime, and the deadline was closing in. The book meant money, quite a lot of money. So why was he going on a wild-goose chase to Vermont?

Because the girl amused him, he thought. Yes, he found her amusing. And he liked the idea of taking this plain-talking Boston intellectual down a peg or two. She might make an interesting conquest. If he had to call her up to Vermont, he might take the trouble to seduce her. It'd probably do her good. He'd never had a Harvard girl before. His taste ran to well-rounded blondes with empty heads and pliant wills. Harvard. Yes, that was something new. He wondered what his old friends in Cellblock 5 would think of that.

P.J. FOUND HERSELF mercifully alone in the elevator that glided toward the ground floor of the building in which Holder had his office. She was shaking and felt faint for the first time in her life.

Only once before had she played out such a scene, acted or spoken in such a way. She blushed to recall it. She had been part of a small group protesting a company dumping toxic wastes into the water system. When the evening shift of workers came on the job, some of them had begun by shouting rude epithets at the protestors, then ended by being rough. They made the mistake of laying hands on a fragile, elderly lady, a retired librarian from a small Boston college. At the sight of two large men converging on one small, harmless and high-minded woman of seventy, P.J. had heard that same snap in her head.

She had knocked one man down with her purse and slapped the other across the face so hard he had actually backed away in fright. She had been arrested, charged and fined. Her father, a lifelong pacifist, had been appalled, and Clarence, her lover then, had said it was a sign that she was a minefield of repressed psychological problems: who knew what else might be lurking down there in her subconscious, ready to explode? She herself hadn't known that so much passion had been buried in her all those years, and it had frightened her.

Now Eli Holder had triggered the same well-repressed urges. He had brought out the worst in her, and perversely, the worst in her was what he had finally responded to. He had snubbed her, bullied her, insulted her, until she hardly knew what she was saying or doing. He had also frightened her in a subtle and incomprehensible way.

And he was *attractive*, she thought, which made things worse. Those slightly mismatched and not terribly distinguished features worked together much better than they should.

The Harvard Business School had given her an enviable education. But she suddenly realized it hadn't prepared her in the least for a man like Eli Holder.

And his remarks about her wanting to be the son her father never had had grated—as had his gibes about her hair and clothing. Her one lover, Clarence, had flung the same charge at her after brooding about it for the two uneasy years of their affair, and it had hurt. He had also grumpily accused her of hiding behind her causes and of shying away from being a real woman. When their relationship had reached that final, crumbling stage, Clarence had sniped that people in P.J.'s family couldn't commit themselves to people, only to issues. To be a Fitzjames, he'd insisted, was to be a head remote from and barely aware of the body beneath it.

The idea of living with Clarence had been cozy and comfortable, but as soon as he was moved in, he was constantly—if unexcitingly—amorous. Sex hadn't been an issue with her previous boyfriend, Michael, but then, of course, their long relationship had ended when Michael went off to become a priest.

With Clarence she had taken the plunge and been disappointed. She kept waiting for things to get better, but they did not. At last she decided sex was the world's most overrated form of recreation. This conclusion made Clarence so sullen he finally sought solace among the livelier female undergraduates of Boston, and P.J. asked him to leave. She missed him. She did not miss sex at all.

Her parents, after all, had loved each other, but there was little, if any, sexual contact between them in their later years. Her mother's long illness had precluded it for one thing; for another, both believed love was a matter of mutual commitment and companionship, not happily frolicking hormones. In the name of inquiry and open-mindedness, P.J. had tried a sexual relationship with Clarence and found it wanting. After that unhappy fiasco she had made up her mind she could live a full and happy life without such nonsense.

Why did Eli Holder make her doubt that eminently sensible decision? Why, in fact, did he make her think about it at all? Why did he make her doubt everything about herself, including the wisdom of trying to retrieve the money that rightfully belonged to SOS?

She exited the elevator briskly, but her knees felt a bit weak. *Never look into the eyes of the wolf,* she thought again. *He will steal your soul. Forever.*

Chapter Two

The next day P.J. tried to slip into the offices of SOS unnoticed. She felt guilty about trying to reopen the Fordyce case without the awareness or approval of the foundation. If the higher powers found out about it, she would be severely reprimanded, possibly even fired. SOS did not believe in vigilante justice. The knowledge of what she had done made her distinctly uneasy.

Illogically she felt even more uneasy about the new blue shirtwaist dress and matching pumps she wore. For some reason that she kept telling herself had nothing to do with Eli Holder and his snide remarks, she had braved the hordes in Filene's Department Store. She kept telling herself that it wouldn't hurt to have a little variety in her wardrobe. It was a perfectly normal impulse, she kept telling herself.

She had never thought much about the way she dressed or her sensible haircut. Fully a quarter of the professional women in Boston sported the same kind of conservative uniform. It didn't mean they were masculine or trying to be masculine but simply that, like many Bostonians, they opted for an understated look. Her own mother had dressed exactly the same way, with the identical easy-to-manage short haircut. The clothes were sturdy, serviceable and never went out of fashion. The haircut was eminently suitable for the woman on the go.

But it certainly wasn't against the law to buy a new dress, P.J. kept telling herself. Or new shoes. What really bothered her was that she had somehow ended up in Filene's jewelry department getting her ears pierced. Maybe the haircut wouldn't look so boyish if she wore earrings. Now her earlobes smarted and tingled from the gold studs, and she felt unnatural and foolish. She kept telling herself none of it had anything to do with Eli Holder. Of course it didn't. That would almost be like admitting the man had hurt her feelings or that she cared in the least what he thought.

She had almost scuttled unnoticed to her office when Henry Emerson, the foundation director, spotted and cornered her.

"My, my, my," said Henry, looking her up and down. "A new look. Very becoming. That dress brings out the blue in your eyes. What brought this on?"

He flashed his most genial smile, which, as usual, was a bit too genial. Henry was fiftyish and the only male member of the staff flamboyant enough to wear a sports coat, although, of course, it was an extremely conservative one. Since his job consisted mostly of trying to wheedle money from people to augment the scanty coffers of SOS, his personality had become ingratiation itself.

"Earrings, even." Henry grinned, radiating beams of sunshine. "Just what's up, P.J.? Have you finally found a man who meets your impossibly high standards?"

P.J. blushed, despising herself for it. "Of course not," she said airily. "I just like a little change, that's all."

"Well, it's a lovely change," oozed Henry in his fondest voice. "And one of these days, young lady—" he shook a plump finger lovingly at her "—you're going to break down and give the male sex a chance. Why don't you show your new self to that handsome young man in the advertising department? I'll bet his eyes would pop!"

P.J. wrestled down the urge to retort, *Because the handsome young man in the advertising department is a flaming gay, Henry. And you're the only one who doesn't know, bless your heart.*

Instead, she smiled feebly. "My burning ambition is to be an old maid, Henry. I'm perfectly happy the way I am."

"Now, now, now!" Henry chortled in admonition, but he let her make her escape. She entered her tiny office, which was next to that of the foundation's lawyer, Gary Wilson, the dour man who had replaced her father. Gary was not a pleasant person or even a very good lawyer. He had simply been the only one willing to work for the meager salary SOS paid.

She sat down at her cluttered desk and sighed. Henry's perpetual jolliness sometimes nibbled at her nerves but never so sharply as that morning. What was wrong with her?

Why was it so earthshaking for her to buy a new dress? And get her ears pierced? She touched the left stud gingerly and muttered, "Ouch!"

Rats, she thought in frustration, it was because of that damned Eli Holder. He'd made her feel like a dowdy frump or a transvestite or something. In less than half an hour he'd reopened every wound that Clarence had inflicted in two years of living together. He'd filled her with a defiant, irrational urge to show the world that she wasn't some sexless freak and that she could be as feminine as anybody. Still, it wasn't as if she'd gone out and bought some sexy frivolous thing. But she fervently wished she hadn't got her ears pierced. They hurt.

She began to sort through the stacks of paper on her desk, then stopped to glance with sad affection at the last snapshot taken of her father. How he had aged in those seven years since her mother's death, she thought, shaking her head. And how hard he had slaved on the Fordyce case. So hard it had killed him.

Well, she thought grimly, turning her swivel chair to the typing table, the only thing she was going to think about Eli Holder from now on was that he was the one man who might be able to get the money back for SOS. She was paying him a veritable fortune to do it, and she prayed he could come up with some results. Heaven knew he was nasty enough to shake information out of almost anybody.

She starting drafting what she thought of as one of her begging letters. She had a list of New England artists she had to beseech to donate artwork to be reproduced on the merchandise the subcorporation hoped to sell. If Holder didn't get the four million dollars back, she and the rest of the staff would probably be out on the streets of Cambridge with tin cups, begging in earnest.

ELI HOLDER RECLINED on the king-size bed in the finest room in the finest hotel in Leaftree, Vermont. The hotel was the Ivory Castle, a Victorian monster so overdone its excess approached magnificence. The Ivory Castle also, as Eli knew, happened to be the headquarters of the Bachelors' Club.

He was rereading the case file that the girl had given him. Her father was a damned good lawyer, he thought, examining the documents. The problem was just that he hadn't been a criminal lawyer. Still, he and his blue-eyed daughter just might have a point. Eli possessed a reliable sixth sense: it was signaling strongly that the Bachelors had probably pulled off a very neat scam indeed. Whether he could prove it was another matter.

He read the notes on the Bachelors themselves. Superficially respectable, something unsavory lurked, with a faint stink, beneath the surface. There was Clive, the retired dentist who drank too much. There was Dirkson, an elderly playboy who thought himself a poet. Eli read a copy of one of his poems and winced. Good thing Dirkson was loaded. He'd never make it on his writing talent. Then there was Bangor, who'd inherited a fortune in a maple syrup company and had gambled most of it away. And finally, there was the doctor, Parmenter, who, gossip had it, had lost a damaging malpractice suit, and possibly more than one. The puzzling thing was that there were no documented facts on the case, only the rumor.

The sixth sense seemed keener when Eli was reading about Parmenter. He tapped the doctor's name lightly with the end of his pencil. "Parmenter," he said to himself. "Parmenter."

This might be more interesting than he'd thought. And if it turned out he couldn't help the girl, he'd probably give her her money back.

He'd never considered returning a fee before, and the notion gave him a rather pleasant sensation. Almost as if he were a nice guy. He might do it. Being a nice guy would be a novelty. And he'd decided not to try to seduce her. She'd be too troublesome and probably no fun, anyway. A nice enough kid, but too uptight.

He shut the file and got up from the bed. He'd go down to the bar for a midmorning potation, just to give the old sixth sense a little alcoholic boost. Besides, there was a barmaid who looked as if she knew a thing or two or maybe a thousand, and she'd given him the eye when he checked in. She was blond and well-rounded but about fifteen years older than she was trying to look.

He sighed. A man in his position sometimes had to make sacrifices. He thought of the blonde's hard face, sighed again and went out to do his duty.

P.J. SPENT A LONG DAY polishing her begging letter and typing copies. She also had to consult four times with Gary Wilson, the new lawyer, on the legal intricacies of establishing subcorporations. Gary was as grumpy as Henry was

overwhelmingly jolly. He was a thin, balding man in his
forties, with a crooked nose and large pointed ears like a
bat's. He was an acolyte in some obscure Eastern religious
group that he claimed gave him inner peace and serenity.
P.J. wondered how evil his temper had been before he found
peace and serenity, then decided she didn't want to think
about it.

She had a late supper at an Italian restaurant with her
friend Barlowe. She and Barlowe had graduated together,
and they liked each other because neither made any demands on the other. P.J. didn't want any more relation-
ships like the one she'd had with Clarence, and Barlowe
freely admitted that most modern women frightened him.
''They're sexual barracudas,'' he'd said with a shudder.
''They expect you to be a combination of Casanova and an
acrobat. What's happened to women? I'm seriously thinking of becoming a monk.''

Barlowe was neurotic and timid and sweet and intelligent
and funny, and P.J. liked him a lot. But that night she kept
looking at him over the flame of the candle on their table.
His eyes were exactly the same light shade of brown as Eli
Holder's. But they didn't look like the eyes of a wolf. Barlowe's looked like those of a pet gerbil.

He walked her home—their apartments were not far apart
in Cambridge—then wended his way back to his bachelor
digs, a lonely figure in the autumn night.

Poor Barlowe, she thought in sympathy. She looked
around in appreciation at her own small apartment. Barlowe had no homemaking instincts whatsoever, and although he made a good salary, his apartment always gave
the impression it housed a starving artist instead of a suc-
cessful accountant.

P.J.'s apartment was furnished in what she thought of as
typical Cambridge chic—a lot of mismatched antiques that
somehow looked good together, a lot of ferns, a lot of

books, a lot of records, a lot of posters and one genuine Picasso print on which she had spent an entire month's salary.

Eustace, her cat, an overweight neutered orange tiger, rubbed against her legs and purred sensuously of his desire for dinner. She changed her clothes, fed him, then, bejeaned and in a faded Harvard sweatshirt, curled up on her lumpy antique love seat to read a law book on subcorporations so that Gary Wilson would scowl at her less often.

Ella Fitzgerald's voice floated comfortingly from the stereo, and Eustace was making himself useful as a foot warmer, albeit an uncomfortably heavy one.

But P.J. had trouble concentrating on the dull book. She kept wondering what Eli Holder was up to. She hoped he wasn't spending her money just lolling around in upper Vermont, drinking expensive Scotch that she was paying for and enjoying the scenery.

ELI HOLDER WASN'T enjoying the scenery at all. In fact, the scenery was pretty pathetic. He set down the half-empty glass of cheap gin and thanked the Fates for giving him a system that could hold any amount of liquor, no matter how bad.

He also thanked them for giving Velma, the hard-faced blond barmaid, the kind of head that cheap gin hits like a sledgehammer. She had just been getting seriously amorous when she passed out on the couch.

He looked down at her and shook his head. Alas, poor Velma, he thought. Her husband was a long-distance trucker who neglected her, and she'd been out for a little fun.

He couldn't afford to be seen with her—he didn't want anybody to know he was asking questions. It had been easy enough to get Velma to invite him to her little bungalow, which was on the far edge of town and semi-isolated—all the better, Eli suspected, for Velma to entertain discreetly.

She had supplied the gin—which tasted as if it could clean bathtubs—the soft lights and what she euphemistically called mood music.

He had waited till Velma was nicely marinated to start asking questions—questions about the Bachelors' Club, questions about Fordyce, questions about the missing witness to the signing of the will, questions about the hotel itself. Questions, if Eli had judged her condition correctly, she wouldn't remember in the morning.

About the Bachelors and Fordyce she hadn't been much help. About the missing witness she knew little. "He just took off." She hiccoughed. "One day he was there. The next day he waddn't . . . wasn't."

But about the hotel Velma had some highly interesting information. Her mother had worked in it and so had her grandfather. Velma was a veritable archivist when it came to the history of the Ivory Castle. So much so that he bent and gave her a little of what she'd wanted all evening—a kiss on the forehead. Unfortunately, she was in no state to appreciate it.

And fortunately, she wouldn't remember whether her desires had been gratified or not. He decided she would be happier if she thought they had.

He found a notebook and a pen and wrote her a note.

Velma, sweetheart,
Can't remember it ever being better than with you. I think you've worn me out for the next three weeks. Thanks for a beautiful evening with a beautiful lady. The least I can do is pay for the drinks.
                                                    E.B.H.

He put a fifty-dollar bill under the gin bottle. He didn't think Velma would object.

He looked at the wasted woman on the couch and covered her with a tattered afghan. He seemed to be full of odd gentlemanly impulses that night, and he didn't know why. Twenty years ago he would have used a woman like Velma, then walked out the door, never looking back.

He shrugged, put on his suit coat and went out to his rented BMW. Now was the time to go back to the Ivory Castle and play Eagle Scout, do a little exploring.

"Sleep soundly, Velma," he said when he got behind the wheel. "And God bless your granddad for knowing that hotel so well."

He wondered if P. J. Fitzjames was sleeping the sleep of the just in Boston or if she was worried about what she was getting into. Untidy little messes such as this one about contested wills could get a young woman into more trouble than she could imagine. He shook his head. No, she could not begin to know. She would be sleeping soundly, her conscience clear. She was, after all, a Bostonian with a cause.

He smiled crookedly to himself. He could almost see her place in his mind. She'd have a cramped little apartment in Cambridge—it had to be Cambridge, he was sure of that. It would be full of books and records and ferns and posters. And a cat. A girl like her would have a cat. One with a funny name. And she probably slept in pajamas. White ones with blue stripes.

Why am I thinking about that? he wondered, driving the winding road back to the Ivory Castle. He shook his head ruefully. *Good question.* If he was lucky, he was about to set the wheels of trouble in motion, then steer them to his advantage as expertly as he had done in the old days. Ah, trouble—he did love it so. It gave him more pressing issues to ponder than what Junior wore to bed.

P.J. GOT UP after a surprisingly good night's sleep, rubbed her eyes, then padded into the kitchenette, still wearing her blue-and-white-striped pajamas. She had slept so deeply she was still groggy, had almost bumped her head on a hanging fern and had almost stepped on Eustace, who was trying to sweet-talk her into an extra large breakfast.

Her first coherent thought, after a cup of herbal tea helped chase the last wisps of sleep away, was *He hasn't called yet.* It sent an odd wave of disappointment through her.

But it was too early for Holder to have found anything, she told herself. Maybe he wasn't even in Vermont yet. But suddenly, as Eustace rubbed provocatively against her pajama leg in a bribe for more milk, she had a strong intuition he *would* call and that he would have found something. She didn't like him, she didn't completely trust him, but she had a peculiar blind faith in him.

She might even have to meet him in Vermont. She shivered at the thought, although the September morning was warm and bright.

For the first time she began to suspect that getting Fordyce's money back to SOS was going to be more complicated than simply hiring a man tough and smart enough to know how to do it. He would want her help. How Holder expected her to help, she had no idea.

She realized she had to prepare Henry for the possibility that she might have to take a short leave. And that meant she was going to have to do something she had little practice in and little stomach for. She was going to have to lie.

ELI SPENT the morning lying. It was something he'd practiced often in the past, and he was good at it. Lying, of course, was difficult work, but it reminded him of the old days, and he was enjoying the nostalgia.

The first person he had to lie to was Velma. She'd nabbed him when he strolled through the lobby, grabbing his sleeve. She looked incredibly hung over but happy and eager in spite of it.

"Psst," she said, "come sit at the bar a minute. I want to talk to you."

He gave her his crooked smile, followed her into the bar and sat down.

"You want a drink?" she asked, smiling through the pain of her headache. "Free. On the house."

"No, thanks," he murmured with a shake of his head. "You hold your liquor better than I do. I don't even want to see the stuff."

"Well, I could use a little hair of the dog that bit me," she admitted. "Don't tell, okay?"

He nodded in promise, then watched her pour a dollop of gin into a glass and drink it straight. He winced slightly.

"There," she said, wiping her lips with the back of her hand. "Better. Say, listen, I want to tell you you were *incredible* last night. I mean, *incredible*."

He shrugged with feigned modesty. "I was all right," he conceded. "You were the one who was incredible." It was, he thought cynically, probably the fifty dollars that Velma found incredible since she couldn't possibly remember what she'd done to deserve it.

"Well," she said, "I think you're incredible, and you think I'm incredible, so why don't you come over again? Like tonight?"

"Velma," he said gently, taking her hand between his, "I don't think we can top what we've already had . . . and I, well, I'm the kind of guy who . . . can't get involved. You know? I'm sort of insecure. I . . . hate to tell you this, but right now I'm not very stable. Business pressures. That kind of thing. I'm here because I'm on the edge of a nervous collapse. I just . . . can't afford to get involved in something new . . . and something that might, well, hurt you.''

"Gee," said Velma, her tired eyes widening. "A nervous breakdown? You?"

"I'm . . . a lot more sensitive than I may seem," Eli lied, staring down seriously at his hands holding hers.

"Oh, gee, yeah," she replied. "I can sense these things. I could tell you're a real sensitive person."

He patted her hand, then released it. "Thank you for understanding," he said softly, not meeting her eyes. He sat for a moment, looking as sensitive as he could.

"And," he continued, "there's somebody else. Another woman. She'll be here soon, in fact. I'm afraid if she ever dreamed about what happened between us last night, she'd never forgive me. And I couldn't bear to hurt her, either. So I think we should be grateful for what we had—and from now on just be . . . good friends."

Velma looked disappointed but admiring. "You're an honest guy," she said at last.

"I try to be," Eli said, again with great humility.

"I like that," she replied with a brisk nod. "And you know what? I'll be proud to be your friend. 'Cause you know what? You're a real gentleman."

"I . . . try to be," he repeated. He cast his eyes downward in the spirit of humble decorousness.

The next person Eli lied to was Harfinger, the tall, unctuous manager of the Ivory Castle.

"Yes?" Harfinger smirked across the desk. "How may I help you?"

"I'm here to rest," Eli said, fingering the buttons of his vest in false nervousness. "I don't want any calls put through to me. None whatsoever. A man deserves time to himself once in a while."

Harfinger nodded enthusiastically, still smirking. "He certainly does, he certainly does," he agreed, scribbling a note that his guest was under no circumstances to be disturbed.

"There's a great deal of pressure when other people's fortunes are in your hands," Eli muttered, fidgeting as he adjusted his silk tie. "They don't understand the responsibility. By the way, do you have a copy of the *Wall Street Journal* around?"

The smirk seemed to freeze on Harfinger's narrow face. Eli admired how the man managed to keep it in place. "Indeed we do," Harfinger said carefully. "But, er..."

"Yes?" Eli looked at him in innocent expectation.

"But," Harfinger said through the pasted-on smile, "you seem to be already carrying a copy." He nodded politely at the newspaper clamped possessively in Eli's left hand.

Eli smiled, conveying slight embarrassment. "So I am," he chuckled in chagrin, then patted the paper self-consciously. "As I said, I need a rest. Wall Street can eat a man alive."

"Oh, I *know*, sir," said Harfinger, as sympathetic as he could be.

"Oh, and another thing," Eli said, fiddling with his tie again. "If the hotel organizes any kind of recreation for the guests—volleyball games, foliage tours, parties where people wear funny hats, that sort of thing—please don't include me. I need time to myself."

"Oh, *no*, sir," Harfinger assured him. "The management of the Ivory Castle has always considered organized activities for the guests to be—excuse the expression—tacky. We think our guests deserve unstructured time during their stay. Ever so much more restful."

"Thank God there are people like you who still have a modicum of taste left," Eli replied in what seemed to be sincere gratitude. "And I trust you host no conventions—no organizations coming in, crowding up the place, making merry. I couldn't stand that."

Harfinger laughed indulgently. "Only the Bachelors' Club, sir. But there are only four of them, and they only meet twice a week in the library. The quietest of gentlemen, I assure you, sir. They'll be no disturbance."

"Disturbance or not, when do they meet? I want no part of any such thing. I don't even want to see them. I'll avoid the library like the very plague, no matter how gentlemanly they are."

"Mondays and Fridays, sir." Harfinger smirked. "And the library is theirs from nine to eleven in the evening. You couldn't get in if you wanted to. You're quite safe. Although, as I say, the old gentlemen are quiet and harmless."

"Fine," Eli said with nervous grimness, "as long as they're quiet and harmless far away from me."

"Oh, they keep to themselves, all right," Harfinger said, nodding, anxious to assure his guest. "They hardly ever mingle with the regular guests."

"Good," said Eli. "And thank you for your consideration. Here's a little bonus for insuring my comfort." He handed Harfinger a crisp one-hundred-dollar bill.

"Oh, sir, I couldn't," Harfinger objected, but his eyes sparkled greedily as he looked at the bill.

"I insist," said Eli, laying the bill on the desk. Then he walked away, looking slightly distracted, like a business genius whose labors have driven him nearly to the edge. The name he had written in the hotel register was Elwyn Brooks Holderman, and he had put down as his occupation venture capitalist. His sixth sense had assured him such a ruse might prove helpful. He didn't know how. He simply trusted his instincts. And Miss Goodboddy had been instructed to call the hotel for Elwyn B. Holderman at least once an hour, giving credence to the charade.

Harfinger had confirmed what Velma had told him. The Bachelors met twice a week in the library. Perfect, he thought, heading back to his room. Perfect. A library, he had discovered last night, is not always the quiet sanctuary people think. The right kind of library, such as the one in the Ivory Castle, could be delightfully treacherous.

In his room he gathered his swim gear to head down to the heated indoor pool. Velma had said one of the Bachelors, Dirkson, the would-be playboy and poet, spent more time at the Ivory Castle than did the others. He breakfasted on the patio, and Eli had no trouble spotting him. He was about sixty-five, slightly obese and wore a jaunty blond toupee that clashed with his gray sideburns. Velma had said Dirkson often hung around the pool, hoping to spot nubile young things in bikinis. Eli would do a bit of lounging himself, in the same spirit of surveillance. Only his quarry would be Dirkson himself.

There was only one woman in a bikini in the pool, and she was the sort who should stay clothed even in the bathtub. She was so thin Eli wondered if she had anorexia. But that didn't keep Dirkson from watching her hungrily over his book of sonnets. When he got tired of ogling her, he feasted his eyes on the plumper dowagers who splashed about in their skirted suits and bathing caps. Female flesh was female flesh to Dirkson. That, Eli thought with satisfaction, will come in handy. By a man's weakness you shall get to him, then gig him like a fish.

At last Eli rose from the lounge chair, shed his terry jacket, strolled to the diving board, executed a perfect jackknife and began to swim lengths.

The women stole glances at his muscles as he stroked through the water. The warmth of their appreciation seemed to raise the pool temperature a degree or two. Eli didn't take much notice. He was thinking. A plan was taking rough but pleasant shape.

He hoped Junior had enough smarts to be paving the way for a graceful exit from SOS if he needed her. He should probably call her, but she was such an uppity little thing it would do her good to let her stew. She might be a Harvard grad, but he could still teach her a thing or two—including how to wait. Making women wait for what they wanted was another of his specialties. He was excellent at it.

P.J. WONDERED IRRITABLY, *Why doesn't Holder call?* He could at least let her know if he'd reached Vermont. For all she knew, he was there doing nothing more strenuous than lounging around a heated pool, lecherously eyeing women in bathing suits.

It's too soon, she told herself for the hundredth time. She tried to concentrate on her marketing study on the feasibility of selling buttons and note cards to raise funds for SOS. Such items reaped nickel-and-dime profits, but SOS needed every nickel and dime it could get.

The office seemed more cramped than usual that day and more nerve-racking. Gary Wilson rankled most of all. Trying to explain the legal intricacies of subcorporations, he had snarled repeatedly at her. He kept appearing in her office like some grumpy spirit of doom. He was still there, in fact, but he wasn't speaking to her.

Gary's explanations were always rambling and garbled, and when she didn't understand his point about Tax Exemption 1556-C, he had snapped unmercifully.

"Please, Gary," she'd said as evenly as she could manage. "Give me a break. I'm a business major, not a lawyer."

"Any decent business major should understand this form," Gary had shrieked. "Oh! You've disrupted my serenity so much I'm going to have to say an emergency mantra!"

With no further ado he had plunked himself on the linoleum by P.J.'s file cabinet, entwined his legs in some impossible yoga position and begun to chant something that sounded suspiciously like "Banana, banana, banana."

P.J. sighed and began to analyze statistics about bumper stickers. She still had to type her quota of begging letters—she had set her goal at twenty a day.

Henry Emerson stuck his benevolent face through the door. "How's it going?" he asked with his ever-present smile. The smile drooped a bit when he saw Gary cross-legged on the floor, his eyes squeezed shut, furiously chanting, "Banana, banana, banana."

"What's wrong with him?" Henry asked, looking slightly alarmed.

"I made him so mad he had to say his mantra to get his serenity back," P.J. said, rolling her eyes at the word "serenity. "Look," she said rather desperately, "could we step out in the hall to talk a minute?"

"Certainly," answered Henry, his smile still stiff with apprehension. He couldn't seem to take his eyes off Gary.

P.J. slipped out the door and closed it behind her. She took a deep breath, knowing she had to have time off if Holder needed her. She was going to have to lie, but with Gary acting the way he was, at least the lie would seem plausible.

"Henry," she said, hoping she sounded convincing, "I...the pressure's getting to me. I...it's getting to us all, I know, but I'm starting to have, uh, migraines. Yes, migraine headaches."

"Oh, dear," said Henry, not grinning at all. He clasped his plump hands together, entwining his fingers. "Are you sure?"

She racked her memory. Clarence used to have migraines. He had claimed P.J.'s lack of enthusiasm for sex was the cause. "Uh, yes," she said nervously. "Uh, pain...very intense pain. Uh, nausea...and, uh, flashing lights. I see lights flashing before my eyes. Uh, that sounds like a migraine, doesn't it?'' she finished hopefully.

"It certainly does," Henry said with deep concern. "Have you seen a doctor?"

"Yes," she replied, feeling lower and more morally vile with every word. "He said if it got any worse...I should probably take...a few days off?"

She looked up at him almost fearfully. Everyone at SOS was overworked, and she knew Henry really couldn't spare her.

"If you need time off, you *take* time off," he said, smiling his kindest smile. "I can't have one of my best heads going around hurting, now, can I?"

Oh, dear, she thought, he was just as understanding as Holder had predicted.

"They may not get any worse," she said guiltily. After all, Holder might not need her at all. She was becoming doubtful again.

"If they do, take time off," Henry insisted. "I mean it, dear."

"Thanks," she said, feeling as if she had done something extraordinarily slimy.

When she went back into the office, Gary's eyes were open, and he was sitting in her extra chair. He glowered at her, sheer malice glittering on his face.

"I am serene again," he snapped. "Let's get on with this, shall we?"

Oh, Eli, she thought in desperation. *Call me! Please! In the name of all that's holy, call!*

BACK IN HIS ROOM at the Ivory Castle, Eli cast a bored glance out the window at the famously flamboyant Vermont foliage. Every year he wondered why everybody made such a fuss about a bunch of dying leaves.

He'd put in a good morning's work. He intended to put in a good afternoon's. There was an elderly woman, a Mrs. Murdock, who was a full-time resident at the Ivory Castle. One look at her sour, critical face and Eli had her pegged as a devout collector of gossip. And people who hoarded gossip, if cultivated correctly, gleefully shared it.

He would have to charm the old biddy, but he was a man cut out for such a job.

But there were some jobs a man wasn't cut out for, jobs that needed a woman's touch. It was time to make a phone call to bring in female reinforcement. But not Junior. Not yet. He smiled his crooked smile, picked up the phone and began to dial.

"Hello?" said a woman's voice.

"Cleo, darling," he said, honest pleasure in his voice for the first time that day. "I'm in Leaftree, Vermont, and I'm overwhelmed with desire for your blond and beautiful company."

That was no lie, either. Cleo was blond and beautiful and, as one of his larcenous uncles used to say of a well-proportioned woman, stacked like the Great Wall of China.

"Eli, you're always overwhelmed with desire." Cleo laughed. She had a sexy voice, and her laugh matched it. "It's got you into trouble before. It's going to get you into trouble again."

He grinned. "You coming down here or not, angel cake?"

"Could I ever resist you, Eli? Of course I'll be down."

Ah, he thought as he hung up the phone, what a woman. He changed into tennis clothes to go down to the patio to the joyless task of charming old Mrs. Murdock.

He wondered idly how long he should wait before giving Junior a call. Certainly not until Cleo, in all her lusciousness, had appeared and departed. Let the little Boston

Brahminette learn a few ways of the world—her turn would come soon enough.

P.J. HAD LOCKED her office door and tried to eat the tasteless sandwich she had brought with her to work. As she struggled to dislodge the whole wheat clod from the roof of her mouth, she fought down the urge to cry. Fretfully she rubbed one of her sore earlobes.

Why doesn't he call? she wondered again. *Why?* Was he even in Leaftree yet? What was he *doing*? Probably, she thought with maximum grimness, he was hooking up with some local beauty and having a fine vacation, complete with fling, at her expense.

AND IN PUTNEY, VERMONT, a lovely blonde named Cleo packed her suitcase, putting in a goodly supply of lacy lingerie, including an absolutely sinful negligee Eli had given her the year before. *Eli,* Cleo thought fondly. *What was that devil up to now?* She smiled. That's what she liked about him. She could never tell what he'd do next. Never. He was always one slightly crooked step ahead of everyone. That, of course, was the secret of his truly dangerous charm.

Chapter Three

Eli didn't call P.J. until two days later. She almost collapsed with relief at the sound of his brusque hello, then went rigid with tension, fearful that he had either no news or bad news for her.

He wasted no time on preliminaries. "Get up here. Tomorrow," he ordered. "I may be on to something. I've made reservations for you at an inn called the Nutmeg Peddler. You're registering under the name Penny Jameson."

"Penny Jameson?" P.J. replied in horror. "A false name? Isn't that illegal?"

He didn't bother to answer. "Take a plane to Putney, rent a car. Don't say you're from Boston, say you're from Amherst. You're a secretary on vacation."

"Amherst? A secretary? Is it legal for me to do that, Holder?"

He ignored her again. "If you see me on the street, you don't know me. Got that? We've never seen each other before. I'll get in touch with you. And go out to Filene's or someplace and buy something more frivolous than that junior-executive suit you run around in. I'm going to need you looking like a girl, not Peter Pan."

The remark about her clothes galled her, reminded her of the stupid shirtwaist dress she'd bought and that her ears still throbbed from the horrid little studs. "This is going to cost me a fortune, Holder," she said. "I'm not made of money, you know. It's taking practically every cent I've got to pay you."

"Hey," he said, his voice dripping with mockery, "it's for a good cause, isn't it, Junior? You've got a lot of fish in the ocean to keep happy."

He sounded so sarcastic P.J. wrestled down the desire to hang up on him. She could have spared herself the struggle. Before she realized it, he had hung up on her.

"Son of a—" she started to say but bit off the last word and simply glared at the phone.

What did he have in mind for her, anyway? she wondered nervously. And she wondered with even greater anxiety why she felt so strangely excited about meeting him in Vermont.

Squirming with guilt, she called Henry Emerson at home and told him the migraines were worse; she didn't know how much time off she might need.

Henry, as befitted a man who ran a philanthropic organization, was charitable about the whole thing, although she could sense the worry in his voice. Things seemed to get rockier every day at SOS. That day they'd gotten word that the pilot whales were starting to beach themselves on the Rhode Island coast again. SOS was helping fund the study to find out why it kept happening, but money was running frighteningly short.

Then she called Barlowe and told him she had to go away. Would he feed Eustace and water her ferns? Barlowe said he would, then, nervous and concerned, asked her what was wrong.

She told the migraine lie again, hating herself for it. Barlowe was one of her best friends. The more deeply she got involved with Holder, the more lies she had to spin, and now he had her impersonating a secretary under an assumed name. What next? Breaking and entering? Arson? Heaven only knew what.

But she squared her shoulders, got into her street clothes and headed for Filene's, where, blessedly, the sales never stopped. All the time she fought the bargain-crazed crowd, however, she couldn't stop worrying. *What does he want with me? What? How much trouble am I going to get into before this is over?*

ELI SETTLED BACK on the king-size bed, putting his arms behind his head. Junior was going to hit the roof when she saw the Nutmeg Peddler. It was the worst tourist dive in town. Too bad, but that's the way it had to be. His intuition told him it could be important to his plans.

Withered and sour old Mrs. Murdock had been a real dream girl. He'd been tempted to kiss her rouged and wrinkled cheek—nasty as the experience might be.

He'd played a quick game of tennis with the hotel's resident instructor, then retired to the patio, drifting casually toward Mrs. Murdock, who was glowering out at the courts from beneath an enormous sun hat covered with straw flowers. Beside her, on a rhinestone leash, was a miniature white poodle that looked as old and unforgiving as its owner.

Eli had stopped to admire it. "What a lovely dog," he said, as if awed by the thing's beauty. He loathed poodles, especially little white ones with ribbons in their topknots.

Mrs. Murdock and the dog both looked up at him suspiciously. She was sipping a large coconut-shaped glass of something that looked potent. Ah, he thought with satisfaction, if the old girl had a bit of a buzz on, his work would be all the easier.

"Lovely dog," he repeated. "What's its name? Would she let me pet her?"

"Foo-Foo," said Mrs. Murdock, still squinting critically at him. "She's a he. And he doesn't take to strangers."

"Oh, I'm no stranger to a beautiful dog." Eli smiled his most charming smile and sat in the lounger next to hers. "Come, Foo-Foo, pretty baby." He stretched out his hand to scratch the dog's wiry topknot.

I've befuddled better brains than yours, you canine goofball, he thought and began to fondle the dog's rather yellowed ears.

Foo-Foo looked offended at first, then blissful. He raised his head for more scratching and licked Eli's hand.

Ugh, thought Eli, but he cooed, "Izzim's pretty boy? Izzim's pretty little Foo-Foo puppy? Izzim's sweetie little fuzzy-wuzzy lovey boy?"

Lord, he thought, *this is the most disgusting goddamned excuse for a dog I've ever seen.*

Foo-Foo rolled onto his back to have his bulging stomach rubbed. Mrs. Murdock gave Eli a reappraising look. "Now that," she said in a gravelly voice, "is amazing. Foo-Foo is usually just his mama's baby. You are one of the few men I've ever seen who knows how to talk to a poodle."

"Well, he's such a *cute* poodle I just had to make friends with him." Eli smiled, rubbing the dog's blubbery belly.

"Say," he added, "what's that you're drinking? It looks delicious. I might order one myself. Could I buy you another? Since you're generous enough to share your dog?"

"It's called a Jamaican Jungle Juicer," said Mrs. Murdock, almost smiling back. He wasn't exactly a handsome man, but he had a certain charming élan about him that made her wish she were forty years younger. "And no, I guess I wouldn't mind another."

A Jamaican Jungle Juicer proved to be one of those pastel-colored drinks that tasted like syrup. Eli sipped it and fought back a grimace. He hated sweet drinks. "Ah, delicious," he lied.

"Aren't they?" asked Mrs. Murdock, almost flirtatiously. "I allow myself one every afternoon, but I guess for once I can be naughty and have two."

And after that things had been easy.

THINGS, P.J. THOUGHT dolefully, were not getting any easier. She looked around her tiny room in the Nutmeg Peddler and wondered how anyone had ever had the nerve to call the place an inn. Her room was no more than a cubbyhole crammed with rickety furniture that looked as if it had last resided in a junk shop. The dresser had a missing leg and was propped at a tilt on a broken brick.

The room smelled dirty, and there was an evil-looking stain running down the ancient wallpaper. She was sure the hole in the woodwork near the bed was the main entrance to a mouse home, or perhaps to a whole subdivision of mice. There was a washbasin with a leaking faucet and a permanent rust mark in the porcelain, but the rest of the bath facilities were down the hall, and she had to share them.

She was tired and nervous and unsure of herself. She had taken a commuter flight to Putney on a plane so small the passengers had to walk at a crouch all the way to their seats. Then she had rented a dented Ford compact and driven another hour before arriving at the uninviting premises of the Nutmeg Peddler.

Writing a false name and address on the hotel ledger had made her feel like a felon, and there was no word at the desk from Holder. She didn't know where he was, but if she'd had money to spare, she would have bet it all that he wasn't staying in a room like this one.

The one luxury her room did contain was an old black phone on a chipped night table. From the moment she'd entered, she'd watched the thing, as if it were some instrument of magic whose ring would restore her world to sanity. So far, she had been in the room for an hour, and the phone only squatted blackly on the table, mockingly silent.

She'd unpacked her suitcase, hung up her clothes and sat with distaste on the edge of the sagging single bed. Its spread was of a splotched graying green, the color and texture of bread mold, and she knew instinctively that the sheets hadn't been changed. There was a suspicious smear on the pillow slip, as if someone had swatted a large bug.

She couldn't believe the price she was paying for this squalid little cell, but then it was foliage season, which meant that the proprietor of the Nutmeg Peddler probably felt the influx of tourists entitled him to practice extortion to the limit.

She would like nothing better than to take a shower and a nap, but she was uneasy at the idea of a shared bathroom, and she really didn't want to recline on the disreputable-looking bed. She glared at the phone again, willing it to ring. It remained silent. She sighed unhappily.

She opened her briefcase and took out the FUTURE paperwork she had brought with her. She tried to sit at the ugly little desk that lurked in one corner of the room, but its spindly chair tilted drunkenly, and she feared it would give way under her. Besides, the desk, too, had a crooked leg and was propped with an old Boston telephone directory.

With reluctance she lowered herself onto the lumpy bed and, using her briefcase for a lap desk, tried to make sense of figures that had looked perfectly logical the day before. As she gingerly adjusted the pillow so the bug spot was facedown, she shuddered slightly. The statistics might just as well have been in Sanskrit.

Why couldn't Holder have left word at the desk for her? she wondered irritably. She got out her pocket calculator and began to try to add a column of numbers. Her stomach complained of hunger. The snack on the commuter flight had consisted of a small bag of tasteless peanuts and a watery cola. In her eagerness to get to Leaftree, she hadn't stopped for lunch. One glance at the greasy and cheerless cave that served the Nutmeg Peddler as a dining room had convinced her that anything she ordered there would be garnished with cockroaches. And she didn't dare go out for fear of missing Holder.

Damn the man, she thought, clearing the calculator because she had punched in a wrong number. Just what had she gotten herself involved in, anyway?

But when she remembered that the tall man with his slightly tilted wolfish eyes might—just might—be able to get SOS's four million dollars back, she felt a tingle of excitement so palpable it tickled her spine and shocked her complaining stomach into silence.

Or maybe I'm just crazy, she thought with a sudden lurch of fear. Maybe SOS's financial troubles and the Bachelors' Club's court victory and her father's death had robbed her of the precious power to reason, and she was embarked on a mad adventure that could lead only to disaster.

She normally had a highly disciplined mind. She tried to shake such confidence-sapping thoughts away. She looked at her statistics, rechecked them and neatly wrote down a number. She forced herself to concentrate on FUTURE and continue her calculations. But she kept making mistakes.

IF ELI'S CALCULATIONS weren't mistaken, and they usually weren't, the girl should have arrived at the Nutmeg Peddler about two hours ago. He hoped she'd had time to adjust to her cubicle in the roach ranch. He hadn't wanted to call her immediately. Let everything seem casual, natural, that was the ticket.

He glanced at his watch. It was four-thirty in the afternoon. Cleo, bless her, who'd left that morning, should have sent the package by now. Lazily he picked up the phone. It was time to give Junior a ring.

When the black phone finally shrilled, P.J. almost leaped off the sagging mattress from alarm and anticipation.

She snatched the receiver up before the second ring.

"Hello?" Again she hated her little-girl voice. It sounded breathless, and her heart was beating so hard her throat felt constricted.

"Hello, Penny," said Holder's amiably indifferent voice. "Glad you made it. How are the accommodations?"

Thank God, she thought, *he's called at last.* But the flippancy of his tone made her pulses thud with anger. She restrained the emotion.

"The accommodations are fine, thanks," she said as evenly as she could. She tried not to look at the nasty stain on the wallpaper. "The accommodations are wonderful. That's not important. Where are you? What's happening? What have you found out? What's going on, Holder?"

"I'm at the Ivory Castle." P.J. could envision his maddening crooked smile, his wolfish eyes. "And I've made loads of new friends. I've found out a lot—but nothing that would hold up in court. And I've got the classic good news-bad news for you."

"What good news?" she demanded. "What bad news?"

"The good news is I found your missing witness to the signing of the will—John Williams. The bad news is he's dead and has been for six months. He won't be telling us anything."

P.J. frowned and rubbed the space between her eyebrows. "*Both* witnesses to the will are dead?" she asked. "Doesn't that strike you as too much of a coincidence?"

"It strikes me as very tidy for the Bachelors. We're going to have to get lucky. And it may have to be tonight. This is almost getting interesting. I want you to meet me."

Her hand tightened on the receiver. "Meet you?" There was no reason for the thrill that uncurled up her spine. Her relationship with Holder was, she reminded herself, strictly business. He was, in fact, in her employ, a hireling. "Meet you where? When?"

"Seven-thirty," he replied. "Wear jeans and something dark. The occasion calls for basic black. Meet me at the west side of the pond, by the old icehouse. To get there take the path that starts about fifty feet behind the Nutmeg Peddler, between a grove of small maples and a tall birch next to a dead birch. Don't use a flashlight unless you have to. When the path forks the first time, go east. When it forks the second time, go north. Leave by the back door of the inn and try not to be seen. There'll be a package delivered for you at the desk just before five. There's a note in it. Read it carefully and do exactly as it says."

There was a beat of silence as she memorized the directions.

"Got it all?" he asked.

"Yes." She took a break, preparing to ask him why the secrecy? What package? Why the icehouse? Where were they going?

He cut her off before she could ask anything. "Good" was all he said, then hung up.

Damn! she thought, staring into the receiver mouthpiece. She wondered again about the package and why she was supposed to wear black. All she could think of was that black was for funerals. She hoped it wasn't going to be hers.

ELI LEANED BACK on the king-size bed and smiled. He had to hand it to Junior. She hadn't complained about her room, and she was quick to understand directions. Maybe she'd been a Girl Scout and was used to roughing it in a citified way.

He corrected himself—of course she had been a Girl Scout. He could see her, twelve years old, at the gangly stage, with a little boy's haircut even then. She would have been cute as hell and strangely lonely for a child.

For some reason he found the image disturbing, so he dismissed it. He resisted the desire to smoke half a cigarette. He inhaled deeply. The ghost of Cleo's perfume still lingered on the air. Ah, Cleo, he thought. There was a woman he could understand.

THE MOON SHONE DOWN, nearly full, and the long New England twilight gave the sky a soft and ghostly glow. P.J., clad in old jeans, a black sweatshirt and her battered Topsiders, made her way carefully down the leaf-strewn path, trying to keep Holder's directions clearly in mind. Thank heaven she had been a Girl Scout and had learned the rudiments of woodcraft. Picking her way through a darkening wood wasn't altogether new to her.

She tried to concentrate on setting her feet down softly, to make a minimum of noise. She concentrated furiously so that she wouldn't think of Holder. She wanted to kill him. It was the first time in her life she'd experienced the urge to kill, and its seductive power surprised her.

The package from Holder had arrived at the desk shortly before five, just as he'd said it would. It had come by Federal Express and was from Putney, and that puzzled her. The contents and the note had done more than puzzle her, they had appalled her.

Falsies? she had thought with horror and disgust when she'd gazed into the opened package. Why in the name of God had he sent her little foam rubber pads to slide into her bra? And a *wig*? And, just as inexplicably, a pair of cheap black gloves. The note instructed her to wear the falsies and carry the wig and gloves with her. The box also contained a black knit sailor's watch cap, with orders to wear it to the icehouse. What kind of melodramatic farce was Holder turning this whole thing into? She felt like someone who had accidentally slipped into a B movie about spies or cat burglars.

The falsies felt unnatural and foolish hovering against her small breasts, and they made her usually shapeless sweat-shirt jut out alarmingly. She felt like a *Playboy* model disguised as a second-story man, and she hated it, wondering if this was Holder's degrading idea of a joke. She found it all unfunny, insulting and humiliating, but there she was, carrying the stupid wig, a curly platinum-blond one in a dark canvas tote bag that bumped uncomfortably against the side of her knee as she picked her way through the leaves.

She came to the first fork and went east, than the second fork and went north. She hadn't used her small purse flash-light yet, and she was already shuddering at the thought of going back through those woods in the dead of night.

At last she came to the pond and saw the dilapidated limestone icehouse, looking forlorn and slightly sinister in the cold light of the moon. The place seemed deserted as she moved toward it as quietly as she could.

She glanced at her sensible digital watch, and the faintly glowing green numbers told her it was 7:29 p.m. She was precisely one minute early, and Holder was nowhere to be seen. She stood uneasily in the swiftly descending darkness and watched a bat swoop erratically over the pond, search-ing for late insects. She shuddered. She wasn't supersti-tious, but the bat reminded her irrationally of vampires and that she was alone in the woods at night, like the classic brainless victim.

As that disturbing thought flitted through the shadows of her mind, a large hand gripped her shoulder from behind. P.J. flinched and wheeled. Holder stood behind her, his face obscured by the darkness. She looked up in alarm. She had forgotten how tall he was.

"Scare you?" he asked pleasantly, as if he hoped he had.

"Of course not," she denied, but her heart had taken off like a frightened animal and still scurried, pounding hard beneath the falsies. "Well," she admitted, "you . . . startled me. How long have you been here?"

"A few minutes," he drawled. "I was watching you. So you don't like bats, eh? I thought someone in your position would love all creatures, great and small. No prejudice against any of our finny and furry friends."

She drew herself up straighter, hating the mockery in his low voice. "Bats don't pertain to the business at hand," she said briskly. She wished she could see his face. She imagined his golden-brown eyes, laughing at her in the darkness. "And I'm not paying you to watch me. I'm paying you to watch the Bachelors' Club. What have you found out?"

"But I like watching you," he said. "I think you're fun to watch. And your—foam-rubber enhancements, shall we call them?—give you an interesting new profile."

She seldom blushed, but since she'd gotten involved with Eli Holder, she seemed to be doing it more and more frequently. Although she couldn't see his eyes, she knew they were resting on her padded breasts. She crossed her arms defensively.

"That's another thing I want to know," she stated, her voice dangerously level. "Why this ridiculous and demeaning . . . padding? And the wig? Are you some kind of sicko, or have you been reading too many mystery novels, or what?"

She saw him tilt his head indifferently. "I suppose the answer is 'or what.' When I get you into the Ivory Castle, I want anyone who sees us together to think you're someone else. If you move fast and keep your head down and your . . . bosom up, you can do it."

"Pass for who?" she asked suspiciously. "And what about the Bachelors' Club?"

"Who doesn't matter at this point," he said, sounding bored. "As for the Bachelors' Club, you're about to see them for yourself. Come on."

He stepped toward the padlocked door of the icehouse, rummaged in his jeans, pulled out a key, deftly opened the door and nodded for her to enter.

"What is this?" she asked, stepping into the lightless dankness. Her heart was starting to canter again. "Where'd you get that key?"

"I have a collection of keys," he replied easily. "A souvenir of my days of crime. It has great sentimental value to me. And occasional practical value. Like now."

He shut the door behind them, and they were together in total darkness. He switched on a flashlight, and P.J. blinked at its sudden brightness. Holder was dressed much as she was, in faded jeans and dark deck shoes. But his shoes were expensive and unbattered, and instead of a sweatshirt he wore a black turtleneck sweater of mohair. He wasn't wearing a watch cap, but she could see one thrust halfway into the back pocket of his jeans.

His brown hair fell over his eyes, giving him an even more rakish look than before. She got a glimpse of his face and decided it wasn't such an ordinary one after all. The slightly tilted eyes were startlingly intense and seemed to be the same coppery brown as oak leaves at dusk. The wide mouth, set in a grim half smile, was hard but also intriguingly sensuous.

"What's all this about?" she asked, watching the shadows play on that disturbing face.

"It's about time to pay the Bachelors' Club a visit," he said, kneeling and brushing away the ancient sawdust that littered the icehouse floor. He uncovered a rusted iron ring and gave it a hard tug. A square door in the floor groaned open.

"A trapdoor." She looked at it in wonder. "Where's it lead?"

"Right where we want to go," he said, starting down a worm-eaten ladder. "The Ivory Castle. To a place where we can eavesdrop. The Bachelors' Club is having a special meeting tonight. I think we might hear something interesting. Come on. Or are you scared of spiders, too?''

She watched him disappear down the ladder, then scurried to follow. She didn't like spiders one bit, and there were enough webs festooning the gloomy interior of the icehouse that she didn't want to imagine what might be waiting below, but it was no time to indulge in squeamishness.

He held the light on the ladder for her, and when he reached up to put his arms around her waist, strange sensations swarmed through her.

''Last two rungs are missing,'' he said gruffly, swinging her to the dirt floor of a narrow tunnel. She imagined—she must have imagined it—that he held her a second longer than necessary.

Then he released her, and to distract herself from the effects of that innocent touch, she looked around. Spiderwebs hung as thick as veiling from some of the beams that supported the tunnel roof.

''Ugh,'' she said with an involuntary shudder. ''Didn't the characters in *Indiana Jones and the Temple of Doom* go through a place like this?''

''You want to talk movies or you want to see if the Bachelors say anything relevant about your four million bucks?'' he asked curtly.

The man couldn't be civil for more than two minutes, she decided irritably. She followed him down the passage, nervously swiping spiderwebs from her path. They stuck to her hands, and long filaments floated, trying to settle on her face.

''What *is* this place, anyway?'' she asked, hurrying to stay close to him and the precious security of the light.

''The Ivory Castle may be white as the driven snow, but its past is shady,'' he said, not bothering to turn to look at her as he spoke. ''During Prohibition a lot of smuggled liquor came through it. Brought in from the coast of Maine. The hotel was the main distribution point in Vermont. They'd bring in truckloads of rum, stash it in the basement, then bring it to the icehouse for delivery to customers. Kept suspicious traffic away from the hotel."

P.J. tried to scrub a nasty strand of web from her cheek. "How did you find out about this in the first place?" she asked. She hated the damp and narrow passage, but she was impressed that Holder had found it.

"You don't want to know," he said bluntly.

"Yes, I do," she insisted, still scrubbing at her cheek. "How'd you find it?"

"I found a knowledgeable barmaid with a headful of history and a weakness for gin," he muttered.

P.J. almost stopped, but he kept moving, taking the light with him, and she was forced to hurry to keep up. "You got some poor woman *drunk*?" she asked in disbelief. "That's disgusting, Holder. That's immoral."

"Yeah?" His tone was sarcastic. "Well, it worked, so spare me the sermon, Junior."

She thought Holder totally unscrupulous, but she kept her mouth clamped tightly shut. She followed him in uncomfortable silence, still swiping and wiping at the dangling spiderwebs.

"Why do you think we might hear something interesting *tonight*?" she finally asked. "And why am I going with you?"

"You're going with me because I want a witness if anything significant gets said. And tonight they're having a special meeting—not one of the regularly scheduled ones."

"What kind of special meeting? How do you know?" she demanded, watching him turn his broad shoulders sideways to make his way through a particularly narrow section of the passage and turn left.

He glanced idly over his shoulder. "I've been eavesdropping. As for what's special, you're from Harvard. Figure it out." He smiled. "What's the date?"

"September seventeenth," she answered, catching up to him. Then once again she nearly stopped. Her mouth opened slightly in surprise. "It's the anniversary of Fordyce's death," she said with a little gasp of comprehension. "He died a year ago today!"

"Very good," scoffed Eli. "Go to the head of the class."

"Good grief," she said, "they're not *celebrating*, are they? That's positively ghoulish."

"I imagine they'll raise a glass or two to the old boy." He shrugged. "And I'm counting on Clive, the dentist, to raise a few too many. Three drinks and the man begins to talk too much. I also want to hear what that doctor, Parmenter, has to say. He's the smart one. Did you know he was treating Fordyce last summer?"

"What?" She reached out and grabbed Holder's elbow, forcing him to stop. He turned and faced her, his face unreadable.

"Dr. Parmenter treated Delmer Fordyce? He had him as a patient? That never came out at the trial. My father never knew that. How did you find out? That means he could have known about Fordyce's heart condition. We could subpoena his records—that alone might be enough to reopen the case!"

He stared down at her a moment. One eyebrow rose, and in the shadowy light the scar on his cheek looked more like a sardonic dimple than ever. "I said he treated him—but Fordyce wasn't a patient. Just a few friendly after-hours consultations—no records. I told you, Parmenter's smart."

"But how did you find out? Why didn't my father find out? That could have helped SOS's case."

He merely shrugged. "Maybe. It's hearsay. I got it from an old woman who hangs around the patio collecting dirt on all and sundry. She doesn't like Parmenter. She doesn't like the Bachelors. She's willing to think the worst of them. Actually, she's willing to think the worst of most people. But she said she once saw Fordyce and Parmenter go into Parmenter's office downtown at about seven in the evening, and the next day she heard Fordyce thank Parmenter for 'easing his mind about the pains.' And she thinks Parmenter's a quack—or worse. Too many of his patients don't get well.''

P.J.'s mind spun. Holder was right: it was far from hard evidence, but it was something, a straw to grasp at, a new straw, one her father hadn't found.

"Why did she tell you all this?" she asked. "My father drove clear up here. He asked all kinds of questions. Nobody wanted to talk.''

"Nobody wants to talk to a lawyer," he returned shortly. "Lawyers mean trouble. And Mrs. Murdock—the woman—isn't too approachable in the first place. It took some doing to get her to talk. Once she started, it took some doing to get her stopped. I know more scandal about this town than you'd ever want to hear.''

"So why was she willing to talk to you?" P.J. demanded, putting her hands on her hips and looking up at him.

"Don't ask," he said, turning his back and continuing down the passage.

"Holder!" She grew more impatient with him each moment. "I asked you a question. I want to know."

The laugh was back in his voice. "I scratched her obnoxious poodle, and I plied her with her favorite 'drinky-poo'— her term, not mine—Jamaican Jungle Juicers. Most disgusting beverage on God's green earth.''

She groaned with distaste. "You've gotten *two* women drunk? Don't you have any scruples at all?''

"No," he said, casting her a brief, cold glance. "I don't. Which is why I may get further on this case than your sainted daddy did. If you don't like it, you can turn around now. Just walk back the way we came. It's no skin off my nose."

She ground her teeth. The remark about her father stung. She could still taste his failure—gall and wormwood to her. She followed Holder wordlessly, watching his back in the darkness. He moved as soundlessly as a cat, and again she felt the danger in him. She disliked him more every time he opened his mouth. But he'd done all these dishonorable things on her behalf, and she realized that made her as guilty as he was. She felt slightly degraded—and suddenly, for the first time, really frightened.

He stopped by an old oak door. "This part gets tricky," he said. "I hope you're in shape."

"I'm in shape," she replied shortly.

He glanced at her padded chest, smiled and said nothing. He eased the door open. The room they entered was eerily black, and something crunched underfoot.

"Old coal bin," he said. "Hasn't been used for years. If we take that door out—" he nodded at a second door, black with coal dust "—we're in the basement. We don't go that way. We go up." He shone his light on a rusted and soot-covered iron ladder that led to another trapdoor. "Put on your gloves. And when we get where we're going, I warn you, it's going to be close quarters."

How close? She was afraid to ask. Whenever she got too near him, her nerve ends seemed to short-circuit, and her stomach got that horrible tingle in the pit. But she donned the gloves as he put on his own and followed him up the narrow ladder. He quietly forced the trapdoor open, then nimbly leaped through. "It's a good jump," he whispered hoarsely, reaching his hand to her. "Give me your hand."

She complied reluctantly. She could feel the strength of his hand and the arm behind it as he hoisted her up almost effortlessly.

She tried to pull her hand away, but he kept it firmly gripped. He had switched off his light. "Watch your step," he warned, "and stay close to me."

"Where are we?" She heard the quaver in her voice and knew he did, too.

"A passage between the walls. And I don't think this has anything to do with rum-running. Some high-stake poker games used to be played here—very high-stake and very private. I think that's what these passages are for—to make sure the house won."

Involuntarily her fingers tightened on his, and she had to keep her other hand pressed against his back to follow him in the pitch-darkness. She could feel the warmth of his body through his thick sweater, but she herself seemed cold all over. Secret passages and high-stake gambling? She'd seen such things only in movies—the furtive, expressionless glance at the cards, the watching for cheaters, the ace up the sleeve. There, in the blackness of the passage, her hand slightly desperate on Holder's hard back, she felt as if she'd slipped out of the ordinary world forever.

"Here," he whispered, his mouth against her ear. "Like I told you, it's going to be cramped. And like I shouldn't have to tell you, don't make a sound."

He slid open a narrow door that she hadn't noticed, then guided her into a tiny closetlike space. Two pinpoints of light pierced the darkness. Peepholes, she realized, to keep watch on those games of long ago. The cramped quarters were thick with dust and cobwebs—she could smell them rather than see them. She prayed fervently that she wouldn't sneeze.

One of the spy holes was lower than the other. By standing on tiptoe, she could see through it. It gave her a surprisingly good view of the wainscoted library. She could see the round oak table with its deeply cushioned chairs, where the Bachelors probably sat, and a white-coated waiter stocking a small bar.

Holder slipped his arms around her from behind. She stiffened, then realized the space was so cramped he had to hold her in order for both of them to see.

Questioningly she turned her face to his but could see nothing but shadows. His arms tightened around her slightly. "Now," he murmured in that same almost inaudible voice, his lips against her ear, "we wait."

Then his mouth drew away from her ear, and she could feel the tension in his body as he looked through the higher of the two spy holes.

And now, she thought with empty fatalism, *we wait.*

She wished his long body didn't fit so perfectly against her own. She wished she was not so conscious of the strength of the arms wound around her body just beneath her breasts. She wished that a frisson hadn't run through her when his lips touched her ear.

She drew in her breath. She resisted the desire to relax against him and draw from his strength. They waited in the darkness in a space no larger than a coffin.

Chapter Four

The confines of their hiding place pressed about them. A faint and musty odor permeated the black air, but P.J. swiftly grew more conscious of the scent of Eli's cologne. It encircled her like a subtle bond, reminding her of autumn and brandy and exotic spices.

She tried to shake off the disturbing awareness of him and kept her gaze focused unwavering on the section of the library revealed by the peephole. She could clearly see the bar, an oak card table, wing chairs covered with tapestry.

Yet she was far too conscious of her forced nearness to Eli to really scrutinize the quiet scene. Men had held her closely before, and from desire, not necessity. But this man affected her differently than the others had.

His arms fit around her body too perfectly. His body molded against hers too well. She could feel the warmth and hardness of his broad chest against her back, the sinewy firmness of his upper thighs pressed against her hips. His chin rested on her shoulder, his face close to hers. If she turned her head even slightly, her soft cheek grazed his rougher one. His breath fluttered against her jaw and throat. And when he pressed his lips against her ear to whisper, the touch and the intimate warmth made her want to leap out of her prickling skin.

Finally, the library door opened, and someone entered. She tensed, and Eli's arms pulled her more firmly against him, as if to reassure her. His mouth was hot against her ear. "Dirkson," he said in a voice so low it seemed almost supernatural. "Our poet."

She bit her lip and nodded, watching Dirkson carefully. The entry of the first of the Bachelors broke the spell of Eli's nearness. As ridiculous—or as provocative—as her position might be, she was here on business, and desperate business at that. She willed her mind to turn into the high-precision machine it usually was.

Dirkson was a short, flabby man between sixty and seventy. He was not much taller than P.J., but he was fleshy in a squat, stocky way. He had a rather large squarish head with impressive jowls and beetling white eyebrows. His sideburns were gray, equally bristling and unstylishly long. They did not match the lavish blond waves of his expensive but obviously outdated toupee.

He dismissed the barman with a broad smile and a pat on the back. Alone, he mixed himself a weak whiskey and soda, then turned to peruse the spines of the books on the library shelves. There was something peculiar about his actions, almost as if he knew he was being watched and was playing it up for the benefit of an audience.

He knows we're here, P.J. thought in sudden panic. She stiffened. But Eli gave her the slightest of squeezes and brought his cheek almost imperceptibly closer to hers. She understood. Dirkson was such a poseur, so used to putting up a front, that he acted self-consciously even when alone.

She watched him closely, memorizing each feature of his large, ruddy face, his every theatrical gesture. That done, her mind veered back to earlier preoccupations—Eli holding her close and his cologne, so understated but intoxicating.

Gratefully she watched the library door reopen. This time two men entered. The first, tall, straight and dark-haired in spite of his age, was surprisingly handsome. He was impeccably dressed in a dark blue suit. If anything he looked almost too natty. He was oddly expressionless, his whole appearance so faultless that he didn't seem completely human. He reminded P.J. of a department-store mannequin that had somehow come to spurious life, then aged.

"Tall, dark and empty-faced," Eli's whisper fluttered past her ear. "That's Charlie Bangor—never worked a day in his life. Spent his nights gambling the family fortune away."

Well-dressed Charlie Bangor, the perfect clothes hanger, she thought. It would be easy to remember Bangor's curiously unappealing perfection.

The man beside him, however, would be memorable for other reasons. Average in build and weight, it was his face that was extraordinary. Beneath a close-cropped cap of thinning gray hair, his face was corrugated with wrinkles. So remarkable were these wrinkles that they overwhelmed his other features with the exception of his nose, which was large, fleshy and purplish red.

"The walking prune is Clive, the dentist," Eli breathed, his mouth so close he seemed to be speaking directly to her mind. "Behold his nose—a sermon against the abuse of drink."

Dirkson turned from his examination of the library shelves and raised his glass in flamboyant salute to the other two men. "What revels are at hand?" he intoned with a self-satisfied grin. "What festivities to celebrate the anniversary of fortune's bright smile?" He drank, as if to toast his friends.

P.J. winced. She did not like to think of Fordyce's death as "fortune's bright smile."

"Hello, Dirky," Clive rasped in a whiskey-roughened voice. "Poetizing so soon? I'll need a drink to face that." He made his way to the bar and mixed himself a glass of bourbon and water with no ice.

Charlie Bangor simply stared about the room and nodded, as if he could think of no greeting. He stood, immaculate, poised and slightly stupid-looking. Slowly a sly look crept across his fine-featured face. "Since it's a celebration," he suggested, struggling to keep his expression blank, "perhaps we ought to do something special tonight—to commemorate the occasion, so to speak."

Clive, the dentist with the nose and complexion by Jack Daniel's, looked at his tall companion and scoffed. Clive was the most casually dressed of the three, attired in baggy wool slacks and an ancient but expensive ski sweater. For all his wrinkles, scruffiness and obvious dependence on drink, he still seemed at least twice as bright as his tall and handsome friend. "Charlie, Charlie," Clive said, shaking his head, "playing for stakes? Don't even suggest it. We have to save you from yourself, you know."

"You should face it," Dirkson said unctuously. He ran his ringed fingers over the sculpted waves of his toupee. "Gambling is a disease. We're your friends. We've no interest in taking your money or—far less likely—giving you ours. Now that we finally have some again."

"To the divine concept of 'money again,'" muttered Clive, his wrinkles sagging downward. He looked meditatively into his bourbon glass and then took a long pull.

Charlie Bangor's lifeless but unlined features managed to look almost sullen. "As if drink isn't a weakness," he said. "I may gamble. But I don't swill."

"To a man who doesn't swill," Clive said sarcastically, raising his half-empty glass to Charlie Bangor. He made a mock bow to Dirkson. "And to a man who both gambles and swills but in moderation."

Dirkson returned the bow with a courtly flourish. "Come, Charlie," he said to the stiff-faced Bangor. "As the song says, 'Come, come, come, and have a drink with me.' None of us is perfect. But what we are, once again, is financially comfortable."

Obediently as a robot, Charlie Bangor made his elegant way to the bar and let Dirkson pour him a small glass of white port. Bangor took it up without tasting it. He held it as if it were a prop.

"Don't sulk, Charlie," Dirkson said jovially, carrying his drink to the card table and sitting down. "We all have our foibles. With me it has been beauty. The beauty of art and the beauty of women. I will be the first to admit I overindulged in both enthusiasms. Yet now, thanks to Delmer Fordyce, we may all indulge our foibles—within bounds, of course. A million dollars can last a careful man a long time. Even if the careful man is somewhat corrupt."

P.J. felt herself jump slightly, like a small animal of prey that has just sensed blood. Dirkson, affected and foolish as he was, had just admitted he was corrupt—not only himself but his unsavory friends, as well. How much more, she thought, her eyes narrowing, would he admit before the evening was over?

Her jump must have been more obvious than she realized, for she suddenly felt Eli's lips moving softly against the nape of her neck. "Steady," he said, his voice very low. "Relax. Slow and easy."

If the unexpected touch of his lips against her sensitive skin was meant to calm her, it was eminently unsuccessful. She did not relax, and there was nothing slow and easy about her response.

She straightened slightly in a futile attempt to lessen the contact between her body and his. In the narrow confines it was almost impossible.

She tried to train all her concentration on the peephole again. This time she was rewarded by seeing the library door swing open and a small, neatly dressed man with beautiful silver hair enter. Unlike the other three men in the room, he radiated a coolness and a control that seemed the product of a highly disciplined intelligence. He was dressed casually but conservatively in gray flannels and a navy blazer. Silver-rimmed glasses framed his pale and observant eyes.

"Good evening, gentlemen," he said and nodded with polite crispness.

"Parmenter," Eli murmured. And with some uncanny instinct P.J. was sure that Parmenter was the one man of the four who might be truly dangerous.

The other men greeted him, Dirkson with a flowery phrase, Clive with a mechanical raising of his refilled glass and tall Charlie Bangor with his mannequin's smile.

Dr. Parmenter walked to the bar. With efficiency and precision he poured a jigger of Pimm's over ice and added a wedge of orange and a dash of soda.

"Friends," he said, looking with cool satisfaction from man to man, "I think a toast is in order—and we all know why."

Unconsciously P.J. clenched her fists and tried to boost herself higher on tiptoe to see better. Her calf muscles were straining from the effort of standing so, and as though he could feel it, Eli automatically pulled her more securely into his arms, taking most of her weight to spare her cramping legs. He adjusted his arms to encircle hers so that she felt half sheltered, half imprisoned by his grasp.

Dr. Parmenter lifted his glass. "To our dear friend Delmer Fordyce," he announced with unfeeling calm, "who one year ago went to his heavenly reward—and kindly left us our earthly one—for which we heartily thank him."

"Here, here!" chortled Dirkson and drank with the doctor. Clive took a hearty swallow, as if he needed it, and even Bangor smiled stiffly as he sipped his port.

P.J. almost gasped aloud at the callousness of the four—actually drinking to the death of poor, kindly Delmer Fordyce.

"May I add something?" Dirkson asked, his face flushing with pleasure. He smiled so whitely P.J. suspected his teeth were as artificial as his mismatched blond waves. He raised his glass. "There was a time when I thought those fool fish lovers at SOS would snatch our inheritance from beneath our noses. But they failed and failed abysmally. I have taken the liberty of paraphrasing a poem by Kipling to commemorate our victory—should I say, our most lucrative victory?"

"Oh, Lord," groaned Clive, his wrinkles writhing in consternation. "Is it worth a million dollars to have to listen to Dirky's poems?" He grimaced and refilled his glass.

"It goes thus," said Dirkson, his voice achieving round and fruity tones.

"Oh, we don't like to gutter fight,
But, by jingo, when we do,
We've got cunning, brains and craft—
Now we've got the money, too."

"Not as bad as most of Dirky's doggerel," Clive said philosophically and took another swallow.

"It helped, of course, that their lawyer was incompetent," Dirkson said with satisfaction. "The fool was completely out of his league. I rather felt sorry for the tired old wretch."

At those words of insult to her father, P.J. took in her breath sharply. She made a small helpless lunge toward the peephole, as if she could climb through it and seize Dirkson by the throat and shake him until his toupee flew across the room.

But Eli had anticipated her reaction, and one long arm encircled her like a bar of iron. His left hand went over her mouth, clamping hard. She wanted to cry out in anger, but his force and firmness brought her back shakily to her senses. She could not untense her muscles, and his hand remained unyielding, pressing to insure the silence of her lips.

"Not yet," he ordered in that eerily soft voice at her ear. "Get mad later, Junior. For now, just listen."

"Ah," said Dr. Parmenter with a self-satisfied sigh. "As soon as I saw their attorney, I knew our troubles were over. The man simply didn't have strength enough. My only fear was that he'd die before the trial was over, which would have been a pity. But fate let him drag it out to the bitter end. Gentlemen, I venture to say that we must live right."

P.J. felt anger taking hold of her again, as if some spirit of vengeance swooped down and seized her by the roots of her hair. But Eli held her with that implacable fastness, and still his hand covered her mouth.

"If we lived right, we wouldn't have needed the money," Clive ventured moodily, staring into his bourbon. "He really was a decent sort, old Fordyce. I regret—"

"Regret nothing," snapped Dr. Parmenter with surprising vehemence. "Fordyce is dead. All men die. His death was simply more fortuitous than most."

"And more timely," Clive said with the same moodiness. "Extraordinarily timely. Too damned timely."

"Well, it's better to die a timely death than an untimely one," Dirkson said jovially. "And better to die a fortuitous than unfortuitous one. And better to leave one's money to fellows than to fish if you ask me—especially fine fellows like us."

"Precisely," said Dr. Parmenter. "Surely, Clive, you can't think the money would have done one whit of good in that pathetic little foundation. I can spot mortal illness in a man, and I can spot it in an institution. SOS is cancerous with debt. Fordyce's estate couldn't save it. I, for one, am glad to let it die badly so I may live well." He raised his glass and clinked it with debonair finality against Clive's. "Cheers," he said. "And never grieve over having taken money from fish. They don't really appreciate it, you know."

He drank, and Clive drank, too, more deeply than he should have.

"Besides," Dirkson put in, stroking his toupee fondly, "look on the bright side, Clive. With SOS gone there's one less charity to clog your postal box with junk mail."

Dirkson laughed at his own wit, Dr. Parmenter smirked slightly and Charlie Bangor seemed to be thinking of something else. "Say," he said finally. "Are we going to play cards or not?" His voice was as perfect and wooden as the rest of him. "I still think a slight wager might make things more interesting, and this *is* a celebration...."

Dr. Parmenter reached up to give Bangor's broad shoulder a friendly pat. "Tut, tut, Charlie," he counseled. "Your betting days are over, remember? No. Certainly not. Especially among your friends. What are friends for, eh, if not to help one another? Especially with their little vices. And more especially with their big ones."

The men freshened their drinks and sat down at the card table. Dr. Parmenter shuffled the cards and dealt out hands of bridge. Chatter was friendly but aimless. All the men except Clive sipped their drinks. He applied himself to his with a sort of determined energy. For the next hour each glass seemed to make the wrinkles of his face sag more morosely.

"Too bad old Fordyce isn't here," joked Dirkson, fondling his sideburns. "He enjoyed a hand of bridge. He was an indifferent player but an enthusiastic one."

"He enjoyed a quiet evening," Dr. Parmenter said slyly, trumping Charlie Bangor's ace. "And now all his evenings are quiet. I trust he's better as a corpse than as a bridge partner."

"It doesn't seem right to talk of him like that," Clive said. He massaged his magenta nose as if new veins were breaking to empurple it further.

"Bah," said Parmenter. "The dead are impervious to insult. It's the living who count. You're as glad to live well as I am."

"Of course, I'm glad to live well," Clive said almost sulkily. "It's just the way that we let him—"

"The way?" crowed Dirkson, flashing impossibly pearly teeth. "Way? I say what we've done proves the old saying—'where there's a *will*, there's a *way*. All one has to do is *forge* ahead.' Do you see? Will? Way? Forge? A clever pun, eh?" He laughed and kept repeating his bon mot to himself, shaking his coiffured head.

"I just—" Clive began unhappily, but Dr. Parmenter cut him off.

"Have another drink, Clive," the doctor said persuasively. He took the other man's glass himself and rose to fill it. He splashed straight bourbon into the glass and handed it back to Clive. "Cheer up," he said smoothly.

As if the doctor had known some magic formula or number, Clive began to cheer up. He became mellow. He also grew quieter and played his cards less skillfully. He and Charlie Bangor were soundly beaten by the doctor and Dirkson.

Then the game was over, a nightcap poured, more small talk made. Clive was nearly drunk and totally silent. Dirkson, flushed with victory, was more florid in face and conversation than before. Charlie Bangor sat listening with a slightly stupefied expression. He looked as if he thought he was probably having a good time.

At last goodbyes were said. Dr. Parmenter, as cool and observant as when he had entered, looked at the more relaxed faces of his fellows.

"A quiet little celebration," he said, smiling a tight-lipped smile. "A tasteful tribute to the departed. But as you know, gentlemen, I think it should be our last celebration. In fact, it will be best to mention Delmer Fordyce as little as possible—and the clever way we outfoxed SOS, even within this room. You all understand, of course."

Charlie Bangor nodded stolidly; Clive's wrinkles rippled with their own gravity, as if he understood all too well and it darkened his mood again. Teddy Dirkson flashed his teeth. "We aren't fools," he said in his affected voice.

"Of course not," Parmenter replied, smiling back. But something in his contained attitude seemed to say the opposite. "It's my turn to drive Clive home," he said. "Good night, my friends."

"Ha, ha, ha." Dirkson laughed, going out the door, slapping Charlie Bangor's elegant back. "Where there's a *will* there's a *way*. Indeed, Charlie. Indeed. And we had a hell of a will drawn up for old Fordyce, didn't we? A real work of art. Let's thank the Fates for sending us so many unhealthy men."

"Dirkson," Dr. Parmenter said sharply. "Didn't I just say such remarks were no longer in order?"

Dirkson only grinned his pearly grin. "I don't think I'm the one you have to worry about talking, Parmenter," he said. He raised his bushy eyebrows and cast a significant glance at the drunken Clive. "A touch of larceny gives no twinge to my conscience. A good thief should never suffer pangs of guilt. And I'm a very good thief, Parmenter. Just like you."

SHAKEN, APPALLED, P.J. let Eli lead her from their hiding place and through the darkened corridors. Somehow they ended up in the basement again. He made her remove the black hat and put on the blond wig, then drew her outside. She obeyed numbly, almost as if she were a bit drunk herself.

The night was cold by that time and wet, as well. Rain drizzled relentlessly from the black sky. Eli gritted his teeth and put his arm around her as if to contain her trembling. "Come on," he said grimly. "Keep your head down. I'll take you to my room."

Again she obeyed without thinking. Her mind spun dizzily with what she had seen and heard. Eli took her in a side door. As instructed, she kept her head down. When they encountered a bellhop in the hall, Eli drew her closer still. He lowered his face in order to block the view of hers. Till the man passed, he kept her face obscured by pretending to be whispering something secret and affectionate.

Then she was in his room, sitting on the edge of his king-size bed. Her heart beat so hard she felt as if it might choke her. She stared without full comprehension at the cobwebs on her jeans.

Then she looked up at Eli. He stood before her, his hands on his hips, staring down. He had an odd crook to his mouth, as if he didn't like what he saw.

"Are you all right?" he asked at last. "You can take off that stupid wig now."

He reached over and plucked the blond curls away as if they were a cap, leaving her own short brown hair in silky disarray. She'd made a cute blonde, and Eli was a connoisseur of blondes, but somehow he liked her better the way she really was. Except she didn't look well at all. She looked disturbed, disillusioned, like somebody who's just realized the world is not actually a pleasant meadow but a minefield of unpleasant surprises.

Her blue eyes held his for a long moment. "They did it. They're not men, they're ghouls. And the way they talked about my father, and poor Delmer Fordyce, and SOS..."

Hell, Eli thought, shaking his head in disgust, *she's practically in shock. She's really never looked evil in the face before.* What the Bachelors had done had been an abstraction to her until that night. She was struggling so hard to control herself he had the nervous feeling she might explode before his eyes.

He went to the bureau drawer, drew out a bottle of Chivas Regal and poured a stiff shot into one of the hotel tumblers. He returned to the bed and thrust it at her almost roughly. "Drink that."

Good Lord, he thought, she was pale as the ivory satin coverlet on the bed. The sparks that he remembered could swirl in her eyes were there but dimmed by something—sorrow. She looked half like a grieving woman, half like a hurt child. More than that, she looked strangely beautiful, like a sad-eyed slender nymph carved out of marble. No, she looked too soft, too fragile to be carved of marble. She looked more like something made of flower petals. He had a sudden urge to take her in his arms, to hold her, to run his hand over her short silky hair, to lay her face against his shoulder, to kiss her cheek until he could warm her back into life.

Instead, he turned away. He recognized the impulse was dangerous—to himself. He'd vowed to leave her alone. She could only mean trouble for him. He'd understood that from the first. Well, it was over now—or almost.

He glanced at her over his shoulder, then turned and paced back to the bed. "I said drink," he ordered gruffly.

But she only held the glass between her clenched hands and stared up at him. "They forged the will. They knew Delmer Fordyce was going to die, and they forged the will. They must have known both those witnesses were going to die. They even knew my father was going to die. And it made them *glad*." Her voice was full of bitter indignation.

He swore softly. He sat down on the bed beside her. He took the glass from her hands and held it to her lips as if she were a child. "I said drink it," he repeated, his voice curt.

Oh, hell, he thought again because he was forced to put his arm around her shoulders to make her drink the Scotch. She fit into the crook of his arm all too neatly, just as she had fit a bit too perfectly into his embrace in the confines of the hiding place. It was damnably distracting to have a woman who fit so neatly into his arms, especially since she was so obviously the wrong kind of woman.

She choked on the Scotch, but he made her finish it. Then he poured her another shot, this one weakened with water, and gave himself a generous glassful.

He sat down beside her on the bed, but he was careful to keep his distance. He supposed he was going to have to break the news. He never should have gotten involved in this case in the first place. It was a long shot, and he'd always hated playing long shots. Now he felt as if he'd failed her, and that made him angry. He wasn't used to failure.

"We weren't as lucky as I'd hoped," he said at last.

The color had returned to her cheeks but only in a dim flush. Her eyes widened. "What do you mean?" she asked. "You heard what they said. They *did* it. You heard them, I heard them, and we can reopen the case. And put them in prison where they belong."

"The hell we can." He gave her a sardonic look and took a hefty drink of the Chivas. "We didn't get one damned thing that'd hold up in court."

She leaned toward him in disbelief, and he wished she hadn't. He stared into his glass because he didn't like looking into those blue eyes with their feathery lashes. They were about to become unhappy blue eyes again. "But they said—" she objected.

"They said nothing," he interjected, cutting her off. "Innuendos. Hints. Sly jokes. Oh, they came close, kid, but nobody came out and actually admitted anything. You and I may know they did it. But we can't prove it. And that's the bottom line. You're not going back to court."

"But," she argued, "we both heard them. Surely..."

He finished the Scotch in one long pull. *Forgive me, great god Chivas, but the woman is making me edgy.* Part of him wanted to tell her to go back to Boston and get out of his life, and part of him wanted to climb on a white charger and play Sir Lancelot for her. The latter impulse mystified and disgusted him.

"Look," he said between his teeth, "you read the transcript of the original court case. What happened every time your father brought up a witness who supported his claim that Fordyce had always wanted the money to go to SOS?"

She shook her head impatiently. "The Bachelors' lawyer screamed it was hearsay evidence and inadmissible. It was the most frustrating part of the whole case for my father."

"Well," he asked coldly, "doesn't that tell you something? The rules of hearsay evidence are complicated, Junior. What people overhear outside a courtroom is hardly ever admissible. If—just *if*—we got lucky and heard one of those guys actually confess—in detail, I might add—it *might* be admissible evidence and you *might* reopen the case. But we didn't get lucky. And if we didn't get lucky tonight, I'm afraid our chances range from slim to zero that we will."

"How can you be so sure?" she challenged, her eyes starting that disconcerting virtuous blazing again. "Dirkson admitted he was a thief. We should have tape-recorded them. You can't know whether what we heard won't hold up in court. You're not a lawyer—"

"We're not law-enforcement people, and judges and juries tend to hate ordinary citizens who sneak around with tape recorders," he shot back. "Dirkson could claim what he said about thieves had to do with winning at cards. It's as easy as stealing candy from a baby. Have you ever heard how a lawyer can sow doubts about what the words on a tape really mean? I know—and I am a lawyer, of sorts. I was a jailhouse lawyer. One of the best, so they told me.''

"Oh," she said in disgust, "now you're falling back on your fabulous years as a criminal. Reading law books in a prison library does *not* make you a lawyer."

"It made me enough of one to get five years knocked off my sentence. I can talk habeas corpus and substantive due process till your head spins, baby," he said roughly. Suddenly he wanted a cigarette. He reached into the drawer of the nightstand and took one out. He thought about breaking it in two, decided he needed the whole thing, thrust it in the corner of his mouth and lit it. He glowered at her through the smoke. "I know what I'm saying," he growled finally. "And unless we have a very convenient miracle, you aren't going to get those old boys back into court."

She had that stunned look on her face again. "Are you telling me you're quitting?" she asked at last. Her voice trembled, although she kept her jaw stoically steady.

He took a second drag on the cigarette, then ground it out. He looked at her, and he realized suddenly that he wanted her. He wanted her a lot. Too much for it to be safe. "Junior," he said as gently as he could, "I hate to resort to clichés, but we've done all we can. I've left no stone unturned. I've checked every avenue. Both witnesses to the signing of the will are dead. Unless one of the Bachelors cracks—and cracks badly—we've got no legal moves left. I'm sorry."

She said nothing, which was disconcerting. Her silences could say more than most women's best speeches.

She had set her second drink, untouched, on the night table. Again she sat, staring down at the cobwebs on her jeans. She felt sick. Eli was right, and she knew it. She had seen her father fight the losing war over hearsay evidence. The system of justice, so carefully designed to protect the innocent, had become a tangle of legal loopholes through which the guilty too often slipped. Technicalities designed to shelter the blameless became the criminal's refuge, as well. Thieves and murderers with clever lawyers walked the streets, jaunty in their freedom.

Eli watched her as the truth sank in. He wasn't in the habit of feeling sorry for people, and he didn't want to start now. She had a smudge on one of her cheeks. He took out his handkerchief and scrubbed it away, rather fiercely. "I'm sorry, kid," he said gruffly.

"Well," she said, her voice still unsteady, "at least I know my father was right. I know for sure now."

Then she sniffed. That's all it was, one small sniff. "I guess if SOS is going to be saved, I have to sell a lot of bumper stickers," she said. "You did what you could. From here on out, it's up to me." She had tears in her eyes, but she tried not to let them fall. She didn't succeed.

She sat so still, so straight, that before he knew what he was doing, he was reaching over, wiping the tears away with the handkerchief. "Hey," he said harshly.

She straightened her back. She set her jaw. "I think I'd better go back to my place now," she said stiffly.

"No." He put his hands on her upper arms and leaned toward her. "I think you'd better come here."

And then he relinquished his damned willpower and kissed her, the way he had wanted to from the first. He could tell almost immediately that nobody had ever kissed her the way she deserved. The touch and taste of her hit him harder than any Scotch had ever done.

My dear Junior, he thought, tasting the surprised softness of her mouth, *you've got the most beautiful lips in Christendom. You've been deprived, but I can make it up to you. And then some.*

Then he kissed her again in a way that made her gasp against his lips. With one hand she tried to push him away, but simultaneously her other arm wound around his neck and drew his face nearer hers.

"Oh," she said at last against his mouth, but he ignored her and kept kissing her.

At last he drew away slightly. He looked down at her with his golden wolf's eyes. "I think you'd better stay awhile," he said. "We need to talk. About how I'm going to get your money back."

"What?" she asked weakly, her lashes fluttering dazedly.

"Your money, Junior," he repeated. "Your four million. I'm going to get it back for you."

He supposed he had always known, too, that it would come down to this. He'd get back in the dangerous old game for her. He kissed her again.

Chapter Five

She drew back from him in alarm. One part of her mind told her she had yielded to his arms because she was confused and frightened and upset. She hadn't had the comfort of a human embrace since Clarence had left. But another part of her was thoroughly dismayed. Clarence had certainly never kissed her like that. He'd never made her feel that way, as if the top of her head was dancing off and her body was exploding into hungry sparkles of need.

So this is what everybody's been talking about, she thought with utter amazement. *But not with him. Oh, good Lord, not with him, of all people.*

He was looking at her with one brown eyebrow cocked and one corner of his mouth crooked cynically. "You look surprised, Junior. Why? Because I kissed you or because I said I'd get your money back?"

"Both," she said, inching away from him on the bed. "And please don't kiss me anymore. We have a . . . a business relationship, that's all."

"I didn't really want to kiss you," he said casually. He inspected his nails. "You just looked like you needed it."

"Well, I didn't," she said with some heat.

"You did. And still do. Stop pretending you didn't like it. That attitude died with Queen Victoria."

"So maybe I'm the last Victorian," she countered, brushing ineffectually at her jeans again.

"I don't think so," he said, a taunt in his voice. "I think you're a kind of nice little peach who's just about ready to turn ripe—and delicious."

"Don't be ridiculous," she said, brushing at her jeans more vigorously. The man was colossally insolent. But he could certainly kiss, and she was still agitated by how powerfully he had affected her. It wouldn't happen again. She struggled to regain her composure.

"Suppose you tell me how you think you're going to get SOS's money back," she challenged, darting him a suspicious look.

He shrugged and leaned back against the headboard. He locked his hands behind his head. "I can get it back fifteen or twenty different ways," he said with maddening confidence. "Remember me? I'm the guy who wrote the book about parting fools and their money."

She turned to stare at him. The sparks were back in her eyes full force now. He smiled slightly.

"What?"

"Do you want your money back?" He pretended to stifle a yawn. "Or do you want to lose it? Parmenter says your organization can't survive even if it gets the dough back, so maybe it really doesn't make any difference."

"Dr. Parmenter's a liar," P.J. countered. "I know its books backward and forward. SOS is tottering, but it certainly doesn't have to die. Fordyce's money would put it in fine shape."

"So?" Eli said and hid another yawn behind his hand.

Damn him, she thought. He looked so long and lazy and smug lying there on the ivory satin in his black clothes that it was like being next to a lounging panther. "So it certainly *does* make a difference if we get the money back. But just how do you propose to do it if the law can't help us?"

"Justice," he said vaguely, "is not always dispensed in courtrooms. There's a fruit bowl on the bureau. Would you peel me a grape?"

"Peel your own grape and stop talking in riddles," P.J. retorted, resisting the urge to hit him—hard—with one of the king-size pillows.

He cast her a languid glance. "What I'm saying is, I know about fifty ways to sting them, con them. It might not be within the confines of perfect legality, but I could put that four million back in your lap."

Amazed, she turned on the bed so that she could glare down at him. He still had his hands locked behind his head, and he was staring at the ceiling. Somehow he managed to look as innocent and harmless as St. Francis of Assisi. It was disconcerting to see that normally cynical face looking so guileless.

"If you're saying you'll cheat to get it back, forget it," she said at last. "I'm not a thief. I won't sink to their level."

"I am a thief," he replied, still staring at the ceiling. "At least I used to be. I never stole for a good cause before, but the idea's got a certain charm. As for sinking to their level, I doubt if it's possible. It's always been fair to trick the trickster. You said it: the men are ghouls, especially Parmenter."

"No," she retorted firmly. "I can't condone anything that breaks the law. It goes counter to everything SOS stands for, that my parents stood for. And everything I believe in. I'm a professional, Holder. I solve problems by using the proper channels, the way a professional should."

He looked at her, his old familiar expression back. "Whose money is it supposed to be?" he asked, his lip curling.

"SOS's," she replied. She continued to stare down at him as if he were some sort of reptile. It didn't phase him in the least.

"And just what," he asked with patience, "are these much-vaunted proper channels?"

"The courts, the law—" she began.

He cut her off. He sat up straight and looked her directly in the eyes. "And how much good have they done you so far?" he demanded sarcastically. "How much good did they do your father?"

The mention of her father took some of the wind out of her sails. "No good. So far. But—"

"No *buts*," he said between his teeth. "What kind of self-absorbed Goody Two Shoes are you, anyway, lady? You saw the men we're dealing with. In the con game we'd call them COD boys—Collect On Death—stiff sellers. Every culture has its hierarchy and so do con men. And the lowest of the low are the guys who play Dead Games. But you're going to let them get away with it because you don't want to put a spot on your immortal soul. Want to know what I think of your immortal soul?"

"No," she said because he was making her angry. He was talking fast, playing games of logic with her, and he was good at it.

"I think it's a selfish little prig of a soul, but it isn't white. It's marred by a wide streak of yellow."

"Yellow?" she demanded. "Just because I don't want to break the law, you're calling me a *coward*?"

He leaned his elbow on the top of the bed's headboard and his chin on his fist. He looked over her face with insulting thoroughness. "You called me a coward once," he said. "Now it's my turn. Yes. You're a coward. And a prude. So wrapped up in your own moral superiority you'll let four old stiff sellers rob you blind. And ruin your organization."

She narrowed her eyes and thrust out her lower lip slightly. She folded her arms across her chest. She searched for an answer that would wither him and leave him as a wizened little scrap on the satin coverlet. She couldn't find one. "I will not," she managed to say at last, "break the law. I am a professional. I have *ethics*."

He touched his forehead and his chest in a mock salute, like a member of the lower castes saluting a Hindu Brahmin. "Please to excuse the humble suggestions of this low-life slime, Most High, but you also have rock in your head. I'm offering to get your money back. Offers like that don't come along very often. And if you turn me down, justice is really going to be violated."

"But I can't!" she countered in frustration. "I just can't. It's a question of morals, ethics, professionalism. SOS would never—"

He suddenly reached out and grasped her by the upper arms. He pulled her close; she lost her balance slightly and was forced to put her legs on the bed to stay upright. And now that he was holding her so emphatically, he seemed too close, dangerously close.

"Look," he practically hissed, "you've made your point. You're a pro. Well, I'm a con. I've been a con man and a convict. Now you've hired me for a consultant, and I'll give you *my* professional opinion. You won't get your money back legally unless one of those geezers slips up badly—and you could wait years for that to happen. All four of them are damned poor excuses for humanity, but they're just about to get away with the perfect crime. And you're going to let them."

She gritted her teeth. She felt tears begin to sting her eyes. She didn't want to cry in front of him again, but the night had been so turbulent she was afraid she would. She couldn't counter his arguments any longer except with the same tired old replies.

"SOS can't be involved in anything illegal," she finally managed to say.

His grip on her arms tightened. "Dammit, they won't be involved. And I don't want to take the chance of going back to prison, either. I guarantee that. But if you want the money where it belongs, you're going to bend the law a little."

"Bend it?" she said, looking up at him hopefully. "Not actually break it?" Her heart was starting to beat very fast again, and she wasn't sure if it was because he was compromising her business principles, her sexual ones or both at once.

He stared down at her face for a long time. He studied her eyes, which were pleading, and her mouth, which was at once both strong and vulnerable. He fought back the desire to brush the soft brown bangs away from her forehead, just to feel her hair beneath his fingers. He didn't want to kiss her again, not there. Because that would mean he'd end up making love to her, and that would make her run away—he sensed that clearly. He didn't want her going away. He was the one who decided when it was time to leave and did the leaving.

His gaze dwelt on her lips a moment longer. "All right," he said at last. "I'll figure out a way to bend the law gently, not break it outright. Will that keep you happy?"

She nodded hesitantly. She felt warm and groggy, as if he had hypnotized her. She had an absurd desire to lift her hand and place her finger on the straight, short scar that marked his cheek.

"I think," he said, his voice very low, "I'd better take you home, Junior. I'm going to have to devote my energies to thinking tonight. Pity."

But he still didn't release her, and his eyes continued to explore her features with that same proprietary interest. She bristled uncomfortably because he seemed determined to arouse her and dismiss her at the same time.

"There's no pity about it," she said quietly, twisting free of his grasp with surprising agility. He let her go without a struggle. "I'm paying you to think—and act—within the limits of the law. Don't delude yourself that I have any desire to spend the night with you. I would far, far rather return to the Nutmeg Peddler where I can sleep to the rhythmic patter of the roaches' feet on the woodwork."

"Ah, maybe that's what gets me about you, Junior," he said, smiling slightly. "You're so terribly moral. And I mean that in the worst possible sense. Oh, well, put on your nice wig and we'll be off. But I don't believe you'd really rather sleep with cockroaches."

"That's because you don't understand me, Mr. Holder," she said tartly. "Nor I you. Because we come from different worlds. The more I see of you, the more I realize how different we are."

He rose from the bed and stretched sensuously. She got up on her own side and picked up the silly blond wig from the nightstand. She jammed it onto her head without looking into a mirror. "I don't see why I have to wear this thing, anyway," she grumbled, refusing to look at him. "Or those horrible, horrible...falsies."

He stepped to her side of the bed and started adjusting the wig. He tucked an errant lock of her brown hair beneath it. "I told you," he said, examining his handiwork. "If anybody sees us together from a distance, they'll mistake you for somebody else. I don't want people to know we're together."

"Mistake me for whom?" she retorted. "You mean, since you've been here—living on *my* money—you've made a point of having a blonde in your room on a regular basis?"

"She's been kind enough to come around," he said smoothly, pulling a few golden curls down around her cheeks a bit more seductively. "She's sort of an assistant."

"Assistant?" P.J. asked, raising a questioning eyebrow. She tried to wave his interfering fingers away. "I thought you couldn't afford an assistant on what I paid you. I thought that's why I was supposed to come up in the first place."

He ignored her shooing gestures and made a few more adjustments to the wig. "Cleo doesn't work for money," he replied with equal acerbity. "She works for love. Some women have real chests—and real emotions. If it's too late to develop the former, don't despair, you can work on the latter."

"Has anybody ever told you," she asked, her voice icy, "that you can be an absolutely nauseating man?"

"Countless hundreds," he replied, adjusting the neck of her sweater. "But they never knew the real me. To know me is to love me. Although on occasion I'll settle for simple lust. A great emotion but one I'm sure you've neglected shamefully."

She ignored the gibe. "How do I know," she asked, suddenly dubious, "that you're not just tired of playing straight and you want to pull one last con game for old times' sake? That you didn't plan this all along? That you want to cheat the Bachelors out of that money for the sheer fun of it—and to prove your own superiority?"

"Ah," he replied, brushing a spiderweb from her shoulder. "An astute question. You don't know. The reason you don't is that you don't trust me—not yet."

"And do you think I will?" she asked, her chin raised in defiance that was partly sham.

"Maybe," he said cryptically. "Come on, Junior, I'll walk you home. The rain hasn't stopped. I've got a raincoat I can throw about us. It'll look romantic and make it all the harder for anybody to realize you're not the usual blonde."

"The usual blonde," she said coldly, watching him take the Burberry coat from the closet.

"Jealous?" he asked, raising one brow teasingly. "Why, Junior!"

"No," she returned flatly. "And please stop calling me Junior. I hate it."

He shrugged the coat around his shoulders, capelike, then came to her and put his arm around her shoulders so that she, too, was protected by the coat's long folds.

"Well, I'm not going to call you P.J.," he said dryly. "It sounds like I'm talking to a pair of pajamas. And to shorten it and call you P seems somehow inelegant. Do you have a real name behind the initials?"

"Of course," she said, suddenly agitated by his closeness, the sureness of his touch around her shoulders. "It's Pemberton. Pemberton Joseph Fitzjames Jr."

He groaned. "And you still claim to love your parents, Pemberton? No, thanks, I'll stick to Junior. You'll have to get used to it."

"I don't want to get used to it," she said rebelliously as he led her out the door.

"Too bad—" he smirked, hurrying her down the corridor "—because that's what I intend to call you—and how I'll think of you—to my dying day. Can't you think of it as a term of endearment?"

"No," she said shortly, knowing he was taunting her again.

"Too bad." He shrugged one wide shoulder. "You're a very hard woman. I suppose you know that."

They made it unobserved to the back entrance of the Ivory Castle and into the dripping woods.

The walk back to the Nutmeg Peddler seemed interminable. Eli had excellent night vision and refused to use a flashlight. But the leaves beneath their feet were treacherously slick, and she was forced to wind her arm around his waist to keep herself precariously upright on the wet and winding path.

When they reached the back door of the Nutmeg Peddler, he turned to face her, drawing the coat more firmly around the two of them. "Good night, Junior," he said, his voice husky. He sounded almost supernaturally quiet in the mist and the darkness and rain. "Sleep tight. I'll be in touch. And work on trusting me a little more, okay?"

Before she could object, he ducked his head and gave her another of those soul-shaking kisses. His arms were around her so tightly she temporarily could not breathe. His lips, warm, yet slightly misted with rain, explored hers for a small, dark eternity. Her hands had instinctively rested on the breadth of his chest, and she fought the desire to wind her arms around his neck.

She became frightened again. She wondered if she were having a mystical experience. She saw suns and moons and planets swimming behind her closed eyelids. Her inner self seemed imprisoned in some crucible that was melting it to warm and pliant gold. She wished he would either stop immediately or never stop.

He stopped. He opened the door for her and slipped the coat from her shoulders. "Good night, Junior," he said.

She hurried inside, unlocked her door and fell onto her lumpy bed. She didn't even bother to turn on the lights.

She felt horribly confused, perhaps terminally confused. She put her fist to her mouth and nibbled nervously at her knuckle. What should she do about the Bachelors' Club? she wondered in despair. Was Eli's solution the only one? Was it really stealing if you took back what had been stolen from you to begin with? Or was she simply sinking more and more deeply into wrongdoing, sliding more swiftly down the primrose path to hell?

And Eli, she thought, biting her knuckle so hard it hurt. Why did he fill her with such tumult? Why was he offering to help her at all? She was not terribly experienced, but she realized he wanted her. If that was the only reason he had volunteered to get the money back, it was bad. Worse, against all her better judgment, she had to admit she wanted him, too. He was unlike any man she had ever met. It was as if all the men she had ever known were tame, amiable woolly ponies, and suddenly Eli appeared on the horizon, as strong and demanding as a stallion. Why hadn't her mother told her about men like him? Or had she even known they existed?

She didn't sleep well. Too many things in her tidy universe had been shaken loose. A short time ago she had been an intelligent, conservative and dedicated young woman obsessed by one problem: the Bachelors' Club appeared to have stolen four million dollars from SOS, an organization the Fitzjames family had served selflessly for years.

That obsession had led her to Eli Holder, and that, she feared, was her undoing. She was already registered in her hotel under an alias, slipping about in disguises and spying from behind secret panels. Holder had her half convinced crime was right under the circumstances. She had the feeling that if he hammered at her long enough, he could make her believe black was white, which made him about as trustworthy as the serpent in Eden.

If SOS knew where she was and what she was doing, she would most certainly be put on probation. If they knew what she was contemplating, she would be fired and probably blacklisted.

And the worst part was that Eli was the man responsible for getting her to bite into this crazy forbidden apple. Not only that but also she had the horrible suspicion that if he had kissed her a few more times, she might have ended up in his bed. She who had never had a casual affair in her life. He was a horrible man, even if he was strangely attractive. He had the morals of an alley cat, but he was probably smarter than anybody she had met at Harvard. And he attracted her on a level so primitive she hadn't even known it existed in herself.

With bewilderment she recalled the feel of his mouth moving expertly upon hers and what it had done to her mind and body. In humiliation she hid her head under the pillow.

Damn, she thought, crushing the pillow down harder around her ears. *Damn, damn, damn, damn, damn, damn, damn, damn, damn, damn.* She must be experiencing lust for the first time in her life—or even sillier, infatuation. If she didn't know herself to be above such things, she would almost think she was falling in love with him. Love him? Him? Oh, really, that was the ultimate madness. *Damn, damn and damn.*

ELI SAT UP most of the night, propped against the headboard of the king-size bed. He allowed himself one more glass of Scotch but no more. He wanted his thinking to be clear.

He'd taken off his sweater and jeans. He was naked except for his black briefs because for some reason he never understood, he seemed to think better almost naked. It was like going into the jungle against the enemy, stripped down to essentials.

He allowed himself half a cigarette, and he went through all the ways he could think of to get the money back.

He hadn't been idly boasting to the woman. He knew at least fifty cons that could get her money back. The problem was settling on exactly the right one, then modifying it.

It was a combination of two cons that ultimately seemed best to him. The first was the Magic Wallet. All he had to do was lose some papers of value, then make sure one of the Bachelors—accompanied by Junior—found it. Then, as a reward for the return, he'd offer the old boy a piece of a business too sweet to refuse. The "business" would be a variation on the old Discretionary Game—an investment that offered interest so high the sucker would pour every available dime into it. It was simple, it had a certain elegance that appealed to him and he had the feeling it could be downright irresistible to the Bachelors.

He'd have to count on Junior to be his capper, his confederate. He couldn't afford to involve Cleo in this scheme; he couldn't even tell her what he was up to, which was unfortunate. He liked to keep Cleo informed because she always returned the favor. It was she who had traced the missing witness, John Williams, and found he had inconveniently allowed himself to be placed in a grave in Milford, New Hampshire. Cleo was a remarkable woman when it came to finding out things. His little return to the ways of old, however, was something he'd just as soon keep from her. She wouldn't understand about Junior at all.

Still, he'd give anything if it were Cleo helping him mulct the Bachelors. Instead, he was going to have to depend on the Junior Miss. The disadvantages were twofold. She had no experience, and she had a conscience as big as a house. But she was smart, by God, and she was quick, and his instincts told him that once she got into it, she might be very good indeed. Who, after all, wouldn't trust a face like hers? He almost did himself.

But she was so damned much trouble. She wanted this operation to be as legal as possible. Which meant he was going to have to keep on thinking because playing the Magic Lost and Found Wallet Con or the Discretionary Game was illegal as hell. He needed a new angle. A brand-new, absolutely unexpected, nearly lawful angle. And that, he thought, scratching the scar on his cheek, was the challenge.

He nursed the Scotch, he stared at the white walls and the ivory draperies and thought. For a half an hour at a time he would sit, as motionless as a statue, hardly breathing, in concentration as intense as an Eastern meditator.

And then, at seven o'clock in the morning, he sipped the last drop of Scotch from his glass. He could see the vaguest pink light starting to glow dimly through a gap in the drapes. And he smiled because he knew what he was going to do.

He stood, put on a black silk robe and padded to the window. He drew the drapes apart slightly. The world was veiled in the palest light, virginal and lovely. He slapped his bare chest in self-congratulation. His plan was beautiful, he thought, it was Nice with a capital *N*. He laughed silently to himself.

He closed the drapes again and went to the shower. He'd get under the cold spray to numb his mind, then he'd grab a few hours of shut-eye. Then he'd call Junior and explain what needed to be done. That, he thought, grimacing as he stepped into the cool, stinging water, was going to be the hard part.

He had avoided thinking about her during the long night because she was distracting. If he was going to think of her at all, a cold shower seemed the most sensible place to do it.

He had promised himself he wasn't going to seduce her. But that was before last night, when all of a sudden she had made him want to be the White Knight and before he had finally yielded to temptation and kissed her.

He was going to have to get her out of his system, all right, he thought, drying off with a massive charcoal-gray towel. Well, he hoped it wouldn't hurt her, and it might do her some good.

He'd done plenty of seducing in his day, and he was good at it. But she was pretty seductive herself, although she didn't seem to realize it. She was a beautiful woman, in a low-key way. She was bright, she was spirited, but the thing that got to him was that she actually made him believe she was good. He liked that.

Good, he thought with self-mockery as he climbed, naked, under the coverlet. What an unexpected word to enter his universe. All her idealism and selflessness, which he had mocked so roundly at first, had started to intrigue him. He was starting to think she was for real. He liked her. And that did weird things to his head.

He'd only felt that way twice before. Once he had been six, and a little black-eyed girl in Chicago had reduced him to a ninny. He'd tried to ride his bike past her without holding on to the handlebars, to impress her. He'd taken a header over the bars, landed on his chin, chipped three teeth and broken his collarbone. All because she'd been such a pretty, nice, good little girl, with such large black eyes.

The other time had been seventeen years later, in Kansas City. She'd been a black-eyed girl, too, and extraordinarily beautiful. She'd been rich, educated, from one of the most prominent Kansas City families. He thought she was everything he wasn't. He wanted to lay the world at her feet. She was coyly grateful, and then she asked for more.

He got it for her—to impress her, to be accepted. But he went a little too far, and that's how he'd ended up in Leavenworth convicted of grand larceny. She'd never written him, of course, or gone to see him. She'd immediately married somebody with a flawless reputation and lots of old money and new presents. Eli decided she hadn't been such a nice girl after all. She'd been a greedy, phony bitch.

He'd stopped believing in nice girls after that. He'd certainly lost any interest in girls with black eyes, no matter how flashing or limpid. He had lost interest entirely in falling in love.

He punched his pillow into a more comfortable shape and settled his head back against it. P.J. was just very different, that was all. At this point. Once he'd had her in bed, he imagined she would fade into that legion of half-remembered women that formed his conquests.

But he frowned, remembering how he'd felt the first time he'd kissed her. As if he'd been poleaxed. He didn't like feeling that way. Yet perversely he did.

He tried to convince himself that what interested him most was playing a con again. He hadn't done it for sixteen years. And nobody knew how hard it had been to quit. Nothing made a man's blood sing the way pulling off a good scam did. You could ask any old con men, including the ones who'd been caught again and again, why they kept it up. They'd answer, "Because of the thrill." The thrill was greater than anything. Even sex.

Well, he thought sleepily and remembered again how strangely exciting Junior's lips felt beneath his own, maybe not sex.

He slept and dreamed of his father. His father had died in prison. Eli dreamed he was visiting him. His father watched him sadly through the visitor's window. "Look at me. You want to end up like this? Stay straight. Find a nice girl. Settle down. A nice girl. Raise a family."

"No," Eli said in the dream. "Not me. You've got the wrong man. I love 'em and leave 'em."

"Ha," said his father in disgust. "You haven't ever loved anybody. You've just left them. There's that much of the con man left in you. That's what we're best at, isn't it, boy? Leaving."

And as if to prove his own words, he vanished.

Then Eli dreamed he was standing by his father's grave. A woman handed him a flower to lay by the tombstone. The woman was P.J. He took the flower and dropped it unceremoniously on the grave.

He didn't look at her. "Go away," he said.

But she didn't. It seemed as if she was there beside him for good.

He stared at the gravestone. It was disturbing. It said Eli Holder. He'd never told the woman he was a junior himself.

Chapter Six

Eli slept through most of the day.

P.J. fretted alone in her room at the Nutmeg Peddler. She left it only long enough for a miserable breakfast in the dark, greasy dining room, then again for an equally miserable late lunch.

By four in the afternoon she was so fidgety that she left to drive around the countryside, staring with unseeing eyes at the flamboyant Vermont foliage. She stopped at a state park and took a long and lonely walk through the crunching leaves, wondering why she didn't just pack up and go home. Instead, she drove back to Leaftree, ate a tasteless hamburger at a nondescript diner and returned to her room and her waiting.

She got out her paperwork for FUTURE and forced herself to concentrate. She pretended it was simply an ordinary work session and that her world contained no fraudulent wills, no Bachelors' Club and, most important of all, no Eli Holder.

By midnight, when she still hadn't heard from him, she decided she hated him and would go home the next day. That he hadn't contacted her was a sign straight from the heavens: *Get out of this mess while there's time.*

She fell asleep out of sheer emotional exhaustion. The next thing that impinged upon her consciousness was someone tapping at her window.

She sat up straight in the darkness, her heart beating wildly. Either the cockroaches at the Nutmeg Peddler were so big they could bang on windows or that vile rat Eli had finally turned up.

She got up without switching on the light, groped for her robe, pulled up the blind and shoved up the stubborn, paint-jammed window.

It was Eli, all right, his elbow resting nonchalantly on the sill. He was dressed in black again, and she could just discern his shadowy features by the light of the few stars that dotted the sky. He gave her his crooked half smile. "Hi," he said.

She leaned over to bring her face level with his. "What is this?" she whispered angrily. "What is this adolescent idiocy?"

"I wanted to talk to you," he said simply.

"Have you ever heard of the telephone?" she demanded. "It was invented by Alexander Graham Bell. It makes stunts like this unnecessary."

"Maybe I ran out of dimes," he said sarcastically. "Maybe I should ask for a raise. Move, will you? I'm coming in."

"Oh, really!" she said and wheeled angrily away from the window. She belted her robe more tightly around her small waist and ran a hand over her hair in frustration. She felt like a naughty teenager letting a boy into her bedroom.

He vaulted up and entered the window with an effortless fluid movement she was forced to admire in spite of herself. He might have spent his youth as a cat burglar instead of a con man.

He closed the window, then stepped toward her swiftly and pulled her to his chest before she knew what he was doing. She felt his height, his warmth, was assailed again by the subtle autumn-and-brandy aura of his cologne. He dipped his head and kissed her, expertly but briefly. The warmth of his lips seemed to say, "Welcome Back to Wonderland." Something within her leaped wildly.

"Hi, again," he said in that maddening low voice. He was obviously pleased with himself. He stepped away from her and pulled the window shade down. Then, moving through the darkness without misstep, he switched on the small battered lamp on her nightstand. She blinked nervously. He must have memorized where everything in the room was in the few moments he'd seen it by the paltry starlight. Once again the quickness of his mind disarmed her.

"Ah," he said, "a little light on the subject." He threw himself easily onto her rumpled bed, cast a disdainful glance at the inelegant pillow and leaned against the headboard, hands locked behind his head. "Why are you standing there with your lower lip jutting out? Aren't you happy to see me?"

"Not particularly," she said, standing more erect and setting her lower lip more firmly. "I'd just decided to leave tomorrow and quit all this craziness. Now here you are, finally, running through the night and leaping in my window like Zorro. I'm surprised you don't pull out your rapier and make the mark of Z on my pillowcase."

"When I pull out my rapier in a lady's bed," he said wickedly, "I am usually not concerned with her pillowcase."

One corner of his mouth lifted as she blushed and glared at him. He patted the bed beside him. "But I didn't drop in to swap Freudian innuendos. Sit down. You're not going anywhere tomorrow except to the Ivory Castle. We, love and dove, have a scam to set. It's a lovely piece of work. You're going to admire this."

"I doubt it," she said darkly. "You're enjoying yourself too much, Holder. You never really got the larceny out of your blood, did you? You're going to cheat somebody, and it turns you on. It actually turns you on."

He shrugged casually. "Sure. It turns me on. It, among other things. But don't look down your nose until you hear the plan. Because, Junior, the beauty of it is that it's almost legal."

"Almost?" she asked suspiciously. "Meaning not quite legal, right?"

"Oh, sit down," he said impatiently. "You look like the Goddess of Justice standing there with her blindfold off, giving me a dirty look. Or don't sit down. Stand there all night if it makes you happy. Are you afraid to sit on a bed with me? Does it compromise your highborn Boston principles?"

"Don't be ridiculous," she muttered. She sat down beside him because there was really no place else to sit except the untrustworthy desk chair.

He immediately put his arms around her shoulders companionably and drew her back to lean beside him against the headboard.

"Don't," she objected, feeling stiff and self-conscious so close to him again.

"Silence is golden, P.J.," he murmured, putting his forefinger briefly against her full lips. He let it linger there a moment longer than he needed to. "Just listen. I'm not going to steal the Bachelors' money—exactly. I'm going to persuade them to give it away."

"Give it away?" she protested, but he laid his finger against her lips again, and this time he let it stay.

"Shh. That's not even the best part," he said, smiling. "They're going to give it to SOS. They're going to hand every cent back where it belongs."

He watched surprise war with disbelief in her face. Yes, he thought with satisfaction, he'd caught her off guard, as he knew he would. He studied her changing expressions. She kept her eyes trained on his, as if she could read some answer there. But he was careful to give her no clue.

At last he took his finger from her lips. Such a beautiful mouth, he thought. He was glad she didn't wear lipstick. It would have been like smearing paint on a flower.

She kept staring at him. Without thinking, she licked her lips, as if she could still taste the imprint of his finger. "All right," she said at last. "How are you going to do it? How can you make them give it all back to SOS?"

He leaned back against the headboard again. "Simple. They won't know it's SOS. They'll send the money back through FUTURE."

"FUTURE?" she said in appalled disbelief. "The subcorporation? It isn't even legally formed yet."

"The Bachelors don't know that," he said easily. "Nobody except people at SOS know much about FUTURE, do they?"

She shook her head. "Well...no. Some artists, some craftsmen, a few manufacturers I've contacted about bids for things like T-shirts. But no...it's never generated any publicity. It won't until we're organized and ready to operate."

"Then it's perfect," he affirmed, his voice still rich with satisfaction.

"For what?" she asked, bewildered.

"For the Bachelors to 'invest' in. For them to think it's a company that's going to make them richer than Croesus. And to serve as a funnel to get the money back to SOS."

She shook her head in despair. "Eli, that's crazy," she objected, her face troubled. "Nobody can invest in FUTURE. It's not like a company with stocks and things. It's just a marketing division for a nonprofit corporation. It would be like trying to invest in . . . in UNICEF Christmas cards or the Red Cross. It's impossible to do.''

Again he said, "The Bachelors don't know that. And they won't know. I'm going to make it sound like a gold mine. They're going to be begging me to pour their money into it.''

"But that's misrepresentation," she said in agitation. "It's still fraud. It's . . . lying.''

He raised a forefinger in admonition. "Not quite. The truth is like the law. It can be bent without being broken. All I have to do is bend it carefully. I don't have to say one untrue thing about FUTURE. I just tell them enough to let them jump to their own conclusions.''

"But, Eli," she said, shaking her head, "that's still twisting the truth. I know this concept is foreign to you, but what you're proposing is *wrong*.''

The arm that he had draped so casually around her shoulders suddenly rose and tightened, although not roughly, about her neck. He had her imprisoned, and he brought his face very close to hers.

"P.J.," he said, his voice dropping to that level she knew meant business, "stealing from SOS was wrong. That crime helped kill your father. That was wrong. Parmenter knew full well that Delmer Fordyce had a heart condition but didn't warn him. I don't know if that's murder, but it's close, and it's sure as hell malpractice—which is wrong. Besides that Parmenter obviously picked two witnesses he knew were going to die. I doubt if he told them, either. And I'd say that's wrong. Now we either do it my way, or they get away with it—scot-free. And that, my dear, is wrong. Don't tell me I don't understand.''

He was almost hissing the words at her, and she could feel his breath warm against her lips, feel his brown eyes boring into hers.

"But," she disagreed, "we can't—''

He tightened his hold on her and brought his face even closer. "Listen," he said, barely louder than a breath, "do you think if we left, walked away, it would be over? No. It'll go on. I have a strong hunch other people are going to die because of this, Junior. Hasn't that thought crossed your mind?"

"What do you mean?" she asked, suddenly frightened.

"I mean I think Parmenter knows somebody else might need to die. And may help him along."

"Who?" He was beginning to overwhelm her powers of protest.

He loosened his hold and drew back slightly. He stared down, the line of his mouth straight, one brow lowered in a frown. "You saw it as clearly as I did last night. There's a weak link in the chain of the Bachelors' defenses. One Bachelor has an unfortunate virtue—a conscience—and a fatal weakness—drink."

Her eyes widened, and she felt a chill creep through her bone marrow. "Clive? You really think Parmenter would...kill Clive?"

She bit her lip nervously. Of the four men, Clive, with his wrinkles and inflamed nose, had been the only one to show any compunction about what had been done. He had grown more garrulous about those pangs of conscience—up to a certain number of drinks. And Parmenter seemed to know exactly how many drinks it took to lull Clive's guilt to sleep.

"He wouldn't be stupid enough to kill him outright," Eli said, watching her face carefully. "But I think he can make certain he dies. Soon. Before he can do any damage. And I suspect there just might be another will made out, this one for Clive."

"You mean, they'd try to do the same thing again?" she asked in horror. "Have a will made for Clive that would benefit them? How could they dare try it twice?"

His face darkened. He looked into her clear blue eyes and shook his head. "You don't know much about greed, kid. What else are they going to do? Take a chance Clive gets plastered and tells the wrong things to the wrong people? And if something happens to him, why let his million dollars slip off to someone else? If you're taking bets, I'll put my money on something happening to Clive—soon. And another fortunate will showing up."

She furrowed her brow and thought for a long time. "Look," she said at last, hope dying hard, "maybe Clive is the key to all this. You said he has a conscience. If he realizes he's in danger, he might cooperate with us and you wouldn't have to try to pull off this crazy scheme. I'm sure if he turned state's witness, he'd get immunity...."

Suddenly Eli looked impatient. "Clive is our worst bet. You've got a lot to learn about human nature, too. Of the four, he's the most complicated. He's also the most desperate and the one with the most at stake."

"Why?" she asked, not understanding.

"Because some forty years ago good Dentist Clive made a mistake. He fell in love with one of his patients, a rather fragile married woman named Mrs. Wiggingdon. Worse, he had an affair with her. Mr. Wiggingdon found out about it and discovered that Mrs. Wiggingdon was with child—in all likelihood not his."

P.J. looked at him, her eyes troubled. "How do you know all this?"

"My friend with the Jamaican Jungle Juicers partly," he said. "And my other... assistant," he added carefully.

The blonde in his room, P.J. thought bitterly and refused to relax against his enfolding arm.

"At any rate, Wiggingdon wasn't the forgiving type. He kicked Mrs. Wiggingdon out of the house, but he wouldn't divorce her. That would make things too easy for her. Rotten guy, Wiggingdon. He wanted her branded as an adultress and the kid a bastard. And he didn't want Clive to have her."

"And?" P.J. probed.

"And," Eli continued, his mouth curled in bitterness, "some thought Wiggingdon was a brute, and some thought the woman deserved it. But she didn't pay for long. She died in childbirth. The child, a boy, was so severely retarded he's been institutionalized all his life. Rumor has it he's the image of Clive. Clive's supported him all these years. But each year the son's health gets frailer and the medical bills get higher."

"That's horrible," P.J. said, aghast. She suddenly felt sorry for ill-kempt Clive and understood why he looked so much older than his friends. "At least he's been decent enough to care for the boy."

"Granted," Eli conceded. "And Wiggingdon was such a bastard that public sympathy finally swung around to Clive. But not before he began to drink. His practice had been a passable one but never lucrative. The more he drank, the less lucrative it became. But three people stood by him through it all."

"The other Bachelors," P.J. guessed. "Parmenter, Dirkson and Charlie Bangor."

"Right," said Eli, "but the point is, Clive would be our hardest mark. He's erratic. You can't tell which way he'll swing. I've got to hook one Bachelor, gig him right through the gills."

"Well, who?" P.J. asked puzzled. "Dr. Parmenter's too cagey, Charlie Bangor's too stupid to convince the others to do anything and Dirkson's loathsome, but he's nobody's fool."

Eli sat up straighter. He looked at her, smiled slightly and ruffled her bangs. "Wrong, Harvard. Charlie Bangor's the key. *Because* he's so stupid. If he can seem to make money hand over fist, the others will jump right in the water, where I, your friendly neighborhood shark, will be waiting.''

"And how do you get to Bangor?'' she asked, realizing that somehow she was going along with him again, in spite of her previous resolve.

"Through Teddy Dirkson," he said, giving her a self-satisfied grin. "Dirkson starts it all off. All I have to do is get him to take the bait."

"What bait?" she asked suspiciously. She leaned away from him slightly. His nearness was keeping her from thinking straight.

The smug grin didn't change. He kept his eyes on hers to gauge her reaction. "You, Junior."

"Oh, no," she said, drawing farther away. She stood and nervously readjusted the belt of her robe. "I think you'd better get out of here, Holder. I don't intend to be bait for anybody. Out, out, out. The window is that way." She pointed, just in case he'd forgotten.

He wrapped his arms around his bent knees. He studied her solemnly. "Is it the word bait?" he asked with false concern. "Does the term make you feel I'm comparing you to a night crawler or a piece of liver? I could change the terminology."

"It's not the word," she said, crossing her arms in irritation. "It's the concept. It's demeaning. I will not play floozy for that old lecher."

He leaned back against the bed again, laughing. "You couldn't play floozy if you tried. All you have to be is yourself. A sweet young thing."

"That," she sniffed, "is also a demeaning statement and sexist. I'm not a sweet young thing. I'm a mature, well-educated person. I don't go around trying to seduce old men in bad toupees."

"Oh, God," he groaned, "another fit of morals. Will you shut up, sit down and listen to what I have to say? What you do is so simple a hamster could do it—provided, of course, Dirkson is interested in hamsters instead of women."

Eventually, she relented and let him explain, which he did, briefly and clearly. She looked at him, reevaluating him for the thousandth time. What kind of mind did he have, anyway, she wondered in alarmed awe, to come up with a scheme like that?

It was brilliant, it was complex, but the part she played was simple. A child would be able to do it.

He finally got off the bed, shut off the lights, raised the blind and opened the window. "Come here," he said softly.

Slowly, wondering why she was doing so, she went to him. "I've got to go," he said, his voice low. "I still have work to do. You're going to do fine tomorrow. Remember that and don't be frightened. You'll be perfect. Now give me a kiss."

"Why?" she asked, her voice small. Her heart was starting to do strange gymnastics again.

"So I don't have to take it," he answered and took her face between his hands. She fought the desire to rise on her toes and touch her lips to his. She fought it so hard it made her chest hurt.

So he bent and kissed her instead. "You'll learn," he said against her lips. "You'll learn it's nicer when both of us can initiate this kind of thing."

He kissed her again, making something deep within her melt and her knees turn weak.

"I always figured you'd wear blue-and-white-striped pajamas," he said softly. And although the room was very nearly dark, she could tell he was smiling at her. "What do you figure I wear to bed?"

"I...never troubled to think about it," she said, her voice shaky.

"What do you suppose?" he teased, running his thumb over the slight cleft in her chin.

"Nothing, I suppose," she said miserably and tried not to imagine it.

"Right," he said cheerfully. And then, to her amazement and confusion, he bent and kissed her between her breasts, a short, hot but possessive kiss.

"Nighty-night," he said in the same cheerful voice and disappeared through the window.

He vanished into the outside shadows as if by magic. She shut the window and put her hand to her chest as if to calm the rebellion in her heart. Her fingers met bare flesh. Her mouth dropped open, and she switched on the bedside lamp. Somehow, without her knowing it, he had unbuttoned the top three buttons of her pajamas.

She buttoned them back up swiftly, threw off her robe and climbed into bed. She pulled the blanket up under her chin as if it could protect her from the world and from herself.

She sat up late into the night, staring at the stain on the wallpaper. His plan was exactly like him—devious, daring and remarkable.

All she had to do was appear tomorrow morning at the Ivory Castle and perform the easiest of tasks. And Eli, like a sorcerer in a three-piece suit, would begin to cast the spell that used greed to bewitch four old men and deprive them of their reason.

He ought to be able to deprive them of their brainpower with no effort at all, she thought darkly. He had already stolen most of hers by casting the oldest spell of all.

THE MORNING SKY WAS a deep and delicate blue, the morning sunshine lucid, and the hills around the Ivory Castle blazed gaudily with autumn color.

P.J. moved self-consciously across the patio of the Ivory Castle, her heart beating hard. She wore a bulky gray sweater and a rather full skirt of wine-and-gray plaid. Eli said the full skirt would make it easier. She carried her largest purse and a copy of the morning newspaper.

She saw her quarry and swallowed hard. Teddy Dirkson was sitting at one of the patio tables and had just unfolded a linen napkin in his ample lap. He had an open book of poems before him, but his eyes weren't on the print. They were on her. He smiled at her with his brilliant white teeth. He patted his false blond curls self-consciously.

She forced herself to smile back. Dirkson positively beamed. She steeled herself, made her way to his table and put her hand on the vacant chair.

"Would you mind if I joined you?" she asked, amazed there was no quaver in her voice. "I'm new around here and—"

"Oh, *please* do," oozed Dirkson. He leaped to his feet so swiftly the napkin fluttered from his lap, but P.J. had already pulled the chair out and started to sit down.

"I'm delighted to have company, especially such beautiful company. Are you staying here by any chance?" Dirkson was saying.

"No," P.J. replied brightly. "At the Nutmeg Peddler. But the food there is so bad I decided to splurge and— Oh!"

She had settled into the chair and now looked startled. She reached under the folds of her skirt to the chair's seat and withdrew a large official-looking folder. She had concealed it in the newspaper as Eli had instructed her.

She produced it and laid it on the table with a flourish. It all seemed remarkably easy. She felt a painful twinge that stung her whole body. *So this is how simple it is to start a life of crime.*

"My goodness, what's this?" she asked, blinking in surprise at Dirkson. "Is it yours?"

"I have no idea what it is," Dirkson said. "Someone must have left it there. Let me see it. Perhaps we can track down the owner."

His voice was as rich, fruity and condescending as she remembered. He flipped open the folder and frowned at it. P.J. knew why his face showed such consternation: the papers within looked important, mentioned extravagant amounts of money and made no sense whatsoever. They were gobbledygook, designed to be impressive but incomprehensible.

She had found the folder on the front seat of her car that morning. Eli must have completed it sometime during the night. It was an astounding creation. She thought again that the entire FBI must have gotten down on its knees and offered thanks when Eli decided to work for it and not against it.

"It seems to be some sort of financial information," Dirkson said, still frowning. He obviously couldn't understand anything about the papers except the startling amounts of money they mentioned. "But it's almost in code or something."

"Mercy," said P.J., "isn't there a name on it anywhere?"

"Let me see," Dirkson said importantly and began rummaging through the papers. "Ah, there's a note."

He withdrew an expensive piece of stationery, squinted at the scrawl and read in his best poet's tones:

"Elwyn,
FUTURE's the thing. Not ready to go public. Room for yourself and possibly four or five more firm backers. Keep confidential.

                                        G.C."

Dirkson looked at her and raised his shaggy brows. His eyes were impossibly blue, and with a start she realized he was wearing tinted contact lenses.

"Sounds very mysterious," he said. "Concerns someone named Elwyn. I'll see if there's anyone by that name around."

He snapped his fingers imperiously to summon a waiter, ordered him to see if anyone named Elwyn was registered at the hotel, then snapped his fingers again to send the man scurrying away.

He sat back in his chair and daintily sipped his coffee. "We'll have this solved in no time," he said smugly. "And then we'll have that waiter take your order. I recommend the shirred eggs. Divine. And might I buy you a glass of breakfast champagne? I'm in the mood to celebrate."

"Celebrate?" she asked.

"Yes," he said, smiling whitely. "I just finished a devilishly difficult poem last night. I'm a poet, you see."

"A poet!" P.J. murmured with appropriate awe. "How wonderful!"

"So far, my reputation is only local," Dirkson said modestly. "I have great hopes that a New York publisher will be interested in my next book. The poem I've just completed will be the title piece. It's called 'Rover Will Roam in the Clover No More.' It's about a dog squashed on the road. I'm very sensitive about such things. Do you like poetry?"

"Very much," she replied. Out of the corner of her eye she saw Eli's tall form approaching. She felt both relieved and frightened.

Then he was at their table, his face haggard. "Excuse me," he said, a barely masked desperation in his voice, "but did you by any chance—" His eyes fell on the folder lying by Dirkson's coffee cup. "You found it," he almost gasped. "Thank God."

Dirkson picked up the folder. "Is this yours, sir?" he asked. He stared up at Eli somewhat suspiciously. This was that rather nervous man who'd been so chummy with the beautiful blonde.

"Yes," Eli said. "Thank God it's not lost—or worse, stolen. If it should fall into the wrong hands..."

Then the waiter materialized. "Mr. Dirkson," he said with excessive politeness, "there's a Mr. Elwyn Holderman registered... Oh, Mr. Holderman, it's you, isn't it?"

Eli nodded nervously and took the folder from Dirkson with so much concern it might have been a tender young child. "Thank God," he said again. He looked at Dirkson with intense respect. "You were tracking me down? You would have had me paged?"

"Certainly," Dirkson said rather haughtily. "It was the logical thing to do."

"You, sir," Eli said with gratitude, "are an honest man. I can't tell you how I appreciate that."

"Tush," Dirkson said dismissively. "The young lady found it."

Eli turned to P.J. for the first time. "You're the one who found it? Bless you, my child."

She shrugged modestly but found it hard to take her eyes off Eli. Somehow, without changing so much as a hair, he had transformed himself. He seemed thinner, paler, a man of questionable health and humorless as a grave.

"I must sit down," Eli said in a shaky voice. "I hope you don't mind if I join you for a moment. When I realized this folder was gone, my life literally flashed before my eyes. I need a drink. And please allow me to buy your breakfasts." He sat down without invitation and looked up at the waiter. "A Bloody Mary, please," he said.

"*I* am buying the young lady's breakfast," Dirkson said icily. He gave the waiter a kingly stare. "She'll have the shirred eggs and the croissant. And bring champagne for the two of us. As well as a pot of coffee."

He cast Eli a measuring glance from beneath his shaggy brows. He didn't like this younger man horning in when he had just captured this fresh-faced little creature for himself. Besides, the man already had that scrumptious blonde.

But Eli disarmed him almost immediately. "Oh," he said, stricken, "I didn't mean to intrude. I can see that you two have a sort of...remarkable rapport. But I'm not exaggerating my concern about this folder. I *insist* on rewarding you."

"I wouldn't dream of accepting a thing," P.J. said with remarkable conviction. "We didn't do anything. I'm just glad you have it back. But I certainly can't accept a reward for just *sitting* on the thing."

She resisted giving a sigh of relief. It was her longest speech, and she thought she'd delivered it well.

Eli looked hurt. "What about you, sir?" he said to Dirkson. "Please allow me to make some monetary compensation for your trouble."

"Nonsense," said Dirkson because he couldn't accept a reward if the woman didn't. It would make him look grasping.

The waiter appeared with their drinks, and Eli gulped his Bloody Mary. He still looked shaken from his experience. With a touch of chagrin he asked for their names, and P.J. uncomfortably gave her new alias, Penny Jameson.

Dirkson sipped his champagne with his little finger extended elegantly. Eli, still looking awkward and embarrassed, stared at his own empty glass. He tried once more to get them to accept a reward. Again P.J. refused. Dirkson followed suit and decided the younger man was really a bit too high-strung to be real competition. In fact, he made a nice foil for Dirkson's own mature poise and confidence.

"Listen," Eli said eagerly, as if he had just had a flash of insight. "If you won't accept money, how about an investment tip? It's my business, you know."

"I'm only a secretary," P.J. said rather pathetically. "I don't have the money to make investments."

"I never invest myself," Dirkson agreed, unsheathing his pearly teeth at her. "It's so...mathematical and materialistic and boring. And I really have quite enough money as it is."

There, Dirkson thought with glee. He sensed the young woman was rather taken with him, and it certainly wouldn't hurt for her to know he was not only handsome, charming and talented but rich, as well.

Eli sank back in his chair in disappointment. He gave every appearance of a man dying to be generous. Then he brightened. "Suppose I make one for the both of you?" he asked, his face practically shining with innocence and gratitude. "I make investments all the time. I know the best ones. Suppose I made a small one on your behalf. And, because I'm indebted to you, I give you the interest. Just one day's interest. That's all. It'd be a bit like buying you a chance in the lottery. You might make nothing...or you might do quite well. Surely you can't object to that."

"Why, that sounds like fun," P.J. said, smiling as she pretended to think about it. "It would be like a lottery ticket, wouldn't it?"

"Exactly," said Eli, almost pathetically grateful for her interest. "How about you, Mr. Dirkson? Would you allow me to do it for you, as well? A simple gesture of gratitude. After all, your lady likes the idea."

"I suppose it makes no difference," Dirkson said gruffly, pleased to have P.J. called 'his lady.' The waiter had brought the eggs, and Dirkson set upon them with passion. P.J., who loathed shirred eggs with all her heart, picked daintily at hers.

"Thank you," Eli said with touching humility. "This information—" he gestured with the folder "—is so vital I must do something to thank you. And now I'll leave you to your privacy." He smiled shyly. "I think I can tell a budding romance when I see one."

Dirkson repressed a smug smile, and P.J. resisted an urge to kick Eli hard.

"Let me meet you here again tomorrow," Eli said with boyish eagerness. "I won't take much of your time or interrupt your breakfast. I'll just let you know if my little investment came through for you. All right?"

"Certainly," P.J. said with enthusiasm. "It'd be fun."

"Why not?" Dirkson said waggishly, deciding he rather liked the young man after all. With his insistence on a reward, he had just arranged another breakfast date for Dirkson with the perky little secretary.

Eli excused himself and left, hugging the folder protectively to his chest.

"Odd duck," Dirkson said, glancing after him. "I think he's here for his nerves or something. But I've seen him with an exceptionally attractive blond woman. Whatever she sees in him, I can't imagine. Probably after his money."

P.J.'s mood darkened at the mention of the blonde.

"Nor," lied Dirkson with considerable ease, "do I understand what he sees in her. I could never abide a gold digger. Given my wealth, I've met a few. Perhaps that's what I find so appealing about you, Miss Jameson. You seem like a woman of breeding—not the type who would be interested in a man simply for his money."

"Money means so little in the ultimate scheme of things," she said, giving him a coy smile. Behind her wide blue eyes, however, a thought struck with stunning vehemence. *You nasty old buzzard, I am going to skin you out of your last red cent and get it back to the rightful owner.*

And then, keeping the smile frozen on her face, she thought, *Now it's begun. It's really begun. And Eli's changed me. But what has he changed me into?*

Chapter Seven

Dirkson insisted on giving P.J.—or "darling Penny" as he called her—a foliage tour along exactly the same route she had taken the day before. Even the lovely autumn leaves of Vermont, she decided, could look dreary when she was in the company of a man as unlikable as Dirkson.

But Eli wanted her to befriend him, just in case he might say something to a woman he might not say to a man. Dirkson, however, fond as he was of talking about himself, avoided saying anything of import. He was also depressingly prone to reciting his own poems.

He insisted on buying her lunch at an extraordinarily expensive roadside inn outside Leaftree. P.J. quickly saw how he, like Charlie Bangor, had managed to run through his family fortune. Everything about Dirkson was expensive, from the large diamond ring on his finger to the restored Bentley he drove. And he seemed convinced he could win P.J. over by lavishing her with goodies. He insisted on the most costly lunch the inn served, the most precious vintage wine. In the small gift shop adjacent to the restaurant, he pressured her into accepting an elaborate music box that played "Autumn Leaves." He stopped at a roadside flower stand just inside the city limits of Leaftree and forced a dozen roses on her.

The afternoon was taking on a nightmarish quality, and at last P.J. begged off, telling Dirkson, truthfully, that hers was a working vacation and she had a small mountain of paperwork to do.

He refused to release her, however, until she had one last glass of champagne with him. "Coffee," P.J. pleaded, having had too many luxuries for one day. Dirkson, of course, knew where the finest and most exotic coffees were served. He drove her to a pretentious little eatery with fifteen blends of coffee and twelve varieties of tea.

But as they sat in its dim recesses, the afternoon suddenly sprang into the realm of the interesting. Terrence Clive slouched through the door, his baggy sweater covered with fuzz balls and his wrinkled face looking sadder than usual.

A look of mild surprise crossed his ruined countenance when he spotted Dirkson sitting possessively close to P.J. He gave them a wry smile and approached.

"Hello, Dirky," Clive said in his whiskey-roughened voice. "Who's this you've captured? How'd you get so lucky?"

"Clive," Dirkson said with mixed pleasure. While Dirkson was glad to show off his new prize to Clive, Clive looked so terribly old that Dirkson was afraid it might reflect badly on him. "Sit down. This is Miss Penny Jameson of Amherst. Penny, Dr. Terrence Clive, a retired dentist. One of my oldest friends. In more than one sense—he's got at least twelve years on me."

"Balderdash," Clive said, not unpleasantly as he sat across from them. "Don't try to fool the nice woman. You're three months older than me, and you know it." He gave P.J. a knowing smile. "We were in first grade together. Back in neolithic times. Teddy's just better preserved."

Dirkson gave his friend a disgusted look, which Clive ignored. The old dentist looked at P.J. with frank interest, as if wondering why she was with Dirkson. "I hope he hasn't been reciting his poems to you," he rasped. "I always tell Dirky he drives off all his ladies with his poetry. It's really awful. But nobody can stop him."

P.J. gave him a guarded smile that said nothing. Dirkson looked offended and disdainful. "You don't understand poetry. You never have and you never will. All you know about is molars and stuff. You wouldn't recognize great art if it spit in your eye."

"Probably not," Clive said, unperturbed. He looked unwell, probably badly hung over, P.J. decided. His hands were slightly shaky, his eyes red rimmed, but he was sober. "What brings you here, anyway, Dirky? I thought you always hung out at the Castle."

"Showing Miss Jameson the town," Dirkson said. "And I wanted her to sample the Gevalia espresso here. It's divine."

"It's overpriced," Clive said. He ordered a simpler blend and, when it came, poured an inordinate amount of sugar into it. "But I come down here almost every afternoon. It breaks up the day, gives me something to do until dinnertime. Retirement doesn't agree with me," he said, looking at P.J. "Dirky doesn't understand because he never worked a day in his life. Except at his 'poems' and his bridge game."

"Ah," Dirkson said, narrowing his eyes craftily. "You're being very sarcastic today. I know what that means. You're depressed about something. Anything you'd care to discuss, or will you just sit there and take it out on me?"

"You know me too well, Dirky," Clive said unhappily. "Yes, I've had bad news. No, I don't think I should discuss it in front of your pretty friend. It's Albert again."

"Miss Jameson is a woman of refined sympathies," Dirkson pronounced. "I'm sure she'll understand. What about Albert? Is he worse?"

Clive glanced at P.J., and perhaps he did see sympathy in her face. "Albert's my son," he explained wearily. "He's severely retarded. He's been institutionalized since childhood. His health is precarious." He turned to Dirkson. "And yes, he's worse. They're talking about another damned operation. Sometimes I wonder why they don't let the poor boy just slip away. He has no life. Only an existence. And a painful one at that."

"I'm sorry," P.J. said. Clive's dilemma was a terrible one, and she couldn't dislike him as much as the other Bachelors.

"Devilish bad luck," Dirkson said and seemed to mean it.

They chatted aimlessly for a while, and then Clive left to take his evening's walk in the park. It passed the time, he said, his loneliness almost palpable. P.J. finally convinced Dirkson that she had to go back to the Nutmeg Peddler, and no, she could not drive to Burlington with him for the most exclusive Chinese cuisine in Vermont.

"Unfortunate fellow, Clive," Dirkson commented as he helped P.J. into the Bentley. "Drinks like a fish, as you can probably tell. Never starts before seven in the evening—and then always alone or only with a trusted friend—but then he'll drink till he passes out. Blighted life, poor chap. Recently came into some money. But it hasn't made him happy."

"And you've been friends most of your lives?" she asked.

"Yes, indeed," Dirkson said. "In fact there are four of us. We call ourselves the Bachelors' Club. We've known one another since childhood. There is nothing more beautiful than friendship—" he tossed her a blue-eyed, leering glance "—unless it's a woman such as yourself."

When he let her off at her own car in the Ivory Castle parking lot, P.J. had never been so happy to escape anyone in her life. But before she could flee, he opened the trunk of the Bentley and lifted the lid of an enormous box of books. He handed her a copy.

"A humble little gift at our temporary parting," he said. "Some of my poems that I've had printed at my own expense. I hope you'll enjoy them."

She glanced down with apprehension at the book, which was bound in genuine calfskin and embossed with what appeared to be real gold, *Beaten to Death by Butterflies: A Collection of Poems by Theodore Dirkson*. The edges of the pages also gleamed with gold. Dirkson had spent a pretty penny to immortalize his work.

"Thank you," she said, "I'm very touched."

Then Dirkson dipped deeply, as if bowing, seized the hand in which she was holding the music box and kissed her clenched fingers with wet passion.

He raised his head and stared into her eyes with great intensity. "Until tomorrow morning, my azure-eyed nymph. I will count the minutes. *Au revoir.*"

By the time she got back to the Nutmeg Peddler, she no longer wanted simply to deprive Dirkson of his ill-gotten money. She wanted to deprive him of his life. But she couldn't stave off a feeling of sadness for unhappy, broken-spirited old Terrence Clive. He alone of the four men seemed to actually need the money for something other than the gratification of his own selfishness. The thought of Clive and his hapless son was not comforting. *What happens to them if we get the money back?* she thought. What would become of poor, helpless Albert if, as Eli suspected, something happened to Clive?

She suddenly thought that it was Clive, not Dirkson, she should be keeping her eye on.

ELI SURPRISED HER with the simple courtesy of calling at about ten o'clock that evening. He kept his message brief, as usual. "Have your lights off at midnight and your window up. We need to talk."

"Eli," she said between her teeth, "is all this melodrama necessary? Do you have to come swooping through my window every night like Don Juan? Isn't there some other way to do this?"

"Yes," he said tersely. "You can go through the woods, take the passage under the icehouse, put on your wig and falsies and come to my room. We need guaranteed privacy. Now are you going to open your window or not?"

"Oh, all right," she assented unhappily. Maybe he was right. Leaftree was so small they might be seen together almost anywhere else they met.

She turned out the lights at precisely five minutes to midnight, but this time she had not changed into her pajamas. She wore the designer jeans she'd bought at Filene's, leg warmers and boots and a cotton turtleneck with a bulky blue sweater over it. She felt safer facing Eli in as many layers of clothes as was possible to wear.

This time he didn't bother to tap at her window. She sat nervously on her bed when she heard the faintest of rustlings, a muted deep breath and a soft movement. Then he was standing in her room. He pulled down both the window and blind, then made his way unerringly to her bed. He threw himself down beside her. Then he reached up and put his arm around her neck.

"Kiss me," he ordered, drawing her closer to him.

"Stop that," she protested ineffectually. "You're always doing that. You don't need to."

"I do. For luck," he said, and the pressure of his arm brought her so near that he brushed his lips across hers with maddening brevity. As usual, his slightest touch sent cold flames coursing through her body. She forced herself to draw away swiftly. He let her, as if it were of no consequence to him.

She sat up straight again, shook her head to clear it, then switched on the light, hoping its dim beams would drive away the primal darkness that always seemed to overtake her in Eli's arms.

He still lay on the bed. He was dressed in black again. He eyed her lazily, smiled slightly. "More new clothes," he said, appraising her thoroughly. "How pretty you look—and how covered up. Why don't you add a down vest and a parka?"

"I'd add a suit of armor if I had one," she said unhappily. "I'm not in the habit of having men climb into my bed demanding kisses—especially men with prison records. Can't you stick to business?"

"It's not such a long prison record," he said, smiling indulgently. "Certainly not compared with those of the rest of my family. But if it's business you want, it's business you'll get. But first, how was your day with Teddy Dirkson, and did you find out anything?"

"It was horrible, and all I found out is that he's more of a jackass than I thought."

"Who likes to give presents, eh?" He cast a cynical glance at the roses, the music box and the gilt-edged book on the scarred dresser.

"Yes," she agreed in disgust. "And you'd better get the money back from him before he spends it all. That happens to be SOS's money that he's throwing around. And just what have you been up to?"

"Me?" He shrugged. "Thinking. Refining things. Setting them up. Talking to people. There are two things I can't get a handle on. The first is how the Bachelors got Fordyce to sign that phony will. There are plenty of possible explanations, but I'd like to know the real one. Second, I want to know more about that malpractice suit against Parmenter. Nobody seems to know much. I have a hunch it's something like what happened to Delmer Fordyce and those two witnesses: Parmenter misdiagnosed—or pretended to mis-diagnose—somebody who was seriously ill."

"What difference does it make?" P.J. asked gloomily. "We know they forged the will. We're not going to court. We're going to have to trick them out of the money."

"I never said we might not be back in court," Eli said with such offhandedness that she knew the statement was loaded.

"What do you mean?" she asked, suddenly wary. She brought up her knees and hugged them tightly, as if the position could protect her.

Eli didn't bother to glance at her. "We haven't got enough evidence to take the Bachelors to court. But once I've fleeced them, they may try to take me. It'd be foolishly bold of them, but they've never lacked for boldness. I'd like to have as much on them as possible."

"What?" she cried in horror. "I thought you said this was legal—or almost! Now you've got me involved, and you tell me we might end up on trial?"

He finally turned to look up at her. His face was serious for once. "I thought you always knew that," he said quietly.

She stared at him, stretched so calmly beside her. She felt numb all over. "I'd thought . . . You kept saying . . ."

"Don't worry. Nobody'd ever convict you of anything. I'd say I conned you, along with everyone else. I bet you've never even got a parking ticket in your life. A paragon of virtue, sucked into this nefarious scheme by the old hustling pro—me."

"Oh, fine!" she wailed, throwing her hands out in despair. "I get a suspended sentence or something, destroy my reputation forever, and you just might go back to prison. Eli, I swear you're doing this because you love flirting with danger. You *want* to pull this con."

He rolled onto his side, bracing himself on his elbow. He cocked his head and stared into her face hard. "Maybe you're right. Maybe from the time I heard your story, I knew the only way to get that money back was to con it back. Maybe I wanted the thrill one more time. Or maybe I just wanted to help you enough that I was willing to chance it—but you'd never believe that, would you?"

She blinked hard in surprise. He'd never before mentioned that he actually wanted to help her—and yet she knew he must. Obviously he hated prison, but what if he was putting himself in danger of going back—and losing everything he had achieved—just to help her?

She looked at him, a sick expression on her face. "I don't want you back in jail, Eli. Not for me or SOS or anything else. We've got to stop."

He gave her a slanted smile, and the scar in his cheek deepened. "Now there's a new twist, blue eyes. Before you were afraid because you thought it was wrong. Now can you possibly be afraid that something might happen to me?"

She looked at him. She swallowed hard. She couldn't bring herself to be less than honest. And suddenly it seemed as if the two of them might not have much time. "Yes. I'm afraid for you. I can't bear to imagine you locked up. It'd make you crazy."

He said nothing for a moment. He studied her face, then reached out and smoothed her bangs. He ran his finger lightly down the bridge of her nose, touched her lips, then let his hand fall away carelessly. "They'd never send me to prison. I'm not taking the money for myself. What jury would convict me? I mean, I'm practically Robin Hood, dammit. Don't worry."

"Don't worry," she moaned. She hugged her knees again and pressed her face against them. She had the feeling he was relying on bravado to comfort her. "You *hope* nobody would convict you, you don't *know* it."

She was right, but he preferred not to think about it. Lazily he straightened to a sitting position and slipped his arm around her slim shoulders. "That's why I want to find out everything about the Bachelors I can," he assured her. "They'd be fools to take us to court. But if they try, I want to be well covered—by knowing every suspicious move any of them has ever made."

She kept her face hidden. She wished he'd take his arm away because by that time she was so confused and frightened she wanted to turn to him, lean against his chest and simply hold on to him for all she was worth.

"Hey," he said. "Don't worry." His voice was surprisingly gentle. He kissed her hair, the tip of her ear. "If you want to get out, you can leave now. Send a note to Dirkson saying your aunt in Poughkeepsie has the weasel pox and needs you at her bedside. You're not really involved yet. I never intended to get you involved more than superficially. You can go back to Boston. I can make it alone from here."

"Don't kiss me," she said in a muffled voice because he was kissing her hair again. She wanted only to sink into his arms and quit the impossible battle to resist him. Instead, she summoned the last of her usually iron control. "And I'm not leaving," she said grimly. "I'm staying. I'm going the whole way. You couldn't get rid of me now at gunpoint. So stop telling me to go home. I'm not a coward."

Gently he made her stop hugging her knees and sit up. He looked into her eyes. Although they were worried, they were devoid of tears, and deep within the blue sparks were struggling to swirl. "Certain?" he asked.

His hands were on her arms, and she very carefully, very deliberately, put her own hands on his biceps. Her touch was soft, tentative, but her voice was sure. "I'm certain."

He gave her his slow smile. "Then act certain. We'll keep our eyes and ears open—just in case. And Cleo's in the wings working her mysterious ways. She may find exactly what we need.''

Her hands tensed on his arms at the mention of Cleo, who she instinctively knew was the lavish blonde who'd been in his room.

If he noticed her reaction, he pretended not to. ''And things will start moving faster than you believe. You won't have time to worry. After I give you and Teddy Dirkson your 'rewards' at breakfast, I'm going to end up in the heart of the Bachelors' Club. They won't be able to get enough of me.''

He sounded so confident she almost forgot her fears and smiled.

''Don't believe me, do you?'' he teased, running the back of his fingers over the softness of her bangs again. ''Wait and see. Tomorrow night I'll be in the library, drinking with them as their honored guest. They'll love me so much they'll practically want to adopt me. And by the next day the money should start flowing back to SOS.''

''How can you be so sure?'' she asked because she needed more than ever to believe him.

He lifted a shoulder. ''I can't explain. I have instincts. When I trust them, I'm fine. When I don't, I'm not. I have them about everything. Even you.''

''Me?'' she asked, almost against her will. His arms felt solid and unconquerable beneath her fingertips. Her heart beat hard under her layers of clothing. She realized she cared for him so much it terrified her. Looking into those golden-brown eyes, she was so frightened it nearly paralyzed her. She felt as if she were poised at the edge of a bottomless chasm.

He kissed one eyebrow and then the other. ''I want to make love to you,'' he said, his voice soft and deep. ''But my instinct says you're not ready. Yet. You don't need another moral issue to confound you—or frighten you. Because in the end everything comes down to a moral issue for you. But my instinct says not to leave you. To stay here as long as possible. And do nothing. Except this. Hold you in my arms.''

Slowly he lowered her so that they lay side by side on the bed. He drew her close. He kissed the tip of her ear again but made no move more intimate. ''Rest, Junior,'' he murmured. ''Just let me hold you. You've got enough to worry about tonight without torturing your pretty head over sex. But one of these days—and maybe one of these nights— you'll learn to trust me.''

She stretched beside him, letting him cradle her in his strong arms. She laid her head against his chest and could feel the beat of his heart beneath the softness of his sweater. She was grateful for his simple human warmth. She was puzzled, almost disappointed, that he made no more demand on her than this. And yet she realized that he was right. Sex at that point would be too horribly mixed up with all her hopes and fears. What she needed most from him was his strength, his closeness, his unexpected gentleness.

And she needed desperately to trust him because tomorrow they would enter the danger in earnest. And together.

It was a long time before Eli felt her relax in his arms, slip into an uneasy doze. Gently he pulled her closer. He ran his hand lightly over her smooth hair again, let his chin rest against her silken bangs as he cradled her slight frame against his length.

He stared into the darkness. He was holding her because for so long a time he had wanted to. He realized that he was trying to protect her, that maybe he would do almost anything to protect her, and he didn't even know why. He realized he didn't simply want sex with her, he wanted to make love to her, and when he did, he wanted it to be perfect, untainted by fear or desperation. He wanted her to trust him completely, as she had never trusted another human being, the way only someone in love trusts.

He knew full well he was not a man to trust, nor one whom it was safe to love. Love was the oldest con of all. When he played it, he played it to win, entirely for his own gain and damn the loser. Let her weep. He had always been able to walk away. Now, perversely, he was playing for keeps again with a woman that he didn't want to hurt. He would, of course, hurt her. And he suspected when he did walk away from her, he was going to be feeling pain himself, for the first time in years. And maybe guilt. For the first time in his life.

ACROSS TOWN, in an immaculate white clapboard house, as colonial as New England itself, another man lay staring into the darkness. Dr. James Parmenter found that the older he got, the less sleep he seemed to need. Perhaps, knowing how few years might be left to him, he did not want to waste them in sleep, not when he could use the time to make plans to protect the precious life left to him, to make it as secure, as comfortable as possible.

He made plans carefully and well, for his was a mind that was scientific to the point of coldness, and he was a man whom the years had made almost perfectly selfish. He was a highly refined creature, a streamlined machine designed for pleasant self-survival.

He was also, as a physician, a man of power. He had learned to wield it ruthlessly, clumsily at first, then with greater and greater artistry. Once, idealistically, he had vowed to save lives, at any price. Now, idealism long worn away, he had learned that some lives were clearly expendable. If a man's death created a greater good for a greater number than his life did, let him die. Perhaps even assist him in that dying, so the benefits of his demise flowed forth more swiftly and without impediment.

Parmenter was not without emotion. He had loyalties, he even had, in his way, affections. But he no longer allowed them to interfere with the most important of his priorities—his own safety and well-being.

He hoped he had his unfortunate friend, the alcoholic Clive, under sufficient control. Clive had enough sense to confine his drinking to the evening, when he was alone or with Parmenter or one of the other Bachelors who could keep his tongue from wagging dangerously. But Terrence Clive had always had such a vigorous conscience—far too vigorous. It was that that had led him to drink in the first place. Such a conscience, combined with the wrong number of drinks, could conceivably pose a problem. And it might be for the greater good if poor, tortured, hagridden old Clive was released from his considerable worldly sorrows, his fortune channeled to some endeavor more rewarding than the support of his idiot son.

So, quite coolly, Dr. Parmenter lay in the darkness contemplating how, if necessary, he would arrange that Terrence Clive, his faithful friend of sixty years, die a convenient death.

And when he thought he had conceived the perfect way to dispatch Terrence Clive from this vale of sorrow, he filed it carefully in his mind under the category Measures: Protective. Then he drifted into a light, relaxing, dreamless sleep, the kind of sleep enjoyed only by those of clear conscience or no conscience at all.

A FEW MILES AWAY, on the outskirts of Leaftree, in a house far more modest and less well kept, Terrence Clive sat on a shabby couch staring at an old black-and-white cowboy movie on his small television set. Clive was having trouble getting sufficiently drunk that night. This happened some nights, especially when he was thinking of poor Albert and of Albert's beautiful, unhappy, fragile mother. All Clive had

wanted to do was to love and protect her, to take her away
from her unhappiness with Wiggingdon and build a new life
for them. He had thought they would marry and be happy,
have years of delight in each other, and children—three,
Clive had thought. Three would be a lovely number.

But instead of his love saving her, it had destroyed her,
and their only legacy was Albert, that poor, suffering boy.
Ironically, Albert's powers were so limited he could not even
understand the concept of "father." He could not remember Clive from visit to visit. He did not know who he was.

Clive poured himself another drink, a stiff one. He stared
at the cowboy movie, where good and evil were so clearly
defined and good was sure to triumph.

He took a hard swallow. He was probably killing himself
with the liquor, he knew, but it hardly mattered, as long as
Albert was taken care of. He had put all the money into a
trust for Albert. He had asked Parmenter to make sure the
bank, the executor of the trust, would ensure that Albert
would always receive the best care money could buy. Where
would he be without Parmenter and his other friends? Clive
thought hazily. He could not have endured as long as he had
without them. Flawed they might be, but so was he. Yes,
Clive thought, thank God for good friends. Without their
loyalty, what reason was there to live at all?

ELI DOZED FITFULLY, but his inner clock awoke him just
before dawn's first false light began to haunt the sky. Gently he drew away from P.J., who had wound one sweatered
arm around his neck and entwined one slender leg around
his longer, muscled one.

She sighed and frowned in her sleep when he moved from
her. He stood for a moment, looking down at her shadowy
form in the darkness.

She sighed again and stretched her arms groggily to where
he had been, as if searching for him. He was certain she

wasn't awake, but she spoke, a groggy little whisper. "Don't go. Stay," she said.

He smiled slightly. It never occurred to him she might talk in her sleep. It touched him oddly. He looked at her, small in the tousled bed, one hand still reaching blindly and ineffectually to find him again.

"I can't stay," he said, although he knew she couldn't hear him. "I never stay."

He left, but he knew already that's how he would always remember her, in the vulnerability of her sleep, reaching out and asking him to stay.

Chapter Eight

Eli was gone when she awoke in the morning. She had no memory of his departure, only a strange sense of loss. Meditatively, almost tenderly, she stroked the rumpled sheets where he had lain. She could smell the lingering scent of his cologne. She wondered, languidly, what it would be like to wake with his arms still around her, to open her eyes and meet that hypnotic gaze. She sighed and stretched dreamily.

Then she went still as a stone as shock prickled through her. What kind of thoughts were those? What was happening to her? It was as if her mind finally realized it lived in a body, and a healthy young woman's body at that.

She sat up with a start, so fast she felt a little wave of dizziness. Why was she thinking about her sexual identity, anyway? More serious things were at stake. She had to hurry to the Ivory Castle to watch Eli move into the second stage of the plan. He would set the hook in Teddy Dirkson. And she would be there to help. Yes, how could she forget? That day was the day she and Eli would begin to liberate the Bachelors of their ill-gotten millions. She had come about as far from Harvard Business School as it was possible to get.

Forty-five minutes later, scrubbed within an inch of her life and looking as fresh as the bright autumn day, she strode with false confidence over the flagstones of the patio toward Teddy Dirkson's table. She wore a flaring tartan skirt, a bulky ivory sweater and her best midheel tasseled pumps. She looked as solidly respectable and New England as the hills around her.

Teddy Dirkson awaited her with a wide and pearly grin. His artificial blond curls gleamed brightly in the morning sun and contrasted more sharply than ever with his grizzled sideburns. He affected jauntiness that morning, with a Donegal tweed jacket and sky-blue turtleneck. Unfortunately, the sweater made him look remarkably like an elderly and lecherous tortoise.

"Darling Penny," he said, scrambling to his feet to pull out her chair. He made an ineffectual snatch to capture her hand in order to kiss it, but she dodged him gracefully. She remembered those lips working wetly on her knuckles the evening before.

"A little something for you, my dear," he said, nodding at a box beside her napkin. He helped her into her chair.

"Mr. Dirkson," she said firmly, "I can't keep accepting gifts from you. It isn't proper. I wasn't brought up that way. You mustn't. Really."

"Tush, tush," he remonstrated, still standing behind her. "It's nothing, a trifle. And not the sort of thing I can return. Open it—you'll see."

Repressing a sigh, she opened the white box and looked inside. A gaudy orchid wrist corsage greeted her wincing eyes. *It could be worse,* she thought. *He could have brought me a pink feather boa and a rhinestone navel ornament, too.*

"It's lovely," she said, "but—"

"Lovely and nonreturnable." Dirkson beamed. "Shall I help you on with it?"

"No," she said quickly, her hand eluding his for the second time. "And this is absolutely the last gift I accept from you, Mr. Dirkson. I mean it." She slipped the corsage onto her wrist quickly and pretended to admire it. Dirkson, still beaming, sat down across from her.

"But I must buy your breakfast," he said smugly. "I thought that was agreed. Besides, I've already taken the liberty of ordering for you—and having it put on my bill. More of those lovely shirred eggs."

She sighed in spite of herself, and when the waiter brought them glasses of breakfast champagne, she accepted with resignation.

She was forced to make small talk with Dirkson for what seemed an eternity. Most of it consisted of her excuses about why she could not spend the rest of the day with him.

The waiter appeared with the shirred eggs, and P.J. picked her way through them bravely, for she hated eggs in any slippery form and chicken livers in all guises. She began to wonder, in a slight panic, where Eli was.

Even Dirkson noticed. He glanced at his gold watch and lifted a shaggy brow in disapproval. "I wonder where our young friend is?" he mused. "Perhaps he's forgotten. He struck me as an immature sort. A bit callow. A man who needs the seasoning of years."

P.J. nodded noncommittally and allowed another bit of egg to slither down her throat. Dirkson tried to capture her free hand, and again she evaded him.

But he simply leaned his chin on his fist and smiled fondly at her. "Speaking of the seasoning of years," he said in a husky voice. "I've been told by women who should know that no one can satisfy a woman's needs like a man of experience. A woman who seeks pleasure with some young mooncalf still wet behind the ears will not know what true pleasure is. I was thinking—"

Oh, dear, here it comes, she thought desperately, *the proposition serious, the seduction attempt flagrant. How am I going to extricate myself from this gracefully? And where is Eli, anyway?*

"Here I am," said a blessedly familiar deep voice. She looked up with relief and saw him standing beside the table. He was wearing a traditional gray wool chalk-stripe suit and a silk tie of a light plum color. He also wore a pair of horn-rimmed glasses that she had never seen before. He had adopted the same nervous air of the day before, and the glasses added a scholarly aura.

"May I?" he asked, pulling out a chair and looking to Dirkson for approval.

"Certainly," Dirkson said gruffly. "I was wondering if you were going to show up at all, you young rascal. As I recall, you said you wouldn't be staying long."

"I wouldn't dream of interrupting you for longer than it takes to drink a cup of coffee," Eli said. He nodded briefly at P.J. "Good morning, Miss Jameson," he said politely. Then he glanced at her wrist. "*Lovely* corsage," he remarked, admiration dripping from his voice.

Again she resisted a desire to kick him smartly in his elegant shins. But he had already turned his attention from her. He signaled the waiter for a cup of coffee, then he reached into his breast pocket and withdrew two envelopes.

He smiled at Dirkson a bit apprehensively. "I said that I wanted to reward you both for your honesty. You're difficult people to reward. So selfless. But you did agree that if I made a little arrangement concerning a fund, you would be willing to take—how shall I put it?—the equivalent of one day's interest, profit, PE ratio, whatever you like to call it. Correct?"

"Correct," Dirkson said dismissively. He supposed the young fool would try to press a check for twenty-five dollars or so on him and expect him to be grateful. He wished he'd deposit his pittance and be off. Dirkson had begun to move in seriously on Miss Jameson. He sensed it was all or nothing at this point, and he had little interest in Mr. Holderman's paltry amounts of cash, no matter how sincerely they were offered.

"Well," Eli said with shy pleasure, handing each of them an envelope. "Here are your rewards."

Dirkson took his with an air of boredom, and P.J. accepted hers with shy excitement. Dirkson tore his open first, just in case the woman should be impressed by the amount. He wanted her to know that *he* could not be impressed by any paltry one-day profit the young man was willing to bestow.

Then he looked at the check, blinked and looked again. His jaw dropped slightly. The amount was not for twenty-five dollars. It was for $1,428.50. In spite of himself, Dirkson paled. This was *one day's* profit from some investment?

"Mr. Dirkson?" P.J. asked politely, "are you all right? Is something wrong?" She neatly opened her own envelope and looked at an identical check—$1,428.50. It was written on the personal account of Elwyn Brooks Holderman of New York, New York. She pretended to be as astounded as Dirkson. She had been forewarned, of course, but the only thing that really astounded her was Eli's formidable set of resources. He told her he kept bank accounts under several names for occasions when it was necessary to remain incognito.

"Goodness," she said in feigned awe. "I can finally afford a down payment on a new car. Oh, Mr. Holderman, thank you! But I had no idea! Honesty does pay, doesn't it, Mr. Dirkson?"

Teddy Dirkson did not manage money well, but he knew a thing or two about its peculiarities. He was astute enough to realize the check he held in his hand was an indication of something extraordinary. He just wasn't sure what. As Miss Jameson said, honesty paid, and now he was trying madly to calculate how high the payment was.

"This amount," he said, pointing with an unsteady finger at the number, "represents one day's interest in this... this fund of yours, Mr. Holderman?"

Eli became the haggard financier again. "I'm actually not at liberty to say that," he muttered. "But in certain enterprises such a profit is not unheard of."

"Let me see," Dirkson said, trying to maintain his calm. The young man obviously played for higher stakes than he had imagined. No wonder he was nearly burned out. "Let's see. If I may be so bold as to ask, just how much did you invest to achieve this interest?"

Dirkson was trying to do the mathematics in his head and finding it difficult. But at ordinary interest rates, he speculated that to achieve so much profit, Holderman must have invested at least five million dollars.

"Again, my information is privileged," Eli said, sipping his coffee self-consciously. "At this stage, the fund does not even speak of investments. We prefer to term monetary speculations as donations. And the fund likes donations to begin in the neighborhood of one hundred thousand dollars."

"One hundred thousand dollars," Dirkson muttered. "But surely your investment was far more substantial. One couldn't possibly make this sort of interest in one day on a hundred thousand dollars."

P.J. swallowed nervously. Eli claimed greed could bring common sense to a grinding halt. Teddy Dirkson was about to have a vision of wealth beyond his wildest dreams.

"Oh, no," Eli said, almost smiling. "It's possible. I'm not a millionaire—yet. I couldn't afford to invest more than several hundred thousand in anything. No, sir, the check I gave you indicates an extraordinary interest rate, that's all."

Dirkson made a small thoughtful rattle in his throat. "How extraordinary?"

Eli fiddled with the knot of his plum-colored tie. "I'm not at liberty to disclose details, Mr. Dirkson, but I'm sure you're quick enough to see that it's roughly in the neighborhood of ten percent a week."

"A week?" Dirkson gasped. He knocked over his empty champagne glass and hardly noticed. It rolled against his plate with a musical clink. "Ten percent a *week*? Good Lord, man! In a year that would come to... to..."

"Approximately five hundred and twenty percent a year," Eli admitted, setting the champagne glass upright again. "I suppose it would be an understatement to say this is not an ordinary fund I'm speaking of."

Dirkson leaned forward, his eyes so wide that P.J. wondered if his tinted lenses would pop out. "Great Scott! At five hundred and twenty percent, at the end of a year, a hundred thousand dollars would be—"

"Significantly increased," Eli admitted. He took a cautious sip of his steaming coffee.

Dirkson was calculating so feverishly now that P.J. could practically hear the gears whirring in his head. "If you started with a hundred thousand, at the end of the year you'd have six hundred and twenty thousand—over half a million dollars!"

"Goodness," P.J. said innocently. "I wish I had a hundred thousand dollars to invest for a year. Half a million dollars—imagine that."

"As I told you," Eli said, his eyes suddenly shifting nervously, "the information in that folder was invaluable. If the wrong people got their hands on it, who knows what could happen? I really can't thank you enough for returning it."

Dirkson had taken out his gold pen. He was doodling on the tablecloth with a shaky hand, checking his figures. His shaggy brows were pushed together in a frown. "Mr. Holderman," he said carefully, "by my estimate, if a man invested a million dollars in this fund—"

"Donate," Eli said just as carefully. "Supposing a man *donated* a million dollars."

"Donate," Dirkson corrected automatically, double-checking his figures. "If a man donated a million dollars..."

Eli cast his eyes heavenward as if mentally doing arithmetic. "At five hundred and twenty percent he would make over fourteen thousand dollars a day interest. At the end of a year, a million dollars would become six million two hundred thousand."

"Gad!" exclaimed Dirkson, his eyes widening again. "And at the end of two years..."

Eli shrugged philosophically. "The million would become nearly forty million. It would be a shrewdly invested million indeed."

"Indeed," said Dirkson reverently. "And Mr. Holderman, just what is the name of this company, this corporation or syndicate?"

"Fund," Eli corrected, looking about cautiously as if he were nervous about divulging such valuable information.

"What do you call this fund, then?" Dirkson asked, hunger in his voice.

"The enterprise I'm most interested in right now is called FUTURE," Eli said with an evasiveness that P.J. found admirable. "It is, alas, not public at this point. Only a select few are aware of its existence."

"But if a man wished to purchase a share—"

"Donate," Eli amended and sipped his coffee.

"If a man wished to donate, you could arrange it?"

"I could arrange it," Eli admitted. "Arranging it is my business. And an exhausting business it's been."

"I can well imagine," Dirkson said, although he didn't even try. Millions of dollars were capering before his eyes. They were blowing him kisses.

"A great deal of confidentiality has been needed," Eli said, a hint of weariness in his voice. "An enormous amount of business savvy has been demanded. Multitudinous things have needed arrangement. FUTURE is a complex endeavor."

"I'm sure it must be," Dirkson agreed. "Mr. Holderman, you are an amazing man. And to think yesterday I turned down a chance for investment advice from you. Certainly the stupidest thing I've ever done. I'd like to ask you to give me a second chance."

"Oh, certainly," Eli said. "If you're interested in a safe stock, I'd say something such as IBM, McDonald's, Procter and Gamble. Or if you're interested in something a bit more daring, I'd suggest Ben and Jerry's Ice Cream—a company with a brilliant future, to my mind."

Dirkson's face fell. "I was more interested in FUTURE," he protested. "That would outdistance any other investment I could make."

"Well," Eli said, frowning slightly, "I'm not in the habit of proposing FUTURE to anyone not interested in venturing extremely large amounts of capital. In fact, one hundred thousand is a laughably insignificant amount, and it's only because I'm, so to speak, in on the ground floor that I take so small a piece of the action."

"Would you consider a million dollars an insignificant amount?" Dirkson asked, hope mingling with impatience in his voice.

Eli gave another thoughtful shrug. "Not exactly insignificant. Not *exactly*."

"Would you be willing to discuss this with me a bit further?" Dirkson asked with a beguilingly frank smile. "And perhaps a few of my friends?"

"Friends?" Eli asked, looking perturbed. "Well, I usually don't. Discretion is still necessary at this point. But since they're *your* friends, Mr. Dirkson, perhaps..."

"I'd like you to be a guest at my club tonight, Holderman. Nothing formal. A few of us meet in the library, have a few drinks, sometimes a few hands of cards, good conversation. We meet, oh, eightish. What say?"

"Well," Eli said meditatively. "I suppose..."

"Fine, fine, fine," Dirkson said happily. "You're a good man, Holderman. Delighted to have found you. I think our acquaintance can be mutually beneficial. My friends and I are... gentlemen of some means."

"A person in my position," Eli murmured thoughtfully, "is always anxious to meet a gentleman of means—as long as he has vision, as well."

"We are," Dirkson said with a pearly smile, "all men of vision. I'll meet you in the lobby tonight at eight. Now I must contact the fellows. This is most remarkable, Holderman. I can't tell you how remarkable."

He shook Eli's hand, and Eli rose, made a polite half bow in P.J.'s direction and took his leave. He gave P.J. the subtlest of smiles and a brief, knowing look.

"Gad," Dirkson said again after Eli's departure. "This may be the most amazing thing that's ever presented itself to me. No wonder the poor fellow is as trembly as an aspen—arranging investments of such magnitude. The responsibility must take its toll."

P.J. had a part to play—the feminine version of a Doubting Thomas. "Sounds too good to be true to me," she said, frowning slightly. "I mean, I never heard of an investment paying off like that."

"Posh, my girl," Dirkson said condescendingly. "What do you know of it? No offense, my dear, but you *are* just a secretary. These things are foreign to your experience. I've been around money all my life. My own grandfather made a fortune just so—in 1908 he invested in a new invention called the Model T Ford. The rest is history. If only the old fool hadn't sold out in 1941 when Ford unionized... How the old geezer hated unions. Enough to seriously impair the family fortune, the senile loon. But now it's my turn.''

"You don't even know what this FUTURE thing is or does," she pointed out. "You didn't even ask."

"My dear—" he chuckled, patting his sideburns fondly "—that's one of the reasons women do not do well in the business world. You think small, are stymied by details. If a goose is laying golden eggs, it makes no difference what color the goose is."

"You don't even know this man or if you can trust him," she said.

Dirkson laughed indulgently. "He's a gentleman. One can see that immediately. And he did not ask me for a single thin dime, my dear. It was he who gave us money, if you'll recall. Now what sort of crook would give over a thousand dollars to each of us?"

An extremely smart one, P.J. thought ironically, *who's about to get four million back for SOS through his little "reward."*

"Darling Penny," Dirkson said, rising and looking extremely important, as if he had already made nearly forty million dollars that morning, "please excuse me. Nothing would draw me from your side except the most pressing business. But pressing business this is, and when it's taken care of, we will celebrate."

This time she did not manage to dodge fast enough, and he clamped his hands on either side of her face and pressed a kiss of surpassing moistness on her forehead. "Aloha, sweet nymph," he said, eager to be on his way. "I'll call you as soon as possible. And perhaps, when I've made my first five million in profits, I'll buy you a bauble to commemorate this day—a Rolls-Royce, how would that be?"

Ridiculous, she thought bleakly, but she made no comment. He gave her an awkward half bow, in imitation of Eli's flawless one, and then he scurried off, a squat little figure moving surprisingly fast.

To call the Bachelors, she thought. To spread the marvelous word. Eli was right. Greed performed a dangerous and perverse magic on people.

She stared with distaste at her unfinished eggs. She raised her champagne glass. It contained just enough liquid for one last sip. She shook her head slightly in wonder. Eli made all his moves as agilely as a high-wire walker. Not once had he actually stated outright that investing in FUTURE would actually bring five hundred and twenty percent interest. He had simply led Dirkson to draw that erroneous conclusion.

To the devious who serve good causes, she thought, making a private toast to Eli. She finished the champagne.

As she made her way through the lobby and toward the parking lot, she saw Eli standing by the picture windows that looked out on the mountains. She pretended to take no notice of him, and he did the same to her.

But that guarded glimpse of him shook her through and registered on her memory as if seared there. He stood, smiling warmly, his arm around a stunning blond woman of about thirty. The woman looked comfortable nestled in his arm, as if she had been there often. She smiled up at him with obvious affection and a wryness that said she understood him well.

Cleo, she thought. She felt suddenly cold and sick inside. She left quickly. And she tried very hard all the rest of the day not to think of Eli. Because if she did, she would have to remember that he just might land them both in criminal court, and that he was a man of no ideals whose principles were light-years from hers.

She would also have to remember that against all reason she was strongly attracted to him. He was the kind of man who would never return love. She would be only another of many women in his life. Last night she had been in his arms. This night, obviously, was Cleo's turn. And unlike herself, Cleo, she sensed with desolation, would know exactly what to do there.

AFTER A DESULTORY TRIP to shop in the overly quaint boutiques designed to lure tourists, P.J. returned to the Nutmeg Peddler. Almost immediately Teddy Dirkson began phoning. In his sudden fit of lust to become rich, he had temporarily forgotten his more ordinary lust for her. Now he had apparently set up the Bachelors' meeting with Eli, and she returned to his thoughts.

His appeals to her were so transparent they made her angry. He told her that he was a rich man, likely to become much, much richer, and that she would be a silly young woman indeed not to try to please him when he had so much to offer.

P.J. had had little experience fending off lechers, but she had been brought up as rigorously as the Puritans of old. She told him at last that she was not used to being propositioned, that her interest and her company weren't for sale at any price and that she didn't care to talk to him anymore if he couldn't act like a gentleman.

She delivered the speech with all the Bostonian moral outrage she could muster, and he immediately began to apologize. If he could only see her, he said, he could show her how sorry he was. She told him no, she needed time to herself. Five minutes after she hung up the phone, he called again, and again she told him no.

When the phone rang again immediately, she cursed, took up her purse and left her room. She didn't want to see any more of Teddy Dirkson, she didn't want to talk to him and she didn't care what Eli thought about it. Eli would probably want her to go to bed with the old fool if he thought something could be gained from it. She thought again of Cleo's sophisticated blond beauty. A woman like her could probably play Dirkson along for months. P.J. didn't know if she herself was made of sterner or weaker stuff, but she couldn't bear to lead on the odious little man for another moment.

She drove to the neighboring town of Featherston, looked at more flamboyant foliage, toured more overly quaint shops. She found that she was getting weary of leaves, no matter how colorful, and wondered if every shop in Vermont was stuffed with folksy things with designs stenciled on blue-painted wood.

When she returned to Leaftree, it was almost seven, and she went to the least fashionable restaurant in town on the theory it was the last place she'd find Teddy Dirkson.

Instead, she was found by Terrence Clive. She looked up from the chipped Formica table and saw him standing, almost shyly, looking down at her. His wrinkles were just as deep, his nose as flaming, his sweater as disreputable as the day before, but once again he seemed sober. She remembered Teddy Dirkson's comment that Clive never started drinking until evening.

"Miss Jameson," he said in his roughened voice. "What are you doing in this dive? I'll warn you, the food's the worst in town."

She smiled up at him. Oddly, she almost liked the man. "I needed a little change." It was a lie, which made her uncomfortable, but since meeting Eli she had told so many lies that one more hardly mattered.

Clive cocked his close-cropped head. "I'll bet you're hiding from Teddy Dirkson," he said wryly. "It's all right. So am I. That's why I'm here rather than my usual haunt."

She couldn't keep a smile from curving the corner of her generous mouth. "Why are you hiding from him?" she asked. "And do you want to join me? I really don't enjoy eating alone."

Clive hesitated for a moment. "Thanks," he said finally, pulling out a vinyl-covered chair and sitting down. "Why am I hiding from Teddy? He's got a new bee in his bonnet. He wants to make me rich."

P.J. studied his wrinkled face. Terrence Clive reminded her of a kindly old basset hound that life had abused too much. She had to remember that he was one of the enemy. Still, she recalled her original instinct that she could learn more from Clive than any of the other Bachelors. Eli had said no, and he was the expert, but she still trusted her feeling.

"Why don't you want to be rich?" she asked, her tone light. "It sounds like a good offer to me."

"I'm rich enough," he said gruffly. Then he looked at her ruefully. "Sorry. That didn't sound very nice. I've got enough money to take care of me and my son and enough to support Albert after I'm gone. I don't need more than that. What would I do with it?"

"I don't know," P.J. mused. "Travel. See the world. Indulge yourself with a few luxuries."

"I've seen the world," Clive said, an edge of bitterness in his voice. "It's not a very nice place, really. As for luxuries, there's only one I'm interested in, and that's liquor. I don't know if Teddy has told you, but I'm an alcoholic."

"Oh," she said awkwardly. She looked down at the table and then directly into his red-rimmed eyes. "You don't have to be," she said with conviction. "You could get help. You could check into a clinic, join a support group..."

"You don't understand," he said with an ironic smile. He let the waitress pour him a cup of black coffee into which he stirred three spoonfuls of sugar. "I like being an alcoholic, Miss Jameson. I don't want to change."

"Oh," she said again. "I'm sorry."

"Ah," he said with a sigh, "I'm not fitting company for a young person like you. Don't let me distress you. The main thing that concerns me is Albert's welfare, and that's assured. I have a will drawn up stipulating everything goes to his welfare and naming the bank as my executor. I will have the consolation of knowing I've done one right thing in my life. But again, I'm being an oppressive, depressive old poot. Tell me why you're hiding from Teddy. Does he want to make you rich, too?"

"People like me don't become rich," P.J. said, raising one of her eyebrows wryly. "But somewhere Mr. Dirkson got the idea I like being showered with presents. I don't. It makes me nervous. I wish you'd tell me a graceful way to deflect his attentions. You know him well enough."

Clive laughed. When the waitress brought P.J. an unappetizing plate of meat loaf and runny mashed potatoes, Clive shrugged and indicated he'd have the same. "Go ahead," he said. "Don't wait on me. How to deflect Teddy's attentions? A good question. The most effective methods have usually been two. Option A: slam him on the head with a hammer. Option B: threaten to report him to the morals squad."

She chewed the tasteless meat loaf meditatively. "You mean there's no graceful way to stop him," she offered sadly.

He gave her a sympathetic look. "Actually, just keep ignoring him. It takes about a week. Poor Teddy. I know he's a pompous ass, and with women he's impossible. But he's not really completely bad. For one thing, as you've seen, he's generous to a fault. He loves giving things away. In fact, he gave away most of his family fortune, much of it to women who, I might add, were not as scrupulous as you."

P.J. looked at Clive speculatively. He was a strange man. He had no pretensions and was remarkably frank. She wondered if he would be suspicious if she probed further. She decided to chance it.

"Mr. Dirkson says you've been friends almost forever," she ventured. "You and two other men. I suppose you're the ones he's trying to get together tonight to meet Mr. Holderman."

"Ah, yes." Clive nodded. "Mr. Holderman and his amazing investments. See? Teddy's generosity again. Some people would have kept all this financial hocus-pocus to themselves. Not Teddy. He has to share it with his friends."

"The four of you have known each other since childhood?" she prodded. "That's unusual nowadays with the way people move around, lose touch with one another."

He took a drink of his coffee. "We're just four old losers," he said, giving her a dryly amused look. "Maybe we hang out together because nobody else wants us."

"I doubt that," P.J. said with a smile. In spite of herself, she found she liked Clive. He was sad, self-deprecating—but honest. His concern over Albert must have been intense to involve him in defrauding Delmer Fordyce.

"You've seen Teddy at his worst," Clive told her, watching her over the top of his coffee cup. "And you know some of the worst about me—not all of it, thank God. Well, there's also Charlie Bangor. I think we've been taking care of Charlie since first grade. Charlie's very loyal, but not terribly bright. His problem has been gambling. He's come close to beating it, but we have to keep our eye on him. It's a full-time job, but he's got a perfect dragon of a sister, and she helps."

"So," P.J. said boldly. "A flirt, a drinker and a gambler, the latter slightly reformed. Who's the fourth member of this illustrious group?"

"Ah," sighed Clive. "The fourth member and our brightest light: Dr. James Parmenter, the kindly old village physician, now semiretired."

"What?" P.J. said, mocking lightly. "No scandal? No deep, dark secrets about the goodly doctor? Why does he keep company with such a motley crew?"

"Oh, Parmenter's a bit motley himself," Clive said, evasive for the first time. "He's not an easy man to know. He was always the brightest of us. But also the most solitary. Locked into himself and satisfied to be there. Yet even the most self-sufficient of men likes company from time to time. And we've known each other—warts and all—for many a long year."

"And Mr. Dirkson wants you all to get together to meet Mr. Holderman tonight," she said carefully. "Won't you be going?"

"Of course I'll go," he replied, giving her his self-mocking smile again. "It's better than spending a long evening watching old movies on television—and drinking alone."

"I hope," she said, and she was serious, "that your friends don't let you drive when you've been drinking. That would be incredibly dangerous—and not just for you."

"You're a serious little thing, aren't you?" Clive said. "No, of course. I had a rather bad crash a few years ago. Someone always drives me home. That's what friends are for, right?"

"I hope so," P.J. said. "Of course, it would be better if they tried to help you stop drinking altogether."

He shook his head. "How did Dirky ever find a little Puritan like you, anyway? You give the impression of being a young woman out to reform the world. What are you, a schoolteacher?"

"No," she said without a moment's hesitation. She forced her eyes to keep meeting his. "I'm a secretary."

"Well," he said, finishing his coffee, "I think I like you, in spite of your urge to reform me. If you want to keep avoiding Dirky for the rest of your vacation and you really hate to eat alone, I'd be glad of your company. I know a little inn on the edge of town where Dirky never goes. He got amorous with the hostess, and she's threatened him with severe bodily harm if he ever shows up again. If you'd like, we could meet and share a dinner or two. Dutch treat, if you're the modern type and don't want to feel compromised."

She looked at him in surprise. He wasn't exactly making a pass, but she realized with a start that he did seem to like her. Perhaps he was simply lonely.

"I wouldn't want to get you in trouble with Mr. Dirkson," she said. "He might get the wrong idea."

"Dirky would sulk for a few days, then he'd be delighted. I haven't asked a woman out to dinner in forty-some years. He'll be mad about someone else by then and glad you're sharing time with a needy old case like me."

She felt a prickle of excitement. Again she sensed she might learn more from Clive than from any of the other Bachelors. Also, she was struck once more by a peculiar feeling of rapport with the man.

"You're selling yourself short, Mr. Clive," she said diplomatically. "I don't think you're quite the lost cause you like to think. I'd be glad to meet you for dinner—if you're sure it won't offend Mr. Dirkson. I just have one question. Because I'm flattered. After forty years, why me? Or do you think you need a touch of Puritanism in your life?"

He looked at her. His face was troubled. The waitress had set his plate down in front of him, but he hadn't touched it. "Because," he said slowly, "you remind me of someone. Someone quite lovely, really. Both within and without. She was Albert's mother."

P.J. felt a stab of sympathy. After forty years he still loved that long-dead woman.

Clive's coffee cup had been refilled. He ignored his food and stirred sugar into the dark brew. "She was as lovely a woman as ever lived," he said, drifting off in grieving memory. "But she made one dreadful mistake." He looked at her, tried to smile and almost succeeded. "She fell in love with me. Which was her undoing. Take the advice of an expert, my dear. Never fall in love with the wrong man. It can destroy you. Literally."

P.J. struggled to suppress a shudder. He could have said nothing that would have disturbed her more because she was falling in love with the worst man she could have picked. And Clive sat there, in his physical and moral ruin, as a living example of what happens when love is wrong.

CLEO LOUNGED IN THE DOOR of the bathroom, leaning against the frame. She was watching Eli shave. For some reason he always stripped to the waist when he shaved, and he stared in the mirror with such intensity he seemed to be performing an operation, not a simple act of grooming.

She felt he was also being intent about ignoring her. She crossed her arms. "Eli," she warned again, "I'm not kidding. Be careful of this Parmenter character. He's dangerous. I was shocked when I found out how dangerous."

He didn't look at her. He drew the razor along his throat with great precision. "I believe you, gorgeous. I'm always careful. You did a great job on your homework. But don't worry about Parmenter. I always look out for number one."

"Usually," Cleo said sarcastically.

He didn't answer her.

"Eli, you're up to something," she accused. "I don't know what, and I think I'm afraid to know. Do *not* take chances, do you hear me? Especially stupid chances."

"I promise not to take stupid chances," he muttered mechanically.

"There's a woman involved in this, isn't there?" she asked, narrowing her long-lashed eyes. "It's the little preppy-looking thing at your table this morning. Can't you tell she's not your kind? She looks like the kind who plays for keeps."

"I'm not involved with her," he said and drew the razor up his throat again.

"I hope not," Cleo said emphatically, "because I also hope you remember Kansas City and what happened there."

The razor stopped in midstroke. He had nicked himself. He never cut himself shaving. But there ought to be a law about anyone mentioning Kansas City when he had something sharp at his throat.

He remembered it all too well—that lovely, oh-so-respectable woman, the too-ambitious cons to get the money to impress her and then five years in the hellhole of Leavenworth.

"I remember," was all he said.

"Good. Besides, dear heart, I seriously doubt if you're cut out for monogamy."

"Nobody knows it better than I do," he replied, still not looking at her.

"You know I worry about you only because I love you." For the first time there was a tremor in her voice.

He looked at her. He smiled his crooked smile. He moved to her side, put his arm around her and kissed her lightly on the cheek. It left a smear of shaving cream. He wiped it away with one of the hotel's expensive towels.

He didn't want her to know how close to right she was. He was taking chances, flirting with danger again after all these years, and it was because of a woman, just as it had been in Kansas City. And once again it was the wrong kind of woman.

Chapter Nine

Eli called at eleven and said he would come to her room at midnight. P.J., still hurt by the reappearance of Cleo, wanted to hang up on him. She did not. She thought about locking the window and not opening it, but she didn't do that, either. It would have been childish and, worse, would show she was jealous.

Jealousy was an emotion so foreign to her that it made her almost ill. *How stupid,* she thought, *to care that he has another woman. He probably has hordes of women. It's not as if he got down on his knees and promised to be faithful to me for the rest of his life. He isn't that type, so why should I care?*

Because I do! answered some private part of her mind. But she couldn't afford jealousy. She and Eli had, first and foremost, a business relationship. It was a tricky and delicate one, potentially hazardous to them both.

She prickled with restlessness, wondering how his meeting with the Bachelors had gone. The game was primarily in his deft hands from then on. Her only job was to learn as much as she could from Teddy Dirkson. She had already violated Eli's orders on that and centered her attentions on Terrence Clive instead. She wondered if Eli would be angry. He was a man who planned carefully and didn't like his plans thwarted.

She turned off the lights and waited. Again she wore jeans, a turtleneck and a bulky sweater. Although she wasn't cold, she sat in the darkness on the edge of her lumpy bed and hugged herself tightly. Her world was turning not only upside down but inside out, as well, and she no longer understood her own thoughts or feelings.

The important thing, she kept telling herself, was to get SOS's money back, to keep alive the cause for which her parents had worked so hard.

But another part of her said Eli had become equally important, and now she had two obsessions instead of one. She still burned to vindicate her father by getting the Fordyce fortune back to where it belonged, but something else was starting to flame within her, and its fuel was Eli. Once again she remembered Terrence Clive's grim advice about loving the wrong man.

Then Eli was there in her room again. Smoothly he pulled shut both window and blind, moved to her bedside and switched on the lamp. She looked up at him. He was wearing jeans and a navy-blue merino sweater with a V neck and nothing beneath. She could see the fine brown hair that curled at the top of his chest. He looked down at her and gave her his one-sided grin, the one that made his scar look like a dimple.

"It went like clockwork," he said. "Almost perfect. Dirkson and Charlie Bangor are hot to trot. Parmenter is cautious. He's made everybody promise to think it over. But he'll bite. I see the dollar signs in his eyes. Clive's the holdout so far. Absolutely not interested. He may be the hardest to get to. I've been afraid of that. They want me to meet with them again tomorrow. So how about a little enthusiasm? Still not giving any kisses—just taking them?"

He put his hands on her shoulders, bent and kissed her briefly. It should have meant nothing, done nothing, been a mere greeting, but it shook through her like an earth tremor. She almost thought she'd seen something strange in his eyes when he drew away.

"That was a bit cool," he said, his gaze on her lips. She hadn't responded at all, and suddenly she did feel cold, as chill as porcelain.

"I feel like I'm part of a quota," she said crisply. "Where's your other assistant? Waiting for you back in your room?"

He cocked a brow and gave a light snort of disgust. "You sound suspiciously like a jealous woman. I thought you, of all people, would be above that garbage. I hate jealous women."

"I don't like hypocrisy, that's all," she said, looking away from him to hide the anger in her eyes.

"Oh, God," he practically growled, sitting down, stretching out and taking his familiar pose of leaning against the headboard. "Cleo's back in Putney. She's a busy woman. She and I go way back, so far back it's nobody's business but ours. You can either trust me or not. And you ought to be nicer about Cleo because she just did us both a couple of big favors, baby."

"Like what?" P.J. asked suspiciously.

"Like this," he said with elaborate casualness, withdrawing a sheaf of folded papers from his back pocket. He handed her one. "This one right here tells how the Bachelors got Fordyce to sign the second will."

P.J. stared at the paper, which was a dim copy of a bill from someplace called The Patterson Clinic in Burlington, Vermont. "What—?" she began to ask.

"Read it carefully," he said. "A bill to Delmer Fordyce for two hundred and twelve dollars. Paid by Dr. James Parmenter. The Patterson Clinic is an optical clinic—examinations and fittings. They replaced a pair of reading glasses for Delmer Fordyce. Look at the date."

P.J. studied it. The bill had been made out over a year ago last July. The date rang a bell, loudly and clearly. "His glasses," she whispered at last. "They must have been broken the week he signed the will."

"Correct," Eli said with satisfaction. "And if he was like a lot of people his age, he couldn't read a word without glasses. But people like that can make a perfectly passable signature—a signature is so automatic it's practically a reflex."

P.J. looked at him, her resentment suddenly fleeing. "When they made Fordyce an 'honorary member,' they must have had him sign something he thought was a pledge or a membership paper," she said.

"Right. Which he did without thinking twice. And chances are the witnesses, who both worked at the hotel, didn't know what they were witnessing, either."

"But why did Parmenter pay for Delmer Fordyce's glasses to be replaced?" P.J. asked, frowning.

He gave her a measuring look, tousled her bangs and muttered, "You just can't think like a crook, can you? Because Parmenter broke them, that's how. He planned it, made it look like an accident, insisted on having them replaced by his own optician in Burlington—which gave him a few extra days to set up his business with the phony will—and kept anyone around here from having a record of the broken glasses."

"Are you sure Parmenter broke the glasses?" P.J. asked.

He grinned again. "I bought Mrs. Murdock another couple of Jamaican Jungle Juicers today. It seems she vaguely remembers Fordyce broke his glasses playing a game of racquetball with Parmenter. She remembers because for several days Fordyce didn't read his paper at breakfast, and she asked him why."

"Eli," she said, "this may be worth its weight in gold."

"It's circumstantial evidence of the flimsiest kind," he said, "but it's better than nothing. So's this." He handed her another set of similarly dim copies.

"What are these?" she asked, frowning at the blurry reproductions of unfamiliar forms.

"Hospital records," he answered. "The first witness, Harvey Berringer, died right here in Leaftree, a month before Fordyce did. Cause, massive coronary. Personal physician, Dr. James Parmenter."

She looked at him and felt horror mixing peculiarly with the elation of discovery. "So he probably *did* know both Berringer and Fordyce had heart problems and didn't tell them. This is like the records on Fordyce—no previous knowledge of cardiac problems."

"Two might be a coincidence," Eli replied with a grim smile, "but three is pushing it. Look at the info on John Williams, the second witness, the one who died in New Hampshire."

The hospital form gave the same cause of death, massive coronary. Clipped to it was a copy of a note in a neat hand.

Eli,
Found Williams's sister. When Williams retired, he went to live with her. She's certain that his doctor was Parmenter, and Parmenter gave Williams a clean bill of health. She's willing to testify to this. Says it made her brother's death all the greater shock.

Cleo

P.S. Am I good, or am I good?

Cleo, thought P.J. with a slightly sinking heart, was not simply good, she was superb. How on earth was she getting all this information? She was certainly doing a lot of work in the name of affection. No wonder Eli championed her with such cool assurance.

As if reading her thoughts, he said, "So will you try to be a little nicer about Cleo?"

"Eli," she said, awe in her voice, "this is amazing. It proves Parmenter probably knew all three men involved in signing the will were walking time bombs, that none of them had over a year to live."

"Careful," he warned. "Williams's sister's testimony would be hearsay again. I doubt if we could get it past a judge. But things are falling into place. And now, my little Harvard hotcake, for the pièce de résistance. Cleo, I have always maintained, does very nice work."

He handed her the rest of the papers. She perused them, frowning. "Court records," Eli said. "A malpractice suit against Parmenter twelve years ago for misdiagnosis of a heart condition. Parmenter's insurance company paid a considerable sum to the family of the misdiagnosed man. Eight years ago another malpractice suit was filed against Parmenter, this time for botching a spinal operation on one Morris Wiggingdon. Mr. Wiggingdon, left paralyzed, finally died of complications. Suit filed by his nephew. Parmenter's insurance company paid."

"Wiggingdon?" P.J. asked, her eyes widening. "Surely not the same Wiggingdon that ruined his wife's life—and Clive's?"

"One and the same," Eli said dryly. "From all appearances it would seem Dr. Parmenter likes to play God from time to time. Wiggingdon was an old enemy. He hated Parmenter because Parmenter was Clive's friend. But the night Wiggingdon cracked up his car, it just happened to be Parmenter on duty in the emergency room. And somehow Parmenter's knife slipped."

P.J. shuddered. This time she felt comforted rather than disturbed when Eli slipped his arm around her slender shoulders. "Parmenter's a . . . a monster," she said with a gasp as the enormity of all he had done sank in.

"This first case was a little scary, too," Eli said, flipping back the pages for a moment. "The victim of the first misdiagnosis, Lionel Hardesty, wasn't an enemy of Parmenter's. But he had something Parmenter wanted desperately—a farm outside Leaftree. Which he cheerfully refused to sell. It had been Parmenter's grandfather's. Parmenter fancied himself retiring to the ancestral digs as a gentleman farmer. Needless to say, he didn't get it, and the family consults another doctor these days."

"So this is the mystery about Parmenter's malpractice suits, but this should have been common knowledge. Why didn't anyone know?"

"Because the insurance company insisted on discretion and that the records be kept sealed. Only the participants know the truth. Anybody else who talks about it just might get himself sued by Parmenter for slander. Some rumors are dangerous to circulate."

"But what's this?" P.J. asked, looking at a third set of papers in the batch. They seemed to consist of private correspondence.

"This," he said with satisfaction, "is what I've been wanting to get all along. The other two malpractice suits are piddling compared to this baby. This is the one the whispers have been about—and again only whispers—but it's the one that ruined Parmenter."

"Eli," she exclaimed in horror, "there have been three suits against him? The man is a psychopath."

"The last suit never made it to court. It was settled outside, again with Parmenter's lawyer insisting on total silence in the matter. It was only three years ago, and Parmenter was semiretired then. His malpractice insurance rates had gone so high he'd let them lapse. Which was a mistake. Because this time he botched another operation, apparently by accident. That's the ironic part. A patient on whom he performed a simple gallbladder operation ended up with peritonitis and jaundice and nearly died. Parmenter was no longer insured, and he ended settling out of court for two hundred thousand dollars—nearly his life's savings. I imagine it was shortly afterward that he started thinking about pulling something like he did on Fordyce. He just had to wait for the right pigeon to come along.''

"How could he?" she asked, shaking her head, sickened. "He's a doctor. He took a vow to save lives."

Eli sensed the depth of her shock, and it bothered him. He'd seen so much of the world's evil that finding out about Parmenter was merely like receiving scientific information. It did not appall him. It simply gave him the satisfaction of having a few more answers.

"Look," he said very softly in her ear, "you're right. He's a monster. He's not typical. Who knows? Maybe he thought if he saved enough lives, he had the right to take a few. The problem is that he's our monster, and he's a little more dangerous than I thought he was. I want you to stay away from him. So you'd better stay away from Teddy Dirkson."

"I intend to stay away from Teddy Dirkson," she said firmly. "I can't stand him. I make a bad spy and a terrible Mata Hari. Besides, I'd never learn anything from him. He talks more and says less than any man I ever met."

He turned to her, putting both hands on her shoulders. "I want you to go back to Boston, P.J.," he said, his voice resolute. "From here on out you can work just as well from there as from here. Better, in fact. Hanging around with Dirkson was a bad idea of mine. So go home."

She looked at him, stunned. Her heartbeats seemed to slow to a dull, dying cadence. "No," she said at last, her eyes holding his. "I said I'd stay to the end. And I will."

"I don't want you to stay," he said between his teeth. "It'll look less suspicious if you're gone. Nobody will make the connection between us."

"Nobody will, anyway," she said. "We're never seen together. We've been careful. And I can do something here. I can keep an eye on Clive."

He gripped her shoulders harder. "Clive? What do you mean?" His golden-brown eyes bore into hers.

"I mean I met Clive tonight. He...he likes me. He trusts me, I think. He's a lonely man. He told me a lot—more than Teddy Dirkson ever did. And he seemed to clam up when the conversation got around to Parmenter. Just like you said, some rumors are too dangerous to circulate. You said he might be in danger. Let me help keep an eye on him. Besides, I always thought he might be the one who'd give us some vital scrap of information. And he might—to me."

He looked into her eyes for a moment longer. "No," he said at last. He said it with great emphasis. "That's just what Parmenter's afraid of. I don't want you involved with Clive. Parmenter will notice, believe me."

"I am *not* going," she said. "I haven't done my fair share."

Oh, good Lord, he thought, he'd heard that tone in her voice before, and the blue sparks were whirling in her eyes like a fireworks display. She'd looked and sounded exactly the same way that first day in his office. The only way he was going to get her back to Boston was to hit her on the head, tie her up, carry her there and deposit her in the offices of SOS with a note pinned to her blouse: Do Not Set This Woman Free Under Any Circumstances. He thought hard about doing just that.

"I don't want you here," he said harshly. "Can't you get that through your head? If you stay, you'll get in my way. You'll slow me down. So go home."

"Before you found out Parmenter helped send at least six people to early graves, I wasn't slowing you down or getting in your way," she protested. "You wanted me to get information from Teddy Dirkson, but instead, I can get it from Clive. And he's the hardest one for you to get through to—you said so yourself."

He glared at her and felt the same paradoxical urge he had the first time they'd met. He wanted to either shake her or kiss her till she begged for mercy.

"Sorry, Junior," he said, his lip curling. "But I'm afraid I just may have put Clive in the hot seat. If he doesn't want to play my game, Parmenter might want to get hold of his money fast—and I wouldn't get in Parmenter's way if I were you."

"What?" She gasped in disbelief. "Eli, what are you saying?"

"You heard me." This time he gave in to the impulse to startle some sense into her. He gripped her arms tighter and gave her a shake, just one, but hard enough to show her how strong he was. "Like you said, Parmenter's helped six people die younger than they should have. If he thinks Clive's going to pass up a chance to turn a million dollars into more, he just may relieve Clive of the million dollars—and his life."

"Do you mean by doing this we're actually putting Terrence Clive in danger?" she asked. She hadn't even seemed to notice his shake, although it should have rattled her teeth.

"Lord, P.J.," he said impatiently, "I don't know. It's possible. With a man like Parmenter anything's possible. That's why I've got to work hard on Clive so he doesn't hold out and tempt Parmenter to get the interest on that money himself. I repeat, don't get in my way."

"I'm not going," she said with all the stubbornness of which she was capable.

"The hell you're not," he said and shook her again, this time harder.

She didn't even notice. He had the sudden conviction that if she had been a man, she would be the sort another man couldn't knock down. She'd stay upright by pure force of will. "It would be *immoral* to leave," she practically hissed. "If we've put Terrence Clive in the remotest possibility of danger, we have a *duty* to protect him."

Eli released her with a flourish of disgust. He threw himself down on his back on the bed, his hands behind his neck. He stared at the ceiling with repugnance. "'*Immoral* to leave,'" he sneered, mocking her girlish voice. "'We have a *duty*.' My God, you make me sick! Don't you ever stop being a Girl Scout? What duty do we have to Terrence Clive? He's a thief and a drunken old thief at that."

"He's a human being," P.J. said hotly. "And if he's a thief, at least he's not as bad as the rest of them. In fact, it might be good to let him keep some of the money because he really needs it for Albert—"

Eli sat up so fast he frightened her. He grabbed her by the shoulders again. Something in his face had gone slightly wild. "You're defending that larcenous old gink?" he demanded. "And now you think he should *keep* some of the money he stole from you?"

"Well, why not?" she said righteously. "It's for a good cause. It would be inhumane to—"

This time he gripped her shoulders so hard she actually noticed it. She winced slightly. He put his face close to hers. He looked angrier than she had ever seen him before.

"That," he snarled, "is the worst goddamned example of fuzzy, eggheaded, pseudoliberal thinking I have ever heard in my entire life. What have you got for brains? Seaweed? That old swindler robbed you of a cool million dollars, lady. It's in his bank account right now. To get it he stood by and watched Parmenter let three men die. He's part of the reason your own father died. And now you feel *sorry* for him? Are you crazy?''

She looked at him with pain in her face, and to his chagrin he realized his grip was probably hurting her badly and tomorrow she would have bruises. It made him feel like a lout. Worse, he could tell by the look in her eyes that it wasn't physical pain that was bothering her.

"You get me so confused," she said at last, her voice trembling. For the second time in his life, he saw tears glint in her eyes, and it unnerved him completely. He eased his grip on her shoulders and rubbed them softly, as if he could absorb the punishment back into himself.

"I want to do what's right," she said. Her voice caught, and she bit at her lower lip to gain control of herself. She was trying to force the tears back, but she wasn't doing a very good job of it. "I want everything to turn out...right," she said helplessly. She looked at him with sheer misery in her eyes. "And you make me so *confused*."

Oh, God, he thought in despair, please don't let her cry. It would be like Joan of Arc crying and getting her armor all rusty. He released her arms as if he had no business touching her at all. He gave her an unhappy look and shook his head. "You're doing a pretty good job of confusing me, too," he grumbled. "I'm not sure I've ever been so confused by anybody in my life. Look, P.J., I want you to go so there's no chance you'll get hurt. I don't want anything to happen to you—and now you've got me in such a state that I'm the one who's hurt you. I don't like the feeling at all, and I'm sorry."

She stared at him, not comprehending. All she understood was that he was apologizing and that was something she had never expected of him. "You didn't hurt me," she said in perplexity. "I said you confused me."

"I hurt you," he insisted. He turned and touched her arm. "You're going to have bruises tomorrow. And I feel lousy about it. You were riding that little moral hobby-horse of yours so hard you didn't even feel it, did you?"

She looked at him a bit defensively. She guessed her shoulders did hurt a little. "I don't want to leave," she repeated. "I want to stay. I have to stay."

He took his hand away because it was as if the touch of her burned through his nerve endings and landed in the pit of his stomach like lightning. He didn't want to look in her eyes any longer, either. They were getting to him again.

"Stay," he said wearily. He realized he hadn't wanted her to go, anyway. If she did leave, he supposed she'd just turn around and come back. What was he supposed to do with this woman?

"I had hoped," he said, the same weariness and self-disgust in his voice, "that this evening would be a bit more festive. After all, I did bring you a present. But instead of giving it to you, I ended up roughing you up." He shook his head and swore again.

She watched him and frowned slightly. "Eli," she said gently, "why are you feeling so guilty? I told you I didn't feel anything. I never imagined you feeling guilty about anything."

He turned and glared at her. "What's the matter? Can't I be as good as Terrence Clive? Can't I be a human being, too? Of course I've felt guilt in my life. Just not very often."

"And what present?" she asked. "Why was this supposed to be a festive night?"

"Because of this," he replied. He reached into his pocket and withdrew an envelope. It bore the crest and address of the Ivory Castle.

He handed it to her without expression. "Open it," he ordered.

Carefully she unsealed it and took out the piece of paper inside. Her heart began to beat so erratically she thought she was having some sort of attack. It was a check made out to FUTURE for half a million dollars. It was signed Charlie Bangor.

She stared at it in amazement. "This is half a million dollars," she said at last.

"Yeah," he said. "Merry Christmas. Or something. It's started. You money's coming back to you, Junior. Parmenter talked everybody into waiting, but Charlie Bangor couldn't. I knew he wouldn't be able to. He came to my room after the meeting. The gambler couldn't resist the sure thing. I'll have the other half million from him within three days."

She didn't know whether to laugh or cry. Half a million dollars of Delmer Fordyce's money back where it was supposed to be, at SOS through FUTURE. Was it wrong to have done this? No, she thought with a sense of wonder. Silly, greedy Charlie Bangor had stolen the money, and Eli had gotten it back.

Again she felt tears springing to her eyes, but this time of joy. She stared and stared at the check. She thought of the good it would do. She thought of Delmer Fordyce and his favorite line of poetry:

He prayeth best who loveth best
All things both great and small.

She looked at Eli, who was staring moodily at nothing in particular. "You did it," she said, repressing the urge to giggle. "You actually got it back."

He cast her a dark glance. "Of course I got it back," he snapped. "That's what I was supposed to do, wasn't I?"

"Of course," she said, grinning down at the check again. "But now it seems *real*. Before it was like a dream or something. But you really did it. Eli, you're wonderful."

Impulsively, she leaned over and kissed him on the cheek. He was clean-shaven and fragrant with that maddening cologne he always wore, but she was surprised at how the rough texture of his cheek made her lips tingle, even after she had drawn away.

"I hope you're happy," he said, not sounding very happy himself.

"I'm ecstatic," she said, but she wished she hadn't kissed him so impulsively. It made her feel suddenly shy, and the air was charged with a peculiar tension.

"Are you?" he asked with maximum sarcasm.

"Yes. Of course. What's wrong with you?"

"Nothing's wrong with me," he snapped.

"Something is so," she accused. "What is it?" Without thinking, she put her hand on his sweatered arm. As she felt the strength and the heat of his muscles beneath her fingers, she realized how much she wanted to touch him. Conflicting emotions surged within her. It seemed natural and good to reach out to him yet somehow forbidden because it set off so many unfamiliar sensations dancing through her.

"All right," he muttered grimly. "Something's wrong with me. You're wrong with me." He turned to face her. Complex emotions played at odds across his features. There was heat in his eyes but a coldness in the set of his mouth. A vein leaped in his temple like a tiny fork of lightning.

She stared up at him. She was powerless to move her hand from his arm, although it seemed to have grown icy and numb from the prickles racing through it. She knew neither of them was speaking, but somehow as they looked at each other, they were communicating intensely.

I'm not the marrying kind.

I know that.

I'm not even the faithful kind.

I know that, too.

I want you.

I know, Eli. I want you, too.

Want me, kid. But don't love me.

It's a little late for that. I can't help it.

I don't want you to get hurt.

It's too late for that, too, Eli. Whichever way it goes from now, it's going to hurt.

This wasn't supposed to happen.

It would hurt most of all to never have you. That would be the worst thing.

I feel the same way.

I'm not asking for any promises from you.

I couldn't make them if you did.

It doesn't matter, Eli.

We'll take it one day at a time. As it comes.

One day at a time.

And this is the first day.

He took her face between his hands. She could feel the pulses in her throat leaping where his fingers touched. He stared into her eyes for a moment longer.

"Are you sure?" he asked at last, his voice low.

She nodded weakly, feeling almost faint with yearning for him. "I'm sure," she whispered.

He reached over with one hand and switched off the light. Then his fingers settled gently against her cheek again. He bent his face to hers and kissed her, lightly at first, then with more intensity, until her head swam and crazy little lights began to dance behind her eyes.

She put her arms around his neck, felt the hardness of his chest against her tender breasts. He pressed more closely against her.

His lips moved to her cheek, then the silky tip of her eyebrow. "I'm sure," she whispered again. He kissed her eyelid, her cheek again, hungrily, as if he had to touch each part of her face, to claim it as intimately as possible.

"So sure," she said with a catch in her voice, and then he took her lips again and his need mingled with hers and burned through both of them with escalating power.

His arms tightened around her, drawing her down to stretch beside him on the bed.

He dragged his lips from hers long enough to whisper harshly to her, "Remember this moment. And don't ever think it wasn't right. Because if anything is right, this is. You know that, don't you?"

"Yes," she said softly. In the darkness she touched his face, felt the scar on his cheek beneath her tracing finger.

"And now I'm going to show you...very slowly...how right," he said, his lips touching hers again. Then his hands began to move over her with a sureness that drove her to the edge of some sweet madness. Gladly she let him take her there.

Later, remembering, it would seem to her that he had led her through a gate and into a new and magical territory whose existence she had never before imagined. It was a paradoxical territory, full of velvet wonder, so large it seemed to contain universes yet so small it contained only the two of them. It was open and without limits. At the same time it was closed to the outside world, intimate and secret to the two of them. It was so right it was perfect.

Just before dawn he turned to leave her, and she drew him close again. "Don't go yet," she said, her hands caressing his bare shoulders.

He paused for a moment, then turned toward her. "Something happens between us that doesn't happen for most people. I don't know why, but it couldn't happen to a crazier combination than us."

"I know." She smiled. "Please don't leave yet."

So he stayed and, pressing over her, took her lips again. Again he taught her how her body made his whole and how his completed hers. He led her back to the magic and took her to the place only the two of them, entwined, could go.

Chapter Ten

It was well past dawn. Still, Eli felt safe as he jogged through the woods toward the Ivory Castle. A moist and pearly fog wrapped the forest, shrouding it as effectively as darkness.

Back in his room he didn't allow himself to think of P.J. or of what had happened. He had to keep his mind clean, clear and uncluttered for his meeting with the Bachelors later that day.

He stripped off his sweater. He did his standard hundred push-ups and hundred sit-ups, a habit left over from prison. It helped wake him to the harsh demands of the world and remind him of the discipline it took to meet them. It also kept his arm muscles hard and his stomach taut and flat. A vagrant thought of the night before flitted through his mind like a velvety ghost. *No,* he thought, almost superstitiously, *don't think of her.* He pushed himself for the lapse with another fifty push-ups and another fifty sit-ups.

He took a shower, colder than usual. He put on clean black slacks but no shirt. He ordered his coffee and eggs from room service, then went into the bathroom and shaved. He ran over what he would say to the Bachelors that afternoon. He could afford no mistakes. It had to be perfect. When unbidden images of the night before surged softly back to haunt him, he forced them away.

He nicked himself with his razor and swore. It was the second time in two days—and him with hands as steady as those of a surgeon. He frowned, concentrating as he reviewed his plans for the Bachelors. He couldn't afford distractions. He had to fan the spark of their greed and quell any hesitation they had. Clive, the old alcoholic, was going to be the stumbling block.

He threw on his shirt but didn't button it. His breakfast arrived, and he sat by the window, his hair still damp from the shower, his shirt still open. He sipped the harsh black coffee and stared out at the fog.

It was not until then, when he was sure he was prepared for what he had to do that day, that he allowed himself to think of her. Remembrance went through him with a pang that actually hurt. The scent of her, the feel of her, the driving need he'd felt for her, all combined with something else to which he did not want to give a name. Even to recall her face sent a shaft of edged emotion through him. The unexpected purity and unselfishness of her passion had surprised him profoundly, making him desire her all the more.

He sat brooding, staring out at the shifting fog. He should have sent her home. Yet he wished she were in his arms right then. He wanted to hold her again. For a long time. To keep her safe in the circle of his arms. He wanted to taste the danger of her lips again, for they did taste of danger, more sweetly than any he had ever known. They made him want to care. Getting her out of his system was going to be harder than he'd thought.

He poured a second cup of coffee and stared out at the fog. When the sting against the Bachelors was complete, he'd deal with her, one way or the other. In the meantime he still had that cockamamie wish that she were there, in his bed, in his arms, in a separate world of their own where all the differences between them made no difference. He could simply love her and be done with it.

Eli, normally the most observant of men, didn't notice he had let so foreign a term as "love" slip into his thoughts.

P.J. AWOKE TO FIND Eli gone. His absence made her feel peculiarly bereft. She tried not to think of it but couldn't help it. Her body tingled strangely. When she whispered his name to herself, all her cells seemed to leap into startling new life.

"Eli," she whispered again, just to see if the feelings would repeat themselves. They did, and odd flickers of happy yearning filled her, uncurling like the petals of an opening blossom.

She hugged her pillow and looked at the rumpled bed. She smiled shyly to herself. She warmed within, remembering his ardor. He had been patient, overwhelmingly strong, yet surprisingly gentle. She realized, with a self-conscious blush of pleasure, that until last night she had only thought she knew the meaning of the words "make love."

Giving herself to him had seemed as natural and necessary as breathing. Yet there had been a dark and lovely intoxication in it, something at once both tremulous and shattering. She remembered the maddening and wholly intimate touch of his hands, his lips. She shuddered with remembered pleasure.

Eli. Making love. Love. She smiled almost helplessly to herself. She loved him. For the first time in her life, she was in love.

She understood a hundred things she did not understand at this time the day before. The fluid warmth of recollection spread through her again.

Of course, it would mean nothing to him, she thought and stopped smiling. But that, she told herself almost fiercely, didn't matter. She had known that from the start. What he had given her was enough. She had no right to expect more or want it. Love didn't mean asking for things. Love meant giving. She would give him anything he wished. That included, she knew grimly, her absence when the time came. He was not a man to be owned or tied down. A woman might as well want to possess the sea or the wind or the high, cold light of the stars. But that would not keep her from wanting him.

She knew she was no longer the same person. Right then she was glad. She hoped she would not come to hate herself for it.

He called at ten in the morning. Her heart fluttered when she heard his voice. But he was strictly businesslike. He had brusque instructions for her, which he shot at her with machinelike rapidity.

She listened hard, memorizing as he talked, nodding in concentration. As he spoke in that curt and professional tone, it was as if the night before had never happened.

"Got it all?" he asked at last, his voice almost harsh.

"Yes," she said, trying to sound businesslike herself. "I think so."

There was a beat of silence. Already she was frightened. Perhaps that's all he had wanted from her—one night. Another battle won in the ancient game of conquest, the war between men and women. Her fragile happiness threatened to evaporate.

But then he said, "Be careful, kid. I'll see you as soon as I can. I miss you."

"I miss you, too," she breathed.

He added something so odd and unexpected it stunned her. "Don't sit under the apple tree with anyone else but me. All right?"

"All right," she said softly with a smile, for the line was from an old love song. A click told her he had hung up, as usual, without saying goodbye.

It wasn't until an hour later that it occurred to her that "Don't Sit Under the Apple Tree" was a wartime song, the request of a soldier going into battle. "Be careful, Eli," she breathed to herself. It was more prayer than warning.

ELI WAS TO MEET the Bachelors at noon in the library for lunch and decisions on high finance. If he knew the kind of men he was dealing with—and he was sure he did—they would gather before he got there. He elected to slip down to the basement of the Ivory Castle and into the secret passages to the spy holes that looked in upon the library. He was right. At eleven o'clock he stood in the cramped darkness watching. All four men were there, talking about him—and FUTURE.

"It's the chance of a lifetime," Teddy Dirkson was saying excitedly. "It's the kind of thing you can't say no to—and it's fallen into our laps."

Charlie Bangor, who was already in the deal to the tune of half a million, said nothing at all. He simply sat in his wing chair, a stupid yet sly expression on his handsome face.

"At first I was suspicious," Dr. Parmenter said, pouring himself a cup of coffee from the silver service. "But I've found such profits have been made. What Mr. Holderman proposes is not out of the question, gentlemen."

"Really?" asked Terrence Clive sarcastically. He was stirring sugar into his coffee, and Eli calculated the absence of liquor on the scene was to keep Clive from daytime imbibing. "Well, dear and glorious physician," Clive continued, "suppose you tell us about them. Because I never heard of profits like the ones the man is talking about."

"Certain software companies at the beginning of the computer boom," Parmenter returned promptly. He'd been reading old financial magazines. "It's been done from time to time in real-estate ventures. It's been done frequently in films—movies—where a small investment can make a thousand percent profit, or more."

"Show business," Teddy Dirkson said with reverence. He loved movie stars and envisioned them gathered around him, adoring him as he lounged in a director's chair. Charlie Bangor just sat, smiling more stupidly and more slyly.

"How nice," Clive said with the same weary sarcasm. He sipped his sugary coffee, but it seemed to give him little satisfaction. "For all you know, you may be thinking about putting your money into one of those horrible slasher movies or one of those mindless teen things with boys falling over each other trying to peek into the girls' locker room. I wouldn't invest in a movie for anything. They haven't made a decent movie since John Wayne died."

"I, personally, think every film Bo Derek has made is a masterpiece," Teddy Dirkson said haughtily.

"I'm using films merely as an example," Parmenter almost snapped. "There are any number of fields where fantastic profits are to be made if you're in the right place at the right time. Medicine, for instance. Miracle drugs, that sort of thing."

"Also illegal drugs," gibed Clive. "For all you know, you may be financing an airlift of cocaine from Bolivia."

In the darkness of his watching place, Eli ground his teeth. Clive was more stubborn than he had feared. For someone who spent half his time drunk, his thought processes were surprisingly sharp.

"Bosh," said Teddy Dirkson, offended. "I've checked Mr. Holderman out with the manager. He's the genuine article. A venture capitalist with offices on Wall Street and in Boston. He's hounded by so many calls he's got a standing order for them not to be put through."

"Clive," Dr. Parmenter said between clenched teeth, "why are you so contrary? Listen to me. I said miracle drugs. Think of interferon. Of White Knight cells. I'm sure that's what Holderman's on to—something biological. When I asked him if it had to do with biology, he wouldn't deny it. What's the hottest thing in science right now?''

"I don't know," Clive answered, pouring out more coffee. "Jalapeño pepper research?"

"No." Parmenter practically seethed. "Gene splicing, you idiot. It's the most exciting concept of our time. The creation of supercells, superstrains of both plants and animals. Miracle varieties. Peaches that bloom in the desert. Cattle that fatten on next to nothing. Healthy cells that eat diseased ones. A special virus that can devour oil spills—and nothing else—cleaning up the oceans. Don't you read, man? It could be the very re-creation of nature."

"I think we've fiddled enough with nature," Clive said mildly, stirring sugar into his coffee. "Someday nature is going to turn around and bop us on the nose for all this meddling."

"Argh," grumbled Parmenter. "You've no vision, Clive. You never had, and you never will."

"You really think that's what Holderman's setting up?" Teddy Dirkson asked, his shaggy brows working thoughtfully. "This gene-splicing stuff?"

"How could we know?" scoffed Clive, rubbing his inflamed nose reflectively. "Holderman's been totally evasive about this so-called fund."

"Because he's had to be," Dirkson said defensively. "Information like this is confidential. You can't broadcast it. But he said himself it was a whale of a deal. If he was trying to sell this kind of inside tip, he could get into a lot of trouble."

Charlie Bangor, sitting in his chair like an elderly male model, sipped his coffee with elegant grace. "I trust him," he said simply.

"He's done none of the things some hustler would have done," Parmenter insisted. "I've been reading up on these things. Listen. He did *not* insist we buy into FUTURE. He constantly suggested less expensive options. Although he projects this five hundred and twenty percent profit, and has proven that it's holding now, he refuses to guarantee it. Furthermore, he gave me his number and I called his Boston office today. His secretary assures me that his firm is a member of the Securities Investor Protection Corporation and the Federal Deposit Insurance Corporation. And he's certainly *not* rushing us into buying anything."

"Except," observed Clive, massaging his nose again, "he's leaving to finalize this whole business within three days, and then he's off to Tokyo to check out the potential of some gizmo that analyzes analogue symbols—whatever they are. Sounds to me like if you want in, you'd better hurry up. And I hardly call phoning his own secretary 'checking him out.'"

"He wears thousand-dollar suits," Charlie Bangor said, a dreamy look on his vacuous face. "I saw one like the one he had on yesterday in *Gentleman's Quarterly*."

"Thousand-dollar suits," Teddy Dirkson said, musing. "I've always wanted a closetful of thousand-dollar suits. I've heard some rich men pay two hundred dollars for their socks. Do you suppose that's true?"

Charlie nodded solemnly and said he thought it was so, Parmenter looked at both men with disgust and Clive laughed. "That settles it, boys," he said, his wrinkles moving in the closest way they ever came to mirth. "If a man wears a thousand-dollar suit, trust him with everything. Give him every dime you've got. Just don't blame me if he uses it to buy himself more thousand-dollar suits and leaves you with nothing more than your long johns to cover your behinds."

"I've ceased to find your cynicism amusing," Parmenter said acidly, looking at Clive with something close to hostility. "Teddy and Charlie are being slightly ridiculous, as usual, but I'm trying to talk some sense into you. Why won't you listen?"

"Why bother?" Clive asked, a bitter tinge to his voice. "You're about forty years too late."

"Clive," Parmenter said, his eyes narrowing, "I'm trying to help you. What's the matter? I'm not recommending any of us put all our money into this—just part of it. Don't you want to be rich?"

Clive poured yet another cup of coffee. His hands were shaking badly now. "I'm too rich now, James. I think we're all too damned rich."

Eli shifted uncomfortably in the cramped space. He didn't like the way Clive was holding out, nor the cold, speculative look that Parmenter leveled at Clive. The old alcoholic didn't seem to notice the malevolence of his friend's gaze. He began shoveling sugar into his cup again.

"Nobody's ever too rich," Parmenter almost hissed. "Why don't you come over to my house tonight and we'll discuss this in private? Without boring Teddy and Charlie to tears."

Clive looked vaguely interested. "Are you buying the drinks?"

"Of course," Parmenter said smoothly.

Mentally Eli cursed. He could almost see the wheels spinning in Parmenter's head, and they were hurtling Clive toward an early grave. If the coldness of Parmenter's stare could kill, Terrence Clive would be dead already.

Hell, he thought, a muscle in his cheek twitching. *We're in trouble.*

All but the most callous con men had a code. Part of it was "Never send them to the river." It meant never leave a victim in such despair that he considers suicide. But what to do when a potential victim considers murder? This situation was something Eli had never encountered, and he was going to have to do some fast talking to save Clive. But the old man was so tired, so played out and burned out, he seemed beyond rising to the bait. It was ironic. Weariness had imbued him with a sort of virtue, and that virtue marked him for doom.

Eli swore to himself again. If he couldn't save Clive, there was only one person left who might be able to—Junior. He couldn't let it come down to that. He didn't want her trying it. She might not be up to it. She was too honest. But she would make herself try it. He sensed that deep in his bones.

He glanced at the luminous numbers on his watch and saw it was time to leave his spying place and meet the Bachelors face-to-face. His mind worked furiously. He had to bring Clive into line and quickly. He could not let the woman get into it any more deeply than she had already. It gave him a sinking, sickening feeling to think of using her that way. Again he admonished himself that he never should have gotten into this scam, and he never should have let her get into it. He left to use every wile at his disposal against Terrence Clive.

IT WAS TWO in the afternoon when her phone rang. Eli's voice sent a frisson dancing through her body, but his tone was so grim she quickly tensed.

"I've got to see you," he said. "Now."

"How?" she asked. "It's broad daylight."

"Go into downtown Leaftree," he ordered. "To the drugstore on the corner of Maple and Main. I want you to come out at exactly two-thirty-seven. It's two-ten now. Pretend you can't start your car. I'll be there and act like I'm helping. Got it?"

"Yes," she said anxiously, "but what's wrong? Something's wrong. I can tell."

"I can't get to Terrence Clive," he muttered angrily. "I've done everything I can without blowing my cover. You're going to have to reel him in."

"Me?" she cried. "How do I do that?"

"Any way you can, sugar," he said roughly. "And I mean any way. By tonight. Parmenter's looking at him with tombstones in his eyes."

His words sank in, and she was shocked. She had planned to befriend Clive, to test him slowly to see what he might reveal in conversation. How could she do what Eli could not, and do it in one night? "But I can't—" she started to say.

He cut her off. "You have to." There was both finality and harshness in his voice. Before she could protest further, he hung up.

She was filled with more kinds of foreboding than she had names for.

At precisely thirty-seven minutes after two, she walked out of Poindexter's Drugstore, got into her rented car, shifted into Drive, turned the key and feigned frustration when the engine wouldn't start. The dash lights lit up a sinister red, and an ominous warning buzz issued from somewhere.

Eli appeared at her door. She rolled her window down slightly.

"Having trouble? Ah, Miss Jameson, isn't it? Want me to have a try?"

She smiled weakly. The day was gray, and the cold had a gingery bite. Eli wore a navy cashmere topcoat, unbuttoned, that made him look like a prosperous young banker, not a man who had spent five years in Leavenworth. He eased in beside her with quick sureness, cranked up the window and pretended to try to start the car.

"Did you do everything I told you?" he asked, fiddling with the ignition key.

"Yes," she said. She felt a bit dizzy. This was the first time she had seen him since they had made love in the predawn darkness. The topcoat made his shoulders look dangerously broad, the wind had rumpled his straight hair and his face was so hard it was adamantine. He wasn't looking at her. He was staring straight ahead, as if all he listened to were the sounds the car made.

She took a deep breath. "I endorsed Charlie Bangor's check with FUTURE's name and initialed it. I phoned the foundation's bank and told them it was coming in and it was absolutely confidential. I drove to the next town and sent it by courier. It should have arrived by now."

"Good," he said shortly. He had been carrying a newspaper when he'd gotten into the car and had set it on the seat between them. He nodded at it. "Look inside the paper. There are three more checks for you. Do the same thing. Endorse them and get them into the bank by courier before these fools wake up."

Her fingers trembling, she unfolded the paper and took out a hotel envelope, which she thrust into her purse. "How much?" she asked. Her heart was beating so hard she thought it would strangle her.

"One and a quarter million dollars," he said between his teeth. "Half a million each from Charlie Bangor and Teddy Dirkson. A quarter million from Parmenter. Nothing from Clive, dammit."

"Eli," she said, and this time her voice did shake. "That makes close to two million dollars. That's almost half of it back."

"I can count," he said shortly. "It's also over two million we haven't got. We have everything back from Charlie Bangor. When the others found out Charlie jumped in early—that his money was already making more while theirs just lay there sleeping—it got them excited. I figured it would. It's like sharks smelling blood. They'll go into a frenzy. And they'll keep thinking about it. They'll want to be in for more. Except Clive."

"Eli," she ventured, "what did you mean when you said I'd have to get to Clive?"

"Just that," Eli muttered, still pretending to fight the Ford's ignition system. "He's too burned out to care about more money. He's got enough to take care of him and that son of his, and he's not taking any chances with it. Nothing, not even the prospect of a fool like Charlie Bangor getting rich, tempts him. Parmenter's invited him over tonight to try to change his mind. If he doesn't succeed, I have the feeling Terrence Clive is on the brink of an accident—guaranteed fatal."

"Eli!" She felt so tense and guilty it nearly made her ill.

He turned to give her a brief and implacable glance. "You're supposed to have supper with him tonight, right? What time?"

"Seven."

"Fine. He's supposed to be at Parmenter's at nine. Talk him into putting that money into FUTURE. Do it any way you can. And if you can't do that, keep him away from Parmenter. I mean that—and use anything you've got."

"What do you mean, 'anything'?" she asked, horrified.

"Just that," he muttered. "Lie to him. Get him drunk. Promise to marry him. I don't care what you do, just do it."

"I can't do that!" Her eyes widened in horror. "What if he wants to... to..."

"If he wants to go to bed with you," Eli said roughly, "I'd say you're as safe as if you were in the arms of your old granny. He's old, he's in bad health, he's used up with booze. He probably couldn't even snuggle energetically. Get him drunk enough and he won't even be able to do that."

"Eli!" she cried, appalled.

He gave her another cold-eyed glance. "Do you think I like the idea?" he demanded. "I don't. I think it stinks. But do you want the man dead instead?"

She bit her lip. She stared down at her driving gloves. "How did we get into this?" she asked bitterly. She stared out the window, unseeing, at the deceptively peaceful buildings of Leaftree's Main Street.

He looked straight ahead. "We got into this because you hired a thief to catch thieves," he said. "We didn't know one of your thieves was also a murderer. Sorry, Junior, I grew up bilking innocent dumbbells, not homicidal psychopaths. This is a new twist for me, too."

She kept staring into the street. "Let's get out," she said, suddenly wanting to desperately. "We've got almost half the money. It's enough. Let's quit."

"We can't," he countered, his lip curling. "The only way I could call Parmenter off Clive is if I admitted the whole thing's a scam. Parmenter can't stand seeing Clive's money not being used. Welcome to the world of the con, sugar. Once you're in it, there's no turning back. You said you wanted in until the end. Well, that's the way it's going to be."

She turned to look at him resentfully. "But what if I can't change Clive's mind?" she challenged. "What if I can't keep him away from Parmenter? What then?"

This time his golden-brown gaze met hers and held it. Again she was reminded of how wolfish his stare could be. He put the car into Neutral, and it roared into life. The sound startled her.

"You can't afford to fail," he said calmly. "Clive could die if you fail."

He put his hand on the door handle to leave. "I have to see Dirkson and Bangor tonight. They're going to want to put more money in. I'll get Dirkson's, but I've got to stop Bangor. I just want Fordyce's money from him. I don't want to send him to the river. And then I've got other business to attend to. For tonight you've got to keep your eye on

Clive. You said you thought you could do it. Now you're going to have to.''

She was frightened, confused and most of all hurt by the turn events were taking. Did he really expect her to try to seduce Terrence Clive, if it came to that? To get the poor man hopelessly drunk? To talk him into risking any security he had for himself and Albert? What did he think she was? And what kind of man was he to ask her to do this?

He tossed her a measuring look. ''What's the matter? Things getting too rough for you? Want to go home after all? Let Clive take his lumps as best he can?''

She clenched her hands, then unclenched them. ''No,'' she said in a combination of stubbornness and guilt. It was she, after all, who had begun this whole muddle.

''Of course,'' he said callously, ''we could both walk away from it. We've got over a million dollars here. I could clean out my bank accounts, and we could go flying down to Rio and forget about everything else.''

She looked at him with amazement and something close to loathing. ''You can't mean that,'' she said, her voice stiff with accusation.

''Maybe I do and maybe I don't,'' he snapped. ''I asked you once to trust me. Maybe that was just another con. When you started all this, you didn't know much about the powers of darkness. Well, kid, you're learning. You wanted to stay in. Let's see if you've got what it takes to do it.''

''I suppose your friend Cleo would have what it takes,'' she murmured unhappily, then wished she hadn't. It sounded childish and jealous.

''Yes,'' he said with that same maddening lack of emotion. ''Cleo could do it with her false eyelashes tied behind her back. But I don't have Cleo. All I have right now is you. So you've got to tough it out.''

She gave him a dark and accusing look. ''I'll tough it out, all right,'' she said.

He gave her the ghost of his crooked smile. "Good," he said in that same nerveless tone. "I'll be waiting for you at your place tonight. And when all this is over, I'm going to take you to a decent hotel where we can sleep in a decent bed for a change."

Did he think she was that shallow, she wondered furiously, that the promise of sex would make everything seem fine? "What makes you think I'd go?" she asked bitingly.

She suddenly felt as if she had been dragged into something beyond her depth, and it was Eli who had pulled her there.

"What makes you think I'd care if you said no?" he asked coolly. His mouth quirked cynically. "There are plenty of women in the world. I'll see you tonight."

He got out of the car, nodded curtly. The chill wind tousled his hair again as he strode down the sidewalk, not looking back at her. He looked like a man perfectly contained and supremely content in his aloneness.

She slid into the driver's seat and stared after him, tears stinging her eyes. *What are you making me into?* she thought, watching his retreating back. *What am I becoming because of you?* By her dispirited calculations she estimated it had taken her exactly seven-and-a-half hours to realize she had fallen in love with absolutely the worst man she could have picked.

He hurried down the street, keeping his back straight in spite of the nipping wind, which had driven most pedestrians into a chilled crouch. He'd hurt her and badly, he thought grimly. He was asking her to do the last thing she was equipped to do, but there was no other choice. If she ever thought she had Clive's death on her conscience, it would kill her.

And maybe she needed to see him, Eli, at his worst and most cynical, he thought. She needed to understand what he had been once, what he could be again if the occasion demanded. Perhaps when he got as much of the money back for her as he could, the kindest gift he could give her was reason to walk away from him, never looking back. It would be best for her. And the quicker the better.

He didn't want to throw her at Clive. But there was no other choice, and he was sure she was smart enough to stay safe until he made other arrangements to protect both her and the old man. Then, if she couldn't forgive him, she could walk out of his life, her moral superiority intact. It would be better for him, too, because he didn't want the responsibility of her. He was already tired of it. He wanted to be free of her.

Liar, he sneered to himself. He didn't want to be free of her. He wanted to keep her. And perhaps that's why he'd forced himself to be so brutal. He kept thinking of the frightened and stricken look in her eyes. It made him sick to his stomach. But he kept walking away from her, and he never looked back.

Chapter Eleven

P.J. sat nervous but determined in the restaurant of the inn called the Green Mountain Manse. She sipped her second cup of tea restlessly. She was dressed in her blue shirtwaist. A new pair of fake sapphire earrings glittered in her earlobes. She wore perfume behind her ears and the faintest touch of blue eye shadow. It was as seductive as she was likely to get, she thought grimly, and it would have to do.

But Terrence Clive was late. He was precisely half an hour late, and she grew increasingly uneasy. He had made reservations for the two of them, which made his lateness all the more disturbing.

She tried to sit primly, projecting an aura of poised control, but her mind spun like some sort of whirling firework. She felt a bit like a maiden preparing to be a virgin sacrifice, although that was technically impossible, especially after last night. She felt like a liar and a cheat, albeit not a very good one. She felt like a fool and a sinner for having set these events in motion.

Yet she was also steeled by a sense of duty. She hadn't liked the rough way Eli had pushed her into this. Yet she had accepted her responsibility for Clive's plight, and she was willing to face it, no matter how much it cost her or how repugnant she found her own actions.

She had asked Eli to get the money back. She had begged, bullied and challenged him to do it. He had taken chances—dangerous ones—to do it. He couldn't have known Parmenter was such a ruthless customer or that Terrence Clive had sunk into some slough of self-loathing where he refused to profit anymore from past crimes. The situation was her creation. Every ethical bone in her body—and most of them were quite ethical indeed—demanded she do as Eli asked: get Clive to change his mind, or keep him away from Parmenter.

Still, she felt inadequate. The mysterious and beautiful Cleo, she suspected, would do the job with cold-blooded efficiency. If P.J. could do it all, it would be from sheer moral compulsion and dogged determination.

As for Eli, he had shaken her to the core. He seemed to be tossing her to Clive offhandedly, as though she were nothing to him. Then he had made the horrifying suggestion that they take the money themselves and run. Had he been serious? Yet all the time he had had the air of a man forcing himself to be as cold and calculating as possible—almost as if he wanted to put her off. She didn't know what to think.

The head waiter was giving her a suspicious look. She glanced discreetly at her watch. Clive was forty minutes late now. Perhaps he had forgotten about her. Perhaps he had started drinking earlier than usual. Her nervousness increased.

She rose, trying to ignore the supercilious stare of the head waiter, and made her way to the phone in the expensive quaintness of the foyer. She looked in the phone book and dialed Clive's number. She waited for fifteen rings. He didn't answer. Perhaps he was on his way.

She went back to her table and ordered another cup of tea, although all the caffeine was beginning to make her shaky. But when Clive was an hour late, she rose and tried to phone him a second time. There was no answer. She was growing panicky. Not knowing what else to do, she phoned the Ivory Castle and asked for Eli. She was informed by a haughty desk clerk that he had just left. *What was he up to?* she thought desperately. *Where was he when she needed him, and what was she supposed to do now?*

The first thing, she reminded herself grimly, was not to panic. She took her notebook from her purse, opened the telephone book again, and copied two addresses—Clive's and Parmenter's. She struggled to remember what Clive's car looked like. She was not good about such details, but she thought he had driven a dark green sedan of not too recent vintage.

She set her shoulders in determination and went back to her table to retrieve her stadium jacket and scarf. It occurred to her, wryly, that the stadium jacket made her look more like someone going to a Harvard-Yale game than a wily seductress, but Eli knew full well she could only work with what she had.

The head waiter loomed near, staring down his nose at her. "Madame," he said in chill tones, "is waiting no longer?"

"Madame," P.J. replied, throwing down a dollar tip, "seems to have been stood up. If Mr. Clive should show up, ask him, please, to wait. I'll be calling to check if he's here."

He gave her a superior sniff, and she put her nose in the air and sniffed back. Two weeks ago she would have been intimidated by such a man. This night she felt as if she could rock him back on his heels with ease. He was the most minor of her problems.

She made her way to the parking lot and got into her car. She opened the glove compartment. Being methodical had its rewards, for she had purchased a street map of Leaftree her first day in town. She studied it for a moment, took a deep breath and started off for Terrence Clive's house.

The fog had returned with evening, and she felt as if she were driving through an unreal world. Patches of it drifted across her path like ghosts trying to impede her. The road to Clive's house curved cruelly, and she had to pass over a rickety bridge that might have looked picturesque in the sunlight but seemed sinister and hazardous by night. Its guardrail was badly dented, as if someone had recently miscalculated its width.

She crossed another such bridge before she came to Clive's house. It was a modest, two-story white house rising into the darkness, all its windows black. Only a yellow porch light glowed. Her car crunched to a halt in the gravel drive, and she got out. She went to the detached garage and stared inside. She could make out no sign of a car.

Where was he? she wondered nervously. She looked up at the dark and misty sky. Where was he? Was he on his way to the Green Mountain Manse? Was he already there? Or had something happened to him?

She tried to stay calm. She thought of trying to check the interior of the house but reasoned that since his car was gone, he would not be inside. She got back into the Ford, drove back across the first of the two rickety bridges, stopped at a service station and called the restaurant at the Green Mountain Manse. No, Mr. Clive had not arrived.

Her heart started to beat harder under her jacket. She wound her scarf more tightly around her neck. She re-checked her map and drove toward Parmenter's house, praying that Clive's car would not be there.

But it was. A break in the fog rolled by, and she could see clearly for a moment. A slightly rusted dark green Mercury of uncertain age was parked discreetly in the double carport, next to a black Buick she took to be Parmenter's. She felt a nasty, sinking feeling. There was a strange taste in her mouth, which she supposed must be that of failure.

Eli, gruff as he had been with her, had insisted on the importance of her either changing Clive's mind or keeping him away from Parmenter. She had failed on both counts. But she had to make sure. She circled the block, parked next to Leaftree's tiny public library, whose lights were now dimmed, then walked back toward Parmenter's house, her hands deep in her pockets.

What now? she wondered dismally. Did she creep across his lawn like a character in a cartoon and peer into the living-room windows? Surely someone would see her and call the police. How on earth did one spy on someone inside a house? She had no idea. What would Eli do?

Half a block from Parmenter's house a large orange cat that reminded her of Eustace sprinted across her path, then down the sidewalk into the fog. *Ha!* she thought. Feeling rather theatrical, she turned up her collar around her face and walked more swiftly after the cat.

"Eustace! Bad cat! Come back here," she called. Thank heaven, she thought, she didn't have to depend on her acting ability to survive. She would starve. But she marched after the cat, who had disappeared in the shadows and mist. "Here, kitty, kitty, kitty," she called softly. "Eustace? Come here. Nice kitty, kitty, kitty."

She was at the edge of Parmenter's lawn. "Eustace?" she said into the darkness. "Is that you in the bushes, you naughty cat? Come here right now. Come to Mama."

She picked her way across Parmenter's lawn as quickly as she could, wondering if anybody was watching her. "Are you in the bushes, Eustace?" she said softly. "*Bad* kitty!"

She walked along a tall hedge of lilacs that ran beside Parmenter's house. Although his front drapes were drawn, the side ones were not. She kept to the shadows and glanced in. At first the room seemed uninhabited. Then, in the far corner by a coffee table, she saw them. Clive sat in an easy chair, his head in his hands. Parmenter stood beside him. He was refilling Clive's glass from a bottle of something brown.

She inhaled sharply. *She was too late. Clive was already with Parmenter, and Parmenter was getting him drunk. It was just what Eli didn't want to happen. It meant that soon Clive would be signing something he didn't realize the importance of, such as another prefabricated will, or he would meet with some kind of accident. Or both. And Clive looked terrible, as if he were weeping. He must already be on a crying jag.*

What now? she asked herself. *Stay calm,* she answered automatically. She glanced back toward the carport. Clive depended on his friends to drive him when he had been drinking. But his car was there. Parmenter might be intending to let him drive home alone. She remembered the winding roads, the two ramshackle bridges. Her heart turned into a cold stone.

"Kitty, kitty," she whispered mechanically, just in case a neighbor was watching. "Where are you, kitty?"

She moved across the lawn to the sidewalk and hurried back the way she had come. Surely Parmenter wouldn't be rash enough to do anything to Clive in his own house. She would get her car. She would wait outside. If Clive tried to drive home, she would stop him, even if it meant rear-ending him with the rented Ford.

And what if Parmenter drives him home and puts him to bed with a lighted cigarette? she asked herself grimly.

Then you break a window, go in and drag him out, she answered silently. *You don't panic. Above all, you don't panic.*

And what if he's too heavy for you? asked the part of her mind seriously considering panic.

He won't be, said the part determined to stay cool. *You count on adrenaline at a time like that. You can always do what you have to do. You have a moral obligation to this man.*

She got into the Ford and drove back to Parmenter's house. The lights in the front room still glowed cheerily. Both cars sat in the carport. She parked across the street at a slight angle from the house. She hunched down in the seat, hoping nobody would notice her or the car or find them suspicious. If a police officer came along, she would say she'd just had a fight with her boyfriend. She would say she was sitting and thinking things out. That was all. She was thankful for the patchy fog.

Slumped uncomfortably in the cold front seat of the Ford, she sat watching Parmenter's house. And she waited.

IT WAS NEARLY MIDNIGHT when P.J., chilled through and numbed with nervousness, straightened in tense interest. A side door into the carport opened. Light fell briefly on Parmenter's erect figure and Clive's slouching one. P.J. slid farther down in the seat. She saw Parmenter guide a shambling, barely erect Clive into the passenger seat of Clive's green Mercury. Then Parmenter got in on the driver's side, slammed the door and started the engine.

She tried to stay calm as Parmenter backed the Mercury down the drive and into the street. She waited until he had reached the stop sign at the corner, signaled left and turned before starting her own car.

She prayed very hard that Parmenter was taking Clive home and started to speed after them. She didn't put on her lights until she reached the end of the first block. When she turned, she could see the taillights of the Mercury nearly half a block ahead, looking ghostly in the fog.

She had never tried to follow another car, and it frightened her. Common sense told her to stay back, but not so far that she would be unable to catch up if necessary or lose Parmenter if he made an unexpected turn.

Parmenter seemed to be heading toward Clive's house, for which she was grateful. But then he took an odd direction. The Mercury headed onto a crooked but deserted highway and stayed on it for half a mile. Then it made a sharp turn and climbed a newly paved mountain road that looked as if it led to an uncompleted subdivision. She followed in the Ford, growing more frightened by the moment. What was Parmenter up to? Where was he taking Clive and why?

She stayed behind at what she hoped was an unsuspicious distance. When she saw the taillights of the Mercury become stationary, she quickly pulled into the driveway of a darkened house to watch. She killed her lights and prayed the owners wouldn't see her and question her.

Then the Mercury was turning around. The driver's door opened. Through the fog she saw a figure step out. He stood for a moment by the door, ghostly in the dim glow cast by the interior light.

Then everything was darkness again, except for a blurry pinpoint of light. Parmenter was doing something, but she didn't know what. Just when she was convinced that she should drive up and interfere, no matter what the consequences, she saw the Mercury's fog lights switched on, but not its headlights. And then the car began to roll crazily down the steep hill.

Damn Parmenter! she thought, her heart vaulting into her throat. He was setting Clive loose in the Mercury when he was dead drunk. He had taken him just enough out of his way to disorient him and throw more sharp turns and curves into the unfamiliar way home.

Without thinking, she started the Ford again, gunned with a squeal out of the driveway and went careering after Clive's weaving car. She worried momentarily that Parmenter would see her, then promptly forgot to think of it. She was too concerned with how to stop Clive.

Somehow he had managed to negotiate the sharp turn onto the highway, but he was driving down the wrong side of the road. P.J. hurried to catch up with him, then dropped back. A semi came bearing down the road, swerved wildly into her lane to avoid Clive and made her spin the steering wheel madly. She was almost blinded by its headlights, which seemed to be on top of her, deafened by the blaring of its horn. She seemed to be all over the highway for an eternal second and barely missed veering into a ditch. She had been forced onto the soft shoulder of the road. A sickening tug seemed to try to pull her even farther off course. She felt something strike the bottom of the car hard.

She managed to get back on the highway and into the correct lane, but she feared she had knocked something off the bottom of the car. It was making a clunking, gasping sound, and she had horrific visions of an exploding gas tank or a blowing tire or an axle that would shiver into two jagged pieces when she was taking a curve.

Clive was not speeding, but neither was he moving slowly. She was keeping a good five lengths behind him, and her speedometer read fifty miles per hour.

Insanely he sped up when he took the sharp turn back into the heart of town, and only at the last minute did he avoid running into a viaduct. She followed him, her teeth grinding together, wondering if she dared try to stop him by hitting him from behind. His driving became more erratic by the moment, and she had visions of him killing them both.

It was then that Clive did something so irrational that only a drunk or a madman would have done it. He stopped at a green light. At one of the few intersections in Leaftree with a light, with no car in sight except hers behind him, he came to a screeching halt that left a trail of burned rubber on the asphalt. He ended up crosswise in the street, his tail pipe smoking. But he was stopped, at least temporarily.

P.J. braked to a squealing stop of her own beside him, leaped from her car and seized hold of his door handle. She flung open the door of the Mercury. Clive blinked at her in bleary confusion.

"Peggy," he said at last. He looked as if he were going to be sick.

"Penny," she corrected automatically, pushing him toward the passenger seat with all the force she had. He was not a large man, but he seemed as slack and nerveless as a heavy bag of grain, and it took all her strength. She felt something odd happen to her right arm and wondered, almost idly, if she'd torn a ligament.

"What...whaddaya doin'?" Clive slurred, trying to focus on her.

"Taking over," she said shortly, seizing the keys. She backed the Mercury up, then put it in Drive again. She was going to park it down the street, then come back for her own car. But as she started forward, the intersection light changed to red. She hit the brakes. They didn't work.

"Oh, my God!" she said. She aimed the Mercury at the curb. It was going slowly, very slowly, but it jumped the curb. It hit the support of a chain link fence, bent it viciously, but stopped. The hood sprang open with a tortured screech.

P.J. was thrown forward against the steering wheel but felt no pain. She had automatically thrown out her arm to keep Clive from diving into the windshield, and her movement broke his momentum. He hit her forearm heavily and struck the dash, but floppily, almost without impact, like a rag doll. He bounced back against the seat and sagged there. He had cut his head slightly.

He turned to her in puzzlement. All his wrinkles looked slack, as if they were pulling his face downward like a melting mask. "What?" he asked again helplessly.

"Your brakes," she said, her mind racing. "He did something to your brakes. The bastard!"

"What?" Clive said again with the same smeary gaze of incomprehension.

"Come on," she said, getting out of the Mercury. "We're going in my car. Come on. Come on!"

But Clive didn't move. She ran to the passenger side, tore the door open and pulled him out. Again she felt as if she were using more strength than she had. He leaned heavily on her, and she felt she nearly carried him to her own car, almost flung him inside as if she were a very small football tackle. Panting, she ran to her own door and got in. She noticed the Ford was leaking oil, but she wanted to get away quickly. If the police showed up now, she had no idea what she would tell them.

Fortunately, Leaftree seemed as deserted as if all its residents had been administered a sleeping potion. She started toward Clive's house, then glanced over at him. He had fallen asleep, his mouth open. Blood from the cut on his head was staining the Ford's upholstery.

Suddenly, fear pierced her. She didn't want to take Clive to his place. She didn't know where Parmenter was. He might have walked back to his own home—it was only a mile and a half, and he had the cover of the fog. But he might show up at Clive's just to make sure the job he'd started was finished. She couldn't face Parmenter after what she had been through. She couldn't.

Heart racing, breathing hard, she turned the Ford and headed back toward the Nutmeg Peddler. How she would get Clive into her room, she didn't know. But it was the only place she could think of where he would be safe. And Eli would be there. They would be safe if she could just get back to Eli.

She made only one stop. She dashed into an all-night doughnut stand and bought several large containers of black coffee to go, hoping she could sober Clive up enough to see if he remembered anything. The young woman at the counter looked at her strangely, and when P.J. glanced at an ornamental mirror on the shop's wall, she was shocked by her own appearance. She was pale, disheveled, and there was a tiny trickle of blood at the corner of her mouth. She must have bitten the inside of her lip when the Mercury hit the fence support. Her eyes had a wild light in them. Her hands were starting to shake.

"You okay?" the counter attendant asked, concern combining with suspicion in her eyes.

"Fine," P.J. lied. She realized if Clive's accident was investigated, she didn't want to be linked with it. "I nearly had an accident," she said. "I was sleepy, and all of a sudden a deer jumped across the road. I nearly went into a ditch trying to avoid it. I've got a long way to go. I need to stay awake."

The woman nodded with sympathetic comprehension. "Yeah. You got to watch out for those deer. They can be in front of you before you know it. One nearly totaled my brother's car. He couldn't avoid it. You were lucky."

"I certainly was," P.J. said with a tremulous smile. She took the coffee and left. She didn't feel lucky at all.

She parked behind the Nutmeg Peddler and struggled to half drag, half carry Clive inside through the back entrance. She prayed no one would see her. She probably looked like a hooker lugging her hapless prey into her seedy room.

She let him sag against the wall while she fumbled for her key. Shakily she inserted it in the lock, swinging open the door and praying that Eli would be there. The room was dark, but some light from the hall penetrated its gloom. She could barely make out a shape sitting on her bed. Her heart bounded with relief.

She grabbed Clive by the lapels of his coat, and again, with more strength than she thought she had, she somehow propelled him into the room and wrestled him onto the bed.

"Watch out," she said to Eli, nearly panting. "You'd better move. He's drunk, he's hurt and he's bleeding."

She closed the door behind her, leaning against it for a moment, breathing hard. She had made it. She was safe. She had an irrational desire to cry but steeled herself against it. "Turn on the light, will you?" she asked. She hated the quaver in her voice. But she wanted to see Eli. Angry as she had been with him, she wanted nothing more than to fall into his arms and let him take care of things from then on.

The light was switched on, making her blink in temporary blindness. "Ah," said an unfamiliar voice. "Perfect timing. Lock the door."

P.J. blinked again, staring into the sudden brightness with terror. For it was not Eli who sat on her bed next to Clive's inert form. It was Dr. Parmenter, and he held a small automatic pistol leveled at her heart.

Chapter Twelve

Instinctively her hand reached for the doorknob behind her, but Parmenter made a slight gesture with the gun that paralyzed her, her back against the door.

"How did you get in here?" she asked, her heart beating so wildly that her voice was barely a whisper.

Parmenter gave her a cool, tight-lipped smile. "I've been behind you most of the way. I had another vehicle up at the construction site, in the garage of one of the unfinished houses. I saw it all, Miss Jameson. And when you wheeled into the backlot to wrestle our friend through the east rear entrance, I simply came, unencumbered, through the west rear entrance. I opened your lock with a slip of celluloid. It's not difficult for a man who's dexterous with a scalpel."

Clive stirred on the bed and groaned. P.J. swallowed hard. "How did you know where my room was?" she asked. The words nearly choked her.

Parmenter raised the gun so that it was aimed at her face. "Your other swain, Teddy Dirkson, called you three or four times from my house. Always asking for Miss Jameson in room 12."

P.J. swallowed again. Nobody had ever held a gun on her before. She was amazed at how effectively it froze her nerves. "What do you want?" she asked, her voice the same helpless whisper.

"Ah," he murmured with the same mechanical smile, "the question is, what do you want, Miss Jameson? Why were you following us—and then Clive? Of what possible interest is he to you? You could even be said to have saved his life. Noble, but misguided. He wouldn't thank you for it. He no longer cares if he lives or dies."

"He was supposed to meet me tonight," she said, playing for time. If this were a movie, Eli would come crashing through the window now and save her. The window remained silent and unshattered. She realized the hour was late, and Eli might have come, grown tired of waiting and now be back sleeping in his own enormous bed at the Ivory Castle.

"Clive was supposed to meet you," Parmenter mocked. "Yes. He remembered that—after a few drinks. I thought it curious at the time. But when I saw it was you who came flying out of that Ford, you who'd been following first us and then Clive, I began to suspect things, Miss Jameson."

"Suspect what?" she bluffed. "He...stood me up. I went looking for him. I knew you were friends. I thought I'd follow him back to his house and give him a piece of my mind. I don't like being left waiting."

"Hmmm," said Parmenter, raising a smooth white eyebrow. "Lied very prettily. But not convincingly. It suddenly occurred to me, Miss Jameson, when I saw you dragging Clive back to your car, that you happened to be in several places very conveniently with several friends of mine—first Teddy Dirkson, then Terrence. You were, in fact, with Dirkson when he befriended Mr. Holderman. Mr. Holderman who has a quarter of a million of my dollars, I might add. And even more of Teddy's and Charlie Bangor's. Who are you, Miss Jameson?" he asked, his tone measured yet filled with understated threat. "If that indeed is your name. For I begin to suspect you're a confederate of Mr. Holderman's. And that neither of you is up to any good. Though why you'd want to risk your life to save Clive's is beyond me. You simply want his money, the same as everyone else. If you hadn't engaged in such amateur heroics, you might even have gotten it—from me. But I'm afraid you've—how would your generation put it, my dear?—you've blown it."

"I don't know Mr. Holderman," she said, lying more desperately than she had all of the past days put together. "I met him and Mr. Dirkson by accident. Through Mr. Dirkson I met Mr. Clive. He was very kind to me. So I wondered why he just abandoned me like that. I told you. I wasn't trying to be heroic. When he crashed, it was simply a reflex to try to help him."

"And flee here, like a thing pursued—which, unknown to you, indeed you were." Parmenter smiled. "Rather than take him home? Or to a hospital? Or call an ambulance? Or the police? Or to stay, sensibly, at the scene of an accident?"

"I was... frightened," she countered, trying not to tremble. "Shaken. I wasn't thinking clearly."

"No," he said. "You weren't. And perhaps if I looked more carefully through this room, I could find out exactly why you weren't thinking clearly. Do you suppose?"

Involuntarily P.J.'s eyes darted to the little desk with its propped-up leg. In its drawers were all her folders and data for SOS and FUTURE. He would know who she was, he would find out who Eli was. From the look in his eyes, she was sure he would kill them both, and Terrence Clive, as well. He would do it as dispassionately as if he were killing moths.

Again she prayed Eli would come crashing through the window like a cowboy in a film. But the window, mute, with blind drawn, simply mocked her.

Clive stirred again on the bed. He made a whimpering sound and rolled over on his stomach, locking his arms around the shabby little pillow. He reminded P.J. of a small, unhappy child who has cried himself into a fitful sleep only to find himself surrounded by nightmares.

"It really would have been a mercy to let him die," Parmenter said, studying her frightened face clinically. "He no longer has any reason to live. You see, Albert died this afternoon."

P.J.'s body went taut against the door. "What?" She was uncertain whether to believe him.

Parmenter nodded without emotion. "Don't be sad, my dear. In terms of IQ, it's rather like the death of a dog. Albert was of no consequence to anyone—except, of course, Clive. Responsibility for that shambling shell kept him going. But now Albert is dead, and Clive, alas, has no more raison d'être. He'll simply drink himself to death now. I planned to make it quicker and easier for him. Now you've complicated things. Pity."

"So what are you going to do with me, with us?" she demanded, looking as defiant as she could. Eli wasn't going to save her, that was evident; he was probably snoring blissfully in the Ivory Castle. And Parmenter, although he frightened her, was starting to make her angry.

"I intend to search your room," he said with false pleasantness. "If I find nothing that connects you with Holderman, I will simply take you out and dispose of the two of you. Perhaps a fire at Clive's house. I'll have to improvise, which frankly makes me cross, but I've always been a lucky man. It won't do much for your reputation, being found dead in the arms of an elderly alcoholic. But such things happen to young women who don't mind their own business. You've seen too much, and you know too much."

"You won't get away with it," she said, but her threat sounded hollow even to her own ears.

"No?" he asked nonchalantly. "We shall see. I imagine the more sordid the little scenario I create for the two of you, the more eager people will be to believe it. Nobody knows what time Clive left my house. I can say you stormed to my door and demanded he take you home with him. He was so distraught, he didn't know what he was doing, and I—even I, his old friend—couldn't stop him. I thought perhaps a night with a little gold digger such as you might even be therapeutic for the poor man. Such a shame you both got drunk, that a careless cigarette started a fire."

"I am *not* a gold digger," she said between clenched teeth. "Nobody would believe it. I'm just a secretary from Amherst, Massachusetts. And I hardly ever drink."

"Many a young lady has a secret life." Parmenter smiled smoothly. "You tried your luck with Teddy, then decided Clive was an easier mark. I can say you even flirted with me. Who's to deny it once you're dead?"

"Everybody who knows me," she shot back, looking him steadily in the eye.

"There is, of course, another alternative," he purred, keeping the gun trained on her chest. "And that is that you and Holderman are indeed linked. If I find out that's so, I'll simply hold you for ransom until I get my money back— with very nice interest. Perhaps all of Teddy's share and Charlie's, too. That would give you a nice reprieve, wouldn't it? Still, I'd have to kill you, anyway. And Holderman, as well. He wouldn't be quite so attractive with a bullet hole in his head. But he and you would both deserve it, wouldn't you? For trying to cheat four kindly old gentlemen. And I'd have to leave—seek a more enticing climate in a place with no extradition agreement with the U.S."

"Search away," P.J. challenged with false bravado. "You won't find anything." If he turned his back on her for a moment, she thought, she would take a chance, try to hit him over the head with the table lamp or the phone. Now she had put not only Clive's life and her own in jeopardy, but Eli's, as well. *Eli, too,* she thought. *No. Not that.* She felt sick with desperation.

"Sit down, my dear," he said in his best bedside manner. "I don't like the look you have in your eyes. And our friend here isn't sleeping deeply. I think I'll tie you together for a while. That way I can make my search without worrying about either of you."

He went to her closet, pulled out her best skirt and quickly tore a number of strips off it. She winced. His hands, though small, were incredibly strong and sure.

"Now," he said, "sit down on the bed and put your hands in front of you, wrists together."

She obeyed, but she was getting an odd feeling, as if the top of her head were about to spin off and fly away. He sat down next to her. Using his left hand, he started to loop the first of the wool strips around her wrists, all the while keeping a tight grip with his right hand on the gun.

With a movement so quick it surprised even her, P.J. raised her own right hand like a child playing cowboy and thrust her forefinger deep into Parmenter's gun barrel.

He froze and looked at her in anger, disbelief and with a tingle of fear. "What are you doing, you little fool?" he snapped. "Stop that! If I pull this trigger, I'll blow your whole hand off."

She could feel it happening to her now, feel the sparks whirling in her eyes and something coursing through her strongly, as if some alien force had seized her body. "Go ahead and pull it," she dared him, her face and voice absolutely controlled. "You'll blow your own hand off, too. The barrel's jammed. It'll explode. See how you explain *that* to everybody.

He tried to whip the gun sideways from her, but somehow she stayed with him, although she was sure he had wrenched her finger half off. With his left hand he swung at her head, but she ducked, and with all the vehemence she had, she slapped him across the eyes with her own left hand.

He swore at her and started to rise, to jerk the gun away from her. But before he could get to his feet, P.J. slapped at his eyes again, so hard he sat down, thumping against Clive.

With a furious throaty growl Parmenter doubled up his fist and started to swing at P.J. full force. But Clive, disturbed and disoriented, had awakened. He threw his arms around Parmenter and buried his face against the man's chest. "Jim!" he sobbed in confused anguish. "Albert! Albert's gone!"

"Let go of me, you fool," Parmenter snarled. He finally managed to wrench his gun away from P.J., and he brought it down savagely on Clive's head.

The descent of the gun seemed to take forever. P.J. felt as if she were floating within a slow-motion movie. As the gun began its leisurely arc down, she reached across for the black telephone on the beside table. She took it into her hands, then she found herself on her feet, slowly raising the phone above her head. She winced as she saw Parmenter strike Clive. Closing her eyes, she brought the phone down with all her force on Parmenter's skull. It seemed to take forever to connect.

The phone made a crunch and a slight ring against his skull. Parmenter himself made an odd noise, like a tire with a slow leak. With a strange, weak hiss he fell over, across Clive's body in a parody of the embrace of friendship.

Her eyes were open now. She stared down at him, half panting, half sobbing. He really was unconscious, she thought. Time seemed to jerk back to its ordinary speed, leaving her weak and slightly dizzy.

She awkwardly picked up the gun and looked numbly at the strips of wool he had torn from her good skirt. She supposed she should tie him up.

She took a deep breath and concentrated very hard, trying to remember her knot-tying class from Girl Scouts. A square knot was left over right, right over left, left over right.

At that moment Eli, clad in black, came crashing through her window like a movie stuntman. He smashed through, curled into a fetal position, and hit the floor in a shower of glass but was on his feet almost immediately. He had a small automatic, and he raised it with both hands, police-style, leveling it at the spot Parmenter had been in only seconds before. "Freeze, turkey!" he half yelled, half snarled.

Then, blinking in surprise at the empty air, he looked down at Parmenter lying peacefully across Clive's chest. He stared in disapproving disbelief at P.J., who stood with a strip of wool in one hand and Parmenter's gun dangling gingerly from the barrel in her fingertips.

She was still trying very hard to think. She was sure a square knot was left over right, right over left . . .

"What the . . . ?" he said, his eyes moving from her to Parmenter's inert form and back again.

Then she felt as if she were waking from a dream. She stared at the broken window and then at Eli. It was about time, she thought pettishly. "Your entrance was dramatic," she said, her voice ragged and accusatory. "But you have a really lousy sense of timing. Just . . . lousy . . ."

She sank to the bed and put her face in her hands. She was so spent she wanted to fall over and lie down, but that meant she would touch Parmenter, and the thought made her flesh crawl.

"Are you all right?" Eli asked, his voice extremely quiet.

"Yes," she said. "Please tie that man up before he comes to. Please! I can't bear to look at him."

Eli moved swiftly to her side of the bed, picked up the wool strips and began knotting them expertly around Parmenter's wrists. He tied the man's hands behind his back and then bound his ankles together. "What's the story here?" he demanded as he worked. "I've looked all over for you. Where were you? I waited over an hour. Then I went out looking for you and saw Clive's car being towed in. I didn't know what the hell had happened. So I tried back here, saw your light on, looked through a crack in your shade and saw you with your finger stuck in Parmenter's automatic, for God's sake! What got into you?"

She stared unseeing at the stain on the wallpaper. "I saw somebody do it once in a Western—jam the gun barrel. It was all I could think of."

"You could have become permanently left-handed," he growled between his teeth. With one rough movement he seized Parmenter by the collar and flung him down on the far edge of the bed so that he no longer touched Clive or was near P.J.

"What did you hit him with?" he demanded. "A cement block? I backed up halfway across the parking lot so I could vault through that window, and when I sail through it, you've already decked him and he's out like a redwood fell on him. Please don't tell me you used your fist."

"The phone," she said dispiritedly. She let her gaze drift to it. It lay on the floor, the cord jerked from the wall.

"And what about Clive?" he asked, examining the wound on the other man's head.

"Parmenter hit him with the gun," P.J. said, still list-lessly gazing at the phone. "Is he all right? Is he alive?"

"He's breathing. His color's good. He should be fine," Eli said. He came and drew her to her feet. She was trembling so hard she could barely stand. He turned her face to look up at his.

"You're bleeding," he said, gentleness in his voice for the first time. He touched the corner of her mouth, where the slight trickle of blood had started again.

She looked up at him, suddenly comprehending that he was there, that the ordeal was really over. "You're bleeding, too," she murmured, almost forgetting her own pain. His eyebrow was cut, as was his chin, and he had reopened the old scar on his cheek.

She stretched her finger up to touch his cheek. "Are you all right?" she asked.

He laughed and smoothed her bangs away from her forehead. "Am I all right? What a question. How are you and what happened? The only thing wrong with me is that I have enough glass splinters on me to feel like a pincushion, which is why I'm not going to hug you, Junior. You look like you've taken enough punishment for one night. I don't think you need to share my shards."

"Yes, I do," she moaned and put her arms around his neck. "Oh, Eli, I ruined everything. I'm sorry. I couldn't get to Clive, and Parmenter nearly killed him. He got him drunk and sent him out in a car that had something wrong with its brakes. I got Clive, but then Parmenter followed us. He was going to kill us both, and probably you, too. He would have found out who you were."

"Hey," he said, keeping her at a distance and shaking her lightly, "get off the Puritan guilt trip. You didn't ruin things—you just bundled the whole mess neatly into a box, tied it with red ribbon and put it under the Christmas tree for us. And I think you probably got the four million back—free, clear and with no scam."

"What do you mean?" Her blue eyes widened, and her arms tightened around his neck in her need for reassurance. He smiled, but he refused to draw her closer in spite of her unspoken entreaty.

"We've got Parmenter red-handed, P.J.," he said patiently. "Certainly for two attempted murders. Between what you can testify and the little I saw, we can get a warrant for a search of his house. If we find another bogus will that Clive signed—but doesn't remember signing—we're home free. We've finally got hard proof relevant to the Fordyce case. And Clive might just throw himself on the mercy of the court and confess to the whole thing after tonight."

"I don't know," she said, shaking her head groggily. She tried to pull him closer again, but his strength was far greater than hers, and he held her away. "It was such a muddle—and tragic, too. Parmenter said Albert, Clive's son, died. That's why Clive didn't meet me. He was too distraught. It would have been easy for Parmenter to make it look like Clive killed himself either accidentally or on purpose. I managed to follow Clive and get into his car and get the wheel away from him just before the brakes gave out, but it was pure, dumb luck. Nothing but luck. Clive almost died—me, too. I couldn't have been worse."

He held her at a distance for her own safety, but it was starting to cost him a good deal of willpower. He could see the splinters of glass glistening on his clothes. But he dipped his head and kissed her briefly. "Nobody could have done better," he said gruffly. "Nobody. Believe that. Nobody could have known Albert was going to die. You were hardly lucky. You were brave as hell. I never met anybody braver. Or quicker. Or smarter. Or—" He stopped because he was veering dangerously close to sentiment. Eli didn't say such things to women and not in such a tone. But he couldn't stop looking into her eyes, and he feared his own were telling her what his mouth refused to say.

Somebody was beating on the door, but neither of them seemed to notice or to pay any attention when a shrill male voice cried out, "Miss Jameson! Miss Jameson! Open up. What's going on in there?"

"Eli," she breathed. "I don't care if you're full of glass. Would you please hold me—I mean really hold me—just till I get a grip on myself again?"

"I don't want to hurt you anymore," he murmured, his voice low.

"What's a little glass between friends?" she asked, her eyes still drinking his in.

"True," he mused, taking her in his arms and lowering his face to hers. "True. Ouch. But so true."

If a few slivers of glass pricked them, neither felt it. Nor did they notice immediately when the door swung open and a horrified night manager stood there, the aging bell captain behind him.

Eli was kissing her as thoroughly as he could under the circumstances, and P.J. paid attention to nothing else.

"Good Lord!" said the night manager in a voice of awed disgust. His eyes were preternaturally wide. "Two men in her bed and she's got a third! And she seemed like such a nice young woman! Murphy, call the police."

Eli raised his head briefly and gave the night manager a brief, cold stare. "Fine," he said, "it'll save me the trouble."

Then he lowered his face to hers again. "Umm," he said. "Ouch. Damned glass. Ouch. Ummm."

"Stop that!" shrieked the night manager. "This is a respectable establishment! One of those men is tied up! Bondage and heaven knows what—in my inn!"

Impatiently Eli raised his head again. Keeping one arm around P.J., he dug into his hip pocket and produced a wallet. "Stop gaping. And don't throw aspersions on the lady's character. My name is Holder, and I'm an honorary member of the New York City police department, the Washington D.C. police department, Boston, Toronto, Philly, Chicago and the FBI. Do you want to call the police, or do I do it leaving you here to guard this would-be murderer?"

The manager took two quick steps toward Eli and examined the wallet with its collection of badges. He looked at the cuts on Eli's face, the drop of blood reappearing at the corner of P.J.'s mouth and the two unconscious men on the bed. "Isn't that...Dr. Parmenter?" he asked hesitantly, then turned his eyes to the wallet again.

"I said call the police," Eli repeated between his teeth. "Tell them it's attempted murder. I also want an ambulance for the other man and the woman here. And I want it pronto. Understand? Or do you want to stand there gaping like a trout while I do it?"

The manager gulped, as did the elderly bellboy, who still stood in the doorway. "Yessir. Nosir," said the manager and was out the door like a shot.

"You!" Eli barked at the bellhop, gesturing for him to come inside the room. "Keep an eye on these two men. I'm taking the woman outside. Get me if the man who's tied starts to come to."

The old bellhop swallowed hard again but went inside and stood next to the bed, staring down apprehensively at the forms of Parmenter and Clive. Then he folded his arms across his chest like an official guard and set his jaw sternly. He looked like an old soldier, called back to duty at last.

Eli hustled P.J. out into the hall, past fellow lodgers who stared in frank curiosity from their doorways. He steered her into the drab lobby. She had started to tremble again and couldn't stop. It made her feel incredibly foolish.

"What are you doing?" she asked in bewilderment. "I don't need an ambulance." She felt dizzy again. He sat her down on a shabby settee, dropped to his knees in front of her and began to rub her cold hands.

"I wanted to get you away from Parmenter and out of that room," he said with rough tenderness. "After the police get through questioning us, we're going to my place. We'll both have showers to get the glass off us, and we're going to sleep in a decent bed, and I'm going to hold you all night long. You're all right now, P.J. Stop shaking. I've got you."

She still couldn't stop shaking. With chagrin she looked down at him bent above her hands. "I ... don't seem to be very good at this," she said in apology, her voice quavering.

"You happen to be terrific at it. I think the bastard broke your finger," he growled, touching it. "Does that hurt?"

"No," she said. "But my right arm is starting to feel funny. I'm sorry, Eli, I really am. I'm a lot of trouble."

He made her strip off her jacket, examined her arm and hand and then unbuttoned the top button of her shirtwaist and examined the base of her throat.

"Hell," he growled at her, sitting beside her now and putting his arm around her carefully. "Your arm is one big bruise, your elbow looks sprained, your finger's either broken or dislocated and I wouldn't be surprised if you've got a crack in your collarbone. I don't know how you made it, kid."

"It's my own fault," she said miserably. "I deserve it." And she was starting to ache all over, in mind and body. The only thing that relieved it was to sink back against the invulnerable strength of Eli's arm.

He stared down at her, contradictory emotions struggling in his face. "P.J.," he said, his voice both tender and harsh at the same time, "all you were supposed to do was either talk Clive into investing in FUTURE or get him so drunk and distracted he couldn't go to Parmenter's. Since he didn't meet you, you couldn't do either one. What you did instead was stake him out like you'd been doing surveillance all your life, tail Parmenter and him through the fog, then follow Clive while he went weaving all over the road, manage to stop him, take over the wheel, survive a car wreck, get him back to your room single-handed for safekeeping, then completely boggle Parmenter's mind by sticking your finger down his gun barrel and finally knocking him out of commission with your telephone. I know strong men who couldn't have done it. Why do you keep thinking you're a failure and you've done something wrong?"

She had closed her eyes, and she kept them squeezed shut so that she wouldn't have to look at him. She had to tell him the horrible truth at last. "It was almost as if I had to do it the hard way," she said. Then for the first time she came close to sobbing. She hid her face against the strong column of his neck. "Eli, I'm not sure I could have done the other thing. I couldn't have talked him out of his money. Or got him drunk and pretended, well, to be romantically interested in him."

He groaned and made her settle more intimately against him. "Why did I know that?" he asked, disgust edging his tone. "Why did I know you couldn't con him and you couldn't get him drunk? Why did that worry me from the start?"

She opened her eyes and stared into his wolf-brown ones. "Eli," she said, near tears, "you know why. You were asking me to do something *immoral*. And I'm not good at that." She shut her eyes again and sank back against the hardness of his chest once more.

"Oh, yeah," he said, rocking her as if she were a child. "That. Immoral. You're right. The immoral—or at least the amoral—has always been my part of the bargain, right?"

"No," she said, shaking her head, but keeping her face hidden against his warm neck. "You weren't immoral—or amoral. You had the courage to do what had to be done. I didn't. If I could have just done what you'd said, it would have been so much safer for everybody. Right and wrong is a lot more complicated than I ever thought it was. If I had it to do over, I would have grabbed him early in the afternoon and gotten him drunk as a lord. Instead, I nearly got him killed."

He was silent for a moment, contemplating the strength of the small woman in his arms and the many paradoxes within her, within himself, within the both of them.

There were a lot of things he might have said to her, but he wanted to think for a long time before he said them. So he merely kissed her ear in an almost brotherly fashion. He held her as tightly as he could without hurting her. "At least it's over," he said at last.

She nodded, squeezing her eyes shut more tightly. A sudden shudder went through her that had nothing to do with the danger she had faced. She realized, slowly, dimly, that Eli smelled of *perfume*. It was not her perfume. And she hazily perceived at the edge of his jaw the faintest trace of red lipstick. She never wore red lipstick.

She felt a wave of sickness, palpable as a blow. She had gone through all this alone because he had been with a woman? He had left her by herself because he had to see another woman? That was the mysterious business that took him away that night? She and Clive had nearly died because Eli couldn't stay away from some *woman*? She felt more betrayed than she had by the whole Bachelors' Club, the cold-blooded Parmenter included.

He felt the sudden stiffness in her body and held her more tightly, cradled in the crook of his arm. "I said it's over. You're safe. I've got you, and I intend to keep you all night long."

The scent of the perfume seemed actually to assault her. Yet, perversely, she savored his closeness. *Yes,* she thought, and the emotional pain cutting through her was more intense than any physical pain she'd endured all night. *Yes, now it's over at last.* He might want her for one last night, and that would be the beginning of the end, if not the end itself. And she supposed she would go with him. It didn't matter. She'd lost everything already. She'd lost before she'd even started. She still couldn't believe it. He'd left her alone to deal with Clive because he had gone with a woman. It was Cleo, she knew instinctively from the possessive way the blonde had smiled up at him that day in the lobby.

She felt ill. She could not bring herself to accuse him, even speak to him. Yet, she thought bitterly, she would go with him this last night. To savor her own consummate foolishness. To remember what he had done to her so that no other man would ever be able to again. This last night would be both her reward and her punishment.

AS IT TURNED OUT, she did not spend that bittersweet night in his arms. By the time the ambulance arrived, all the fight seemed to have drained from her. She had gone totally silent. She had a dislocated finger, torn ligaments in her right arm, a chipped collarbone, two cracked ribs and a slight case of shock. The examining doctor insisted she spend the night in the hospital.

They gave her a sedative and tried to kick Eli out of her room. They found it a job not within the capabilities of a merely mortal hospital staff. He sat the night beside her bed, holding her left hand. Once in a while he reached up and pushed her smooth bangs back from her pale forehead. He kept shaking his head. She didn't have the stomach to get Clive drunk, but she could go through all she had without blinking an eye.

How different they were. How impossibly different. And it was his fault this had happened to her. If Cleo hadn't been meddling so dangerously, he would have shadowed P.J., kept his eye on her. But Cleo was so ready to make trouble he had to go up to Putney and lie his head off to her, to buy time. Now he wished he'd told her to go to hell. P.J. had nearly died. Because of him.

He sat there the whole night, her hand gripped in his large one, watching her face as if he could not see enough of it. He should let her go, he knew. He didn't seem to be much good for her, and she must have started to realize that herself, after she got her bearings back, since she had retreated into herself, shutting him out. He could understand that.

He never should have asked her to do what was so foreign to her. He should let her go, but he was no longer sure he could. At the same time he did not know how to ask her to stay, or even if she would. If she herself asked, well, that would be something else.

By dawn he saw she was tossing, getting ready to wake. He felt guilty as hell that she was in a hospital bed in the first place, yet, contrarily, he didn't want her to know he had stayed by her side all night. Just before he was sure she was going to awaken, he left and, tired, unshaven, walked down the hospital corridor alone. He was almost forty years old. He had never said "I love you" to anybody in his life. He was too old to start now. Still, he thought moodily, if she asked him if she could stay, he could handle that. He'd look as if it might amuse him and say, "Sure, kid. But remember it's your idea." But he had an intuition that, different as they were, they were two of a kind in one way: loners who didn't admit easily that they needed anybody or anything.

Chapter Thirteen

The police wanted P.J. to remain in Leaftree for the nex
few days while they questioned Parmenter and the othe
Bachelors. Eli made her move into his suite, and she agree
only because she had no more money, and she couldn't g
back to the Nutmeg Peddler; it would give her nightmares
On the way home from the hospital, she said hardly any
thing, except that she wanted to talk to Clive before she left

Back at the hotel Eli watched her uneasily and with a kin
of cynical resignation. She had bandages around her fin
ger, her elbow, strapped across her collarbone and wrappe
around her ribs. The sight of her carrying her small body s
carefully hurt him more than anything ever had in his life
He didn't tell her he'd spent the night by her side. Sh
seemed lost, wandering somewhere deep within herself. I
was as if she were telling him she was glad she'd be throug
with him soon. He kept up a facade of uninterest but wa
glad Cleo wasn't around because he might have cheerfull
strangled her.

He felt sufficiently rotten about the whole mess to try t
apologize. He wasn't good at saying he was sorry; nor
mally he'd rather receive a swift punch in the jaw than de
liver an apology.

"I'm sorry I wasn't there to keep an eye on you," he said. He had brought her things from the Nutmeg Peddler and was watching her unpack them. She was so unnaturally silent that the air between them felt frosty.

"I had an important appointment. I couldn't avoid it. It was crucial to us." His voice was gruff, and his head was cocked at an angle that seemed anything but apologetic. "It had to do with... the law. Meeting with the law." He realized he shouldn't even tell her that much.

Liar, she thought bitterly. She finished unpacking her suitcase but refused to look at him. *Meeting with the law indeed. Since when did the law leave lipstick on a man's jaw and perfume on his clothes?*

"Finding out more crucial information, I suppose," she said coolly.

Dammit, he thought, he felt god-awful, couldn't she tell that? Couldn't she meet him halfway? "Not exactly," he said, not liking the militant set of her shoulders.

"You don't owe me any explanations." Her tone was clipped. "You're an adult. You're free to come and go as you please."

He frowned, and his mouth twitched dangerously. The expression was wasted on her because she still refused to look at him. "That's not the point," he practically growled.

"It most certainly is," she said with her most maddening Bostonian aloofness. "I haven't the faintest interest in how you choose to spend your evenings."

Make love to every blonde in the northeast, she thought rebelliously. *See if I care.* But she did care, and it made her so sick with jealousy she almost hated herself more than him.

I thought you, of all women, might be forgiving, he thought ominously. *I did what I had to do, dammit. Well, forget it, Junior. Go to hell.* But he didn't want her to go to hell. He just wanted her to turn around and be her old self again. When she didn't, he turned his back and went to the police station. He came to get her in the afternoon, to take her to give her statement, but she seemed sadder and more distant than before.

"What's wrong with you?" he finally burst out as he drove her back to the hotel. "Can't you even talk, for God's sake?"

"I just spent two hours talking to the police," she said wearily. "I'm tired." She refrained from reminding him that she hadn't exactly spent the previous night lounging about. She didn't have to. He remembered all too well. He wondered if he should tell her the truth about where he had gone and why. He decided against it. It was dangerous and probably wouldn't do any good, anyway. He returned to the police station to help the detectives prepare to question Clive the next day. Then he went out and unsuccessfully tried to get drunk.

She was still up, staring out the window at the blackness when he returned to their room. He insisted she have the bed to herself. A dark certainty was forming within him: she really was through with him. She had decided he was something she couldn't afford. It was just as well, he told himself. She was an all-or-nothing woman; she would give a man everything she had or nothing whatsoever. He was a man who'd never wanted all that any woman had to give. He'd made a specialty of avoiding emotional commitments. She was a woman who needed them.

He lay awake on the white leather couch, wrapped uncomfortably in the extra blanket, staring across the darkness toward her form on the bed. Sometimes she slept quietly. But often she was restless, and she made odd little moans. Sometimes he knew she was awake. If once she had asked him to come to her, he would have. If that happened, he didn't know how long it would take him to turn from her again. So he spent long hours lying in the darkness, thinking of all the reasons he could never make a go of it with her. There were so many that enumerating them was worse than counting sheep.

The only thing that gave him any ease was his satisfaction that Parmenter had gone too far at last. The case was keeping both Eli and the police busy. He tried to keep P.J. out of his thoughts the next day but had little success. She was in his suite, but it was as if she'd left him already. He missed her. It was crazy. It made him angry half the time and sick the other half.

He welcomed the trudging thoroughness of investigation. A search of Parmenter's house uncovered exactly what he suspected: a handwritten codicil to any will of Terrence Clive's that came forth. It was in Clive's hand, although an unsteady one and was signed by him. Doubtless Parmenter planned to find or forge witnesses' signatures later. The codicil was sweet and simple: in the event of Albert's death, James Parmenter became Clive's sole heir.

Parmenter, Eli told detectives, would have borrowed against the inheritance and placed Clive's million dollars in FUTURE while the opportunity presented itself—blood money invested for a fat profit.

When Clive himself was brought in for questioning, he remembered few events of the night. He had a bandage on his forehead and despair in his eyes. He was still torn with grief and guilt over Albert's death. But he recognized his signature on the codicil Parmenter had concocted. He sat in the office of the Leaftree CID, staring at the document for a long time.

"Do you want to tell us about it—the whole thing?" the detective sergeant finally asked while Eli sat, arms crossed, watching from across the room.

Clive's wrinkled face was impassive, his body immobile for almost a full minute. At last he said, "Enough evil's been done. Enough lies have been told. Parmenter knew Fordyce was going to die. We tricked Fordyce into signing a document he thought was a membership paper. Parmenter claimed there was safety in numbers. Nobody would suspect all four of us. As long as nobody got greedy, we'd get away with it—and Fordyce would die eventually, anyway. We all needed the money—or at least wanted it. I don't want it anymore. I'm turning my share over to SOS. That's where it was meant to go in the first place."

"A wise move," the detective sergeant said calmly. "Turn the money back, plead guilty, testify against Parmenter and I think you'll get off lightly."

Clive glanced at Eli without hope. But Eli, once the finest jailhouse lawyer in Leavenworth, nodded at him in encouragement. The old man should get off easily. Eli was almost glad. Maybe some of P.J.'s feelings had rubbed off on him. Clive had suffered enough.

But when Eli opened the door of the CID room to let Clive out, he was disturbed to see P.J. standing by the stairwell, unhappiness on her face. He closed the door, feeling the familiar combination of anger and sickness.

P.J., her jacket collar turned up and her hands in her pockets, looked apprehensively at Clive. He looked at her with equal discomfort.

"I suppose they told you," she said finally, "who I really am. What we—I—came here for."

He nodded. He looked older and more tired than ever. "Miss Fitzjames," he said in his wry, raspy voice. "Lord, how you must despise me. I don't blame you, my dear."

She raised her chin, partly in surprise and partly in embarrassment. "I don't despise you. I came to say I was sorry

I lied to you. And that I hoped you'd cooperate with the authorities. I think they might let you off."

Clive studied her. She looked young and tired and vulnerable standing there. Again, with a twinge, he thought how much she reminded him of Mary Wiggingdon. "I've told them everything," he said simply. "And I'm giving the money back to SOS. Don't worry about them letting me off. It doesn't matter what happens to me now. Whatever they do is fine."

"That's not true!" she denied. "What happens to you *is* important. I'm...I'm very sorry about Albert. But you need to start living for yourself, Mr. Clive."

He looked away from her for the absurd reason that she made tears come to his eyes. He merely shook his head.

P.J. lifted her chin higher. "Do you forgive me?" she asked.

He gave a choked little laugh. "Of course. Even for saving my worthless life. And you, I take it, have found it in your heart to forgive me. Quite amazing, actually."

She moved quickly to his side while her courage was still high. She linked her arm with his. "Let's go for a cup of coffee," she beseeched him. "I think maybe your whole life could be starting over. You know, you don't have to stay in Leaftree. You could come to Boston. I know a free clinic. It serves a poor community, and it's staffed almost entirely by retired people like you—doctors, nurses, dentists. It always needs good people. And there are plenty of fine support groups to help you control the drinking. Would you come have a cup of coffee and talk...please?"

And because she reminded him so much of Mary, of Mary young and untouched and free and full of possibilities, Clive went. It was almost as if Mary herself whispered, "Go, Terrence. Start again. For me."

FROM THE WINDOW of the interrogation room in the CID, Eli stood, staring out moodily. He watched P.J. cross the street in the fading light, arm in arm with Clive's stooped figure. *Watch out, Clive,* he thought to himself ruefully, *she'll save you from yourself before you know what's happened. You haven't a prayer of escaping her.*

The sight of her walking into the darkness with the old man, talking to him so earnestly, wrenched something deep inside him. He swore under his breath. He had known from the first he shouldn't have gotten involved with her.

"What?" asked the sergeant of detectives.

"Nothing," Eli returned curtly. "Let's get on with it." He broke a cigarette in half.

THAT NIGHT HE SLEPT on the couch again, but he didn't sleep much. Once he heard P.J. whimper, then saw her sit up straight, as if from a bad dream. He could make out her dark form, see her put her face in her hands. He watched her for a moment in silence.

"Are you all right?" he asked roughly, filled with tension. He resisted the impulse to go to her side, to take her in his arms. She had given every indication she did not want that.

"I'm fine," she lied. She lay down, her heart beating hard, wishing he would come to her. But he did not. At last, exhausted, she fell asleep again. He lay awake.

WHEN TEDDY DIRKSON and Charlie Bangor were hauled in for questioning the next morning, they broke almost immediately when they heard of Clive's confession. Eli, all jailhouse lawyer again, suggested they consider their checks to FUTURE as reimbursements for defrauding Fordyce in the first place. A jury might go easier on them. Petulantly both men agreed. Eli figured at their age, and with the restitution they'd made to SOS, they might get a few years in a country-club prison. There, conceivably, they might learn an honest trade, such as stamping out license plates. He could only trust nobody would knife Dirkson to stop him from writing poetry.

As Eli had suspected, James Parmenter was the hardest to break, coldly denying everything. The detectives escorted him into the interrogation room, but his composure seemed set and brittle.

"I know who you are," he said to Eli at last, smiling with superiority. "Law enforcement. You and the woman both. This is entrapment of the vilest sort. It'll all be tossed out of court."

What broke the ice of his restraint was Eli's calm and smiling revelation of who he and P.J. really were. "I'm not official law enforcement," he said, staring down at Parmenter with satisfaction. "And the woman's from SOS. Their lawyer's daughter, in fact. And she's got the goods on you. You're gone. You're through. You're history."

"SOS?" asked Parmenter with a short laugh that had an angry, hysterical edge. "That Micky Mouse outfit? I thought the two of you were together—my God! But I never thought she was from that pack of fools. I wish I had the satisfaction of having killed her when I had the chance, the little—"

It took both burly detectives to restrain Eli from smashing his fist into Parmenter's face. "He's an old man—you'd kill him," the lieutenant said, gasping, struggling to hold Eli's arm back. "It's too good for him. Let him rot in prison."

The cold rage in Eli's face turned to mere coldness. "Prison," he said between his teeth, staring down at Parmenter. "Yeah." He shrugged the two men away. The stare he sent boring through Parmenter was more dangerous than physical threat.

Parmenter, desperate, capitulated and gave a partial confession. He insisted on returning SOS's money in hopes that a jury would find mercy in its heart. Eli doubted it. Parmenter would probably get at least fifteen years, and not in any country-club prison, either.

Parmenter, in a panicky last-minute attempt to better his situation, threatened to drag Eli and P.J. into court for misrepresentation and fraud. The large, cigar-chomping detective sergeant told him no jury would convict them. "Old blood-suckin' weasels like you," the detective said with vengeful glee, "we get any way we can. Forget it, Parmenter. Holder and Miss Fitzjames will get medals before they get jail sentences. You're the villain here."

Parmenter's confession took place on the third day after the attempt on Clive's life. It took another day of questioning, bargaining, statements and transcripts before Eli felt it was wrapped up. By then all four million dollars had been couriered back either to the account of FUTURE or to SOS itself. He was confident the Bachelors would get due justice.

He was sure his own career was undamaged by his brief return to the world of the con; it would probably even gain a little added luster. God knew it was the first thing he'd ever done for a charitable cause. He felt a bit like Robin Hood. Normally, it would have made him cocky, as if once again he'd flirted with the law and left it blushing, dewy-eyed and grateful for his rather roguish attentions.

But he was starting to worry about P.J. It wasn't simply that she kept her emotional distance from him but as if he were watching something die in her. At first he thought she was understandably angry and disillusioned with him for nearly getting her killed, even though she had been glad to see him at first. Now he began to suspect it was something deeper still, and she was hurt in ways he didn't even understand.

Evenings, he would come back from the CID to find her staring out the window pensively. The weather had been lousy; it had rained for three straight days, and the skies were a lowering gray with the constant cold downpour dealing early death to the sodden foliage.

He ached because he wanted to make love to her, but she obviously didn't want it. She had made no move toward him since the night he'd held her in the shabby lobby of the Nutmeg Peddler. He had the disturbing intuition something different from anything he'd ever known was happening—or about to happen. It made him edgy and silent with her.

All they could talk about with any ease was the case against the Bachelors. She kept saying that she had to get back to Boston soon. She still hadn't told the authorities at SOS what had happened, and the thought made her nervous. She also worried about her cat and her ferns.

She slept a lot, which he supposed was unusual for her. She seemed to spend the days when he was at the CID working feverishly on her papers and projections for FUTURE, as if she were driven by some dreadful, final deadline that only she could see. The only breaks she took were to go out for coffee with Clive. He envied the old man.

ALTHOUGH P.J. HAD BEEN too exhausted to protest, she really hadn't wanted to move into Eli's suite at the Ivory Castle. It made their entanglement seem official, semipermanent, when it wasn't at all. She was still shaken by all that had happened and didn't quite believe her strange adventure was drawing to a close, and a quiet close at that.

But since the morning Eli had brought her back from the hospital, he had seemed removed, drawn into himself. She would catch him looking at her strangely, as if she were either something too breakable for him to touch, or possibly something that could break him beyond repair.

He had looked at her with her bruises and bandages and never made a move toward her, except a chaste kiss in the evening when he came back from sitting in on the CID's sessions. She supposed she looked fairly terrible, and she felt drained of energy, but most of all she was frightened because everything was ending.

As soon as Eli's work with the police neared its end, she knew she would have to call Henry at SOS. She would tell him that the four million dollars was back in the bank for SOS, but she would have to tell him how it got there. Now, after it was done, she realized that she would have to resign. If she didn't, in all probability Henry would ask her to. Eli had ventured perilously near the wrong side of the law. But he had done it for her and for SOS, and she was confident it would finally enhance his reputation.

Yet she was the one who had asked him to cruise so near the limits of the law. She had helped him set up a fraud. Even though they hadn't completed the sting, she had been dishonest. She had inadvertently put Clive's life in danger. Through a series of accidents she had been able to keep on the right side of legality and get the money back. But she had gone too far. Publicity would bloom, whole weed patches of it. SOS could not afford a person of such questionable morality on its staff. She was about to lose her job—the only job she had ever really considered having. She doubted if Henry could even find it in his conscience to write her a letter of recommendation. She didn't know what would become of her.

She was certain to lose her job. Worse, she felt Eli turning farther from her every day, and she was afraid she would never get over him. Once she had wanted to be a spinster—safe from the pains of loving and caring. Now she was going to spend the rest of her life comparing every man she met to Eli, every empty day to those charged and blazing ones she had spent with him, every long night to the few she had spent in his arms. She didn't know why she still loved him—she couldn't forgive him for leaving her alone to deal with Clive while he had been with another woman—but she did. And it hurt.

On the fourth day she spent at the Ivory Castle, the day Eli said was the last he'd have to work with the police, she finally found courage to call Henry at SOS and tell him what had happened. As she feared, his answer was the longest telephone silence she had ever heard.

At last, his voice oddly flat instead of self-consciously jolly, he said, "I could not be more pleased that the money's come back to us, P.J. I could not be more grateful." There was another interminable silence. "But," he finally continued uncomfortably, "I'm afraid you've violated any number of principles that SOS stands for. P.J., I can't believe you actually hired this . . . this con artist to get the money back any way he could."

That, P.J. thought bitterly, hadn't been the way it had happened at all. Eli was no longer a con artist, and he had suggested the sting only when he saw how upset she was that no other path was open. She had come to see things his way: right and wrong were not as simple as she had always believed.

But she didn't want to argue with Henry. "I know there were irregularities. I'm prepared to turn in my resignation," she said, struggling to keep her voice steady. "I'll do it immediately. I've also finished most of the paperwork for subcorporating FUTURE. I'll see you get everything. And I won't embarrass you by asking you for references, Henry.''

There was another of his loaded silences. ''This seems a hell of a way to show my gratitude, P.J.,'' he said at last. ''I want to buy you dinner and a drink when you get back. You understand. I know. And I think, in a strange way, your parents would be proud. Especially your father.''

''I hope so,'' she said, and for the first time her voice broke a bit. She said a hasty goodbye and hung up. That was that. She'd got the money back to SOS. Her parents' work would go on. Without her.

She lay down on the large white bed, curled up on her side and watched the gray rain batter the dying leaves. Everything was ending, and now winter was coming. Eli would be back soon. She would have given anything if within the past few days he had simply taken her in his arms and made love to her, for the human warmth of it. But he hadn't because they were bringing whatever had been between them to an end, as well. And that was best.

She stared at the rain and thought of all the reasons a relationship between them could never work. She'd gotten her degrees at Harvard. He'd been educated on the streets and behind bars. She was poor, and he wore suits whose cost would pay her rent for two months. Her head was full of ideals about the world as it should be, and his was full of knowledge about the way it really was. A computer couldn't have picked a man more different from her.

HE UNLOCKED THE DOOR and came in shortly after six in the evening. He looked at her apprehensively. She was sitting in the white armchair, watching the rain. She looked paler than usual, and he had a sudden desire to go to her, draw her to her feet and take her in his arms. Except, he thought, that was probably just what she didn't want.

"We're done," he said. "All wrapped up. We can go home tomorrow. Are you glad?"

She turned and gave him a weak smile. He supposed she'd be happy to get back to Cambridge. He suspected she had a boyfriend there, a nice safe one. He'd heard her once talking on the phone to somebody named Barlowe about her cat and her plants. He thought a man named Barlowe had to be a wimp.

"I'm glad it's over," she said, but there was an odd look in her eyes.

"I figured we could fly back tomorrow," he said, hanging up his damp Burberry. "I'm chartering a plane. It's faster and more comfortable."

"Fine," she said without much emotion. She couldn't afford half the fare for a chartered plane, but she'd figure a way to pay him back. She supposed she owed him expenses for this week, as well, and she didn't have money for that, either.

She was, she realized, being morose, and it was childish to keep taking it out on him. Everything that happened had been her own doing. "I suppose you have a lot of work waiting for you in Boston," she ventured, for the sake of polite conversation. The words sounded stilted.

He stood watching her from across the room. He wished he knew what the hell was going on under that sensible haircut, and he wondered if she had any idea what it did to him when she looked sad. She was a classy little scrapper, ready to take on the world. She reminded him of the old poem about the knight who had the strength of ten because his heart was pure. She should never look as defeated as she did now.

"No," he said noncommittally. "I can't stay in Boston. I'm going up to my place in Rhode Island. I'm behind on the book. I suppose you're anxious to get back to SOS and be the conquering hero, eh? Excuse me, heroine. Have you told them yet? That you got the money back?''

She nodded. "I told them this afternoon," she said, keeping all emotion out of her voice.

He gave her his crooked grin, but it was a little stiff. "So are they going to greet you with a parade? Promote you? What?''

She shrugged slightly, stared out the window at the rain. "Neither. They want my resignation. I was expecting it.''

Eli had been loosening his tie. "What?" he cried in disbelief. But he could tell by the disciplined straightness of her back that what she said was true. He swore and threw the tie on the floor. "Are the bastards crazy?''

"No," she said as calmly as she could because the violence of his outburst surprised her. "They're grateful— truly. It's just that my conduct throughout this whole thing wasn't exactly officially approved, and at some points it was a long way from the ideals SOS stands for.''

He swore again and came to stand beside her. "And you're just going to accept it?" he asked, cynicism sharpening his tone. "I don't understand you people. I'll never understand you—any of you.''

"Don't try then," she said wearily. She wished he wouldn't stand so close. She could feel the heat of his thigh next to her arm, and she could smell the rain on him.

He did some more expert swearing. "You practically get yourself killed getting their money back, and they're happy as clams at high tide—so they fire you. And you accept it? This is supposed to be easy to understand?''

She stood and walked to the window because he was making her nervous. She cradled her arms around herself.

"Just what do you intend to do?" he asked, the same cynicism in his voice. "You loved that job. I bet they won't

ven give you references, right? What do they expect?
You're supposed to sell pencils on the street corner?''

"I'll get along," she said, wishing he didn't sound so angry. His anger made him seem concerned, and she didn't
want to slip back into that illusion.

She had her back to him. She heard him pace toward the
door, then return to stand behind her.

"Look," he said finally. He put his hands gently on her
shoulders because he didn't want to hurt her. He said what
he never intended to say but supposed, wearily, he had been
destined to say from the start. "Why don't you come with
me to Rhode Island? You could use a break. It's a nice
place. Right on the ocean. If any of those damned pilot
whales beach themselves, you can push them back out to sea
single-handed—show SOS how it's supposed to be done."

His touch stirred her tumultuously, far more than she
wanted to admit. "What would I do in Rhode Island," she
asked, "besides push whales off your beach?"

Slowly he turned her to face him. He put one hand behind her neck and let the fingers of the other gently trace the
edge of the bandage over her collarbone. "What would you
do? Anything you want," he said softly. "And nothing you
don't want. You decide."

She looked up into his eyes and saw something flickering
there she had no longer expected—sexual invitation. Why?
she wondered. Maybe because she didn't look quite so bad
today? Or because he felt sorry for her? Or perhaps he
hadn't been able to get to the rest of his harem and she'd do.

"No, thanks," she said. She deserved to get out of this
relationship with a few scraps of her pride. And yet part of
her wanted to say, *Yes, I'll go to Rhode Island with you, or
Outer Mongolia, or Timbuktu, or Mars.*

He was looking into her eyes, studying them hard, and he
thought he could read something in them that made his

blood start to pound hard. He thought maybe she st
wanted him as much as he wanted her. And the thoug|
struck him like a hammer—maybe she was just as wary
caring for him as he was of caring for her. But they bo
cared, and they were probably going to care for a long time

He put both hands on either side of her face, her beaut
ful, unadorned face. "Why not?" he demanded, dete
mined to brazen it out between them this time. "Afraid
come? Afraid you'll end up in my bed again? For the pa
few days I didn't think you wanted to be there—and regre
ted you ever had been—but from the look in your eyes, I'
not so sure. So come to Rhode Island and find out. Give n
three good reasons why you shouldn't."

She looked up at him, and her senses seemed to have d
clared war on her intelligence. Her pulses hammered, h
lips parted without her volition, and she felt her eyes grov
ing dreamy with desire. But she reached deep within for h
considerable willpower, and she found it, shaky but intac
"I'm not interested in a casual fling," she managed to sa
"If you want the truth, I suppose it's because I like you to
much—in spite of everything...."

"Ah," he said softly. "You care too much for a casu
affair. You're a brave little thing to say that. But it's on
one reason. I asked for three." He had brought his fa
closer to hers now, and the cool golden brown of his ey
seemed to fill her vision. "Three reasons—or else you ha\
to come."

She took a deep breath. She looked away from his ey
because they made her feel drugged, but then she was sta
ing at the sensual curve of his mouth, and that was wors
"I don't want to be dependent on anybody," she said, a
most panting out the words. "I wasn't exactly cut out to
anybody's kept woman—long- or short-term."

"Kept woman," he said with a slow mocking smile. "Has nybody used that term since the nineteenth century? Two easons—I can answer them easily enough. But you need iree. Have you got a third? I don't think so. I think you eed to come with me to Rhode Island."

She was experiencing a bad case of butterflies in her tomach, and a few of them seemed to be scouting out her iind, as well. His hands, gentle as their touch was on ei- ier side of her face, seemed to be burning through her flesh nd turning it to pure yearning need of him. "Cleo," she ianaged to say at last. "Cleo and your other women. I was n only child. I never learned to share things I liked."

Suddenly, he threw his head back and laughed. "Cleo?" e asked, then laughed again. He looked down at her and rinned. "P.J., I can't believe it. You're really jealous of er. You shouldn't be. I thought you were bright enough to gure that out long ago."

"You lied to me," she said, her anger coming out at last. You said you had business with the law the night Parmen- er tried to kill Clive. You were with her. Don't deny it. I nelled her perfume on you. And her lipstick was smeared ll over you. Some business. Some law."

"Ha!" he said triumphantly. "So that's it—you weren't mply jealous, you were crazy jealous. I don't know hether I should be amazed or flattered."

"Don't be either," she said, her chin going up in the old ay. "You have your character flaws, I have mine."

"If you knew I'd been with Cleo, why didn't you say omething? Or is sulkiness another of your character flaws don't know about?"

"I hated being jealous," she said, tears starting to sting er eyes. The admission cost her a good deal. "And why idn't you say you were with her? You didn't have to make worse by lying. I could almost stand it if you had the

courage to be honest about it—almost. But I will not tole⌐
ate being lied to.''

He looked down at her, his face expressionless for a mo
ment. They both stood very still. "I said once," he mur
mured, "that I hate a jealous woman. This is why."

She stiffened, and although he still touched her, his hand
were ominously still.

"I hate jealousy because it makes stupid messes like th⌐
one. And you're right not to like it, either. You should b
above it. I didn't lie to you. I never lied to you. I just didn
tell you the whole truth. I'm fond of Cleo, but she's m
cousin. My Uncle Leo's daughter. My only living relative
And she just happens to be one of the finest undercover FI
agents around. She's in Vermont on special assignment—
interstate transportation of stolen goods."

P.J.'s head snapped back, and she blinked hard up ⌐
him. "Cleo is your cousin?" she asked in disbelief. "She'
in the FBI? That's how she could get all that informa
tion?"

"Precisely," he said, smoothing her bangs away from h⌐
forehead. "And I don't talk about her because she *is* u⌐
dercover. It could be dangerous for her. Extremely dange⌐
ous, in fact. But she and I help each other out—unofficiall⌐
of course—from time to time. And one way she helped w⌐
by playing decoy—if the Bachelors thought I was involve⌐
with a flashy blonde, they were less likely to suspect I w⌐
really with the proper little thing from Massachusetts."

"But," P.J. said suspiciously, "she stayed here wit⌐
you."

"I slept on the couch. I told you she was a decoy—that
all."

"Your cousin?" she said again, not quite convince⌐
"Really?"

"Really." He nodded. "Cleo Marietta Holder. Neither of us wanted to end up like our fathers, and we went over to the other side. But she was catching on that I was pulling a scam. She suspected I was flirting with the old ways. She didn't like it. It scared her. That's why I had to let you take care of Clive that night. Cleo insisted I come to Putney. She was sure something was going on and if she didn't stop me, I'd end up back in prison. And believe me, she could stop me. Cold in my tracks. Nothing can slow you down faster than a suspicious FBI agent. I couldn't let her do that. I had to blow a little smoke in her eyes. Of course, now she's not speaking to me, but she will in a month or two. I know her."

"Well, you could have told me," P.J. said, trying to hide how much the news gladdened her. "I mean, it certainly seemed as if she was your... mistress."

"Cleo's profession," he said, kissing her irreverently on the tip of the nose, "isn't the kind of thing you let get outside the family. And since Cleo and I are all that's left of the family, we keep it to ourselves. The only reason I didn't tell you was that I've never told anybody. I feel strange telling even you—even though I know I can trust you. I'm sorry I hurt you, but all you had to do was say you were bothered. So now your third reason for not coming with me to Rhode Island doesn't hold water. Neither do the other two."

"What do you mean?" she asked, afraid to hear him out. He was too good at fooling people, and she knew it well.

"Because," he said, suddenly serious, "I've watched you for the last four days, thinking you probably were sick of me for getting you into this mess and that you'd never forgive me. But I forgot, you're an idealist. You have to forgive me—just the way you did Clive. You already have, in fact, haven't you?"

"I never . . ." She hesitated, looking for the right word "I never blamed you for anything. I care more for you tha you do for me. It hurts, but it isn't your fault."

He looked down at her, frowning. "Don't you think me are human, P.J.?" he asked, watching her face intently.

"Of course," she said immediately and almost, in h nervousness, started to tell him she believed in the equali of the sexes and of men's rights to have feelings. He saw coming and put his hand softly over her mouth.

"Don't you think the idea you didn't want me couldn hurt? It's been so long since I hurt over a woman I didn even recognize the feeling at first. I hate to admit this— mean I *hate* to admit this—but I don't want a casual affai either. I care too much about you. I just can't decide if it in spite of our differences or because of them."

She only looked at him, her eyes widening with surpris If he was lying, this was his boldest fabrication yet. Sl continued to gaze up at him with a mixture of hopef wonder and mistrust.

He stared back warily, watching the puzzlement on h face. Finally, he frowned and slapped his forehead in a ge ture of frustration. Then he gripped her shoulders again gingerly so as not to hurt her. He brought his face close hers. His eyes were so intense they frightened her. "Yc could make this a lot easier for me," he accused, his ga: level with hers. "I mean, you've got to know how hard th is for me. You could say you loved me or something."

"What?"

His mouth took on an impatient crook. "I said you cou say you loved me," he repeated in agitation. "Then I cou say, 'well, okay, I guess I love you, too, so let's get marrie or something.' And you, being you, could say, 'let's g married or nothing.' And I could say, 'well, okay, if you i sist.' And then we could get on with it."

"With what?" Her eyes grew wider. She could feel the tension in the hands that lightly gripped her shoulders, but she wasn't sure she was not dreaming.

"Just get on with it," he said restlessly. "Look, you want to reduce me to groveling? You're not going to give me any help at all except that look in your eyes? All right. I guess I love you. All right. I suppose I should marry you. Do you want to get married? Or what?"

"Married?" she asked, her throat constricted. She put her hand on one of his and squeezed it slightly to assure herself he was really there. "You and I?"

"No," he said impatiently, his eyes flashing. "You and the carpet. Of course you and I. I mean, I'm at an age where I suppose I should think about this sort of thing. And I...can't imagine life without you. That is, I can't imagine it being much good. If we get married, it's a sure bet we'll never bore each other. So are you going to say yes, or have you just been conning me all along?"

"Eli!" she exclaimed in protest, but happy protest.

"Yes or no?" he insisted, his fervor growing. "I sat beside you all night in the hospital and thought that if anything happened to you, all the important parts of me would die. I lay on this damned couch for three nights watching you sleep, wondering if you'd ever forgive me for what I'd gotten you into. I tried to convince myself I didn't want or need you. It didn't work. You're the only woman I've ever loved in my life, and now that I've found you, I want to keep you. So what do you say? And don't try to make me beg because I don't know how."

"Eli," she said tremulously, "you know how different we are...."

"Which means," he said, his eyes penetrating hers, "we can teach each other the lifetime of things we've learned, right?"

The intensity of his gaze dazzled her, intoxicating her with joy. She slipped her arms around his neck carefully because her shoulder still hurt slightly. "Maybe," she ventured, "the more different we are, the more things we have to share. But I'll always have my causes—and probably want a job. I was raised that way."

"Have all the causes you want," he muttered, pulling her close, "as long as I'm one of them. And till you find something else, work for me. Keep my books. Manage my money. I trust you with it. I know you're honest. To a fault."

She smiled up at him. "I think I'd like that. Maybe it's time I got away from the whales. My parents' work will go on. Maybe I'll get involved with people for a change—alongside you."

"Alongside me day and night," he said, kissing her ear.

"Eli," she said, tightening her arms around him and straining closer to him, "I do love you. So much. So hard. I knew from the start, I think."

He cocked his head. "I suppose I knew fairly early myself. I just hated to admit it."

"Why?" she teased gently, but she knew. He was a proud and solitary man to whom love had not come easily.

He shrugged and smiled down at her. "I had to think through the pros and cons of it," he said. He scooped her up easily into his arms. "Know what?" He grinned. "You Bostonians talk too much. There's more to life than discussion. Don't you ever get to the action?"

"Eventually," she replied, leaning her face against his neck and closing her eyes. "If we can find the right type to inspire us."

"I'd like to inspire you," he said in her ear. "Very much."

He lay her carefully on the large white bed, then bent over her, kissing her long and passionately, as he had wanted to do for the past four days.

He drew back momentarily, remembering the punishment she had taken that long night he'd almost lost her. "I don't want to hurt you," he said, looking deep into her eyes.

Her gaze met his with honesty and desire. "You could never hurt me," she said softly and drew him down beside her. "You make me complete."

He smiled as he lowered his face to hers. "Likewise, Junior. Likewise."